THE

SECOND

BOOK

A novel by

D. R. Evans

© Copyright 2012 by D. R. Evans.

First Edition

ISBN: 978-1-936211-04-3

Author website: *www.sff.net/people/N7DR*

www.enginehousebooks.com

DEDICATED TO THE MASTERS –

GRAHAM GREENE AND ANDREW BARCLAY

PART I
SUMMER

The Gringa

It was afternoon, the hottest part of the day on one of the hottest days of the year, and Tecimal was at siesta. On the south side of the *Calle de Generalissimo Javier Felipe Duarte* Barclay sat under the awning of Montoya's barbershop, rocking slowly, watching from beneath his wide-brimmed hat the cloud of dust that presaged the arrival of the bus. On the table between Barclay and Montoya were two glasses holding the smooth curving remnants of ice and a centimeter-deep layer of water.

"I'll get the next one if the bus doesn't stop," said Barclay, breaking the torpid silence.

Montoya made a kind of snort, perhaps because he had been asleep or, more likely, because he didn't think much of Barclay's offer.

"It's the first Monday of the month," Montoya said.

"So?"

"So it's Isabella's day for visiting Chiclahan. She'll have been there since this morning. So the bus will stop to let her off."

"My friend, you malign me. It's St. Mary Magdalene's feast day, and Isabella hasn't left Tecimal all day. I saw her not an hour ago. Go knock on her door if you don't believe me."

"It's too hot." A lacuna followed while Montoya conjured images of Isabella. Then he continued, "To see Isabella after the sun has set, I would travel to Chiclahan on bare feet. But now? In this heat? I'll take your word for it. After all, don't they say that an Englishman's word is his bond?"

3

"A myth promulgated by the English. Take my advice, Montoya, never trust an Englishman. He'll always give you cause to regret it."

Montoya mulled this advice as the cloud of dust rumbled up the *Calle*.

"I accept the bet but not the advice, Señor Barclay."

"You'll regret both," the Englishman replied.

A moment later the bus emitted a high-pitched screech, and the vehicle slowed noisily to a halt. The dust dispersed, revealing an American school bus of uncertain vintage and indefinite color. On the side of the vehicle, visible through several intervening coats of dilute paint, the two men could just make out: *Yuma County School District #1 — Yuma County — AZ*.

"Son of a bitch," said Montoya, honoring the phrase by rendering it in what passed in Tecimal for English: "Zunuva beech. How did you know the bus would stop if Isabella is still in Tecimal?"

Barclay delicately lifted his glass off the table with the thumb and middle finger of his left hand and handed it to Montoya. "The same again, my friend. And here's another piece of advice: never bet against an Englishman. After all, God may be Catholic, but He's an *English* Catholic. There aren't many of us left. Can you blame Him if He plays favorites?"

"Zunuva beech," repeated Montoya, halting his rocking and getting to his feet.

Barclay's eyes rested on the bus while Montoya went inside to get the drinks. A shadow moved inside the bus, making its way from rear to front, then disembarking on the far side of the vehicle.

The driver exchanged a few words with the shadow. When the driver turned back toward the road, he spotted Barclay and favored him with a brief wave. Barclay returned the wave unenthusiastically.

The driver revved the engine and engaged first gear with a crash; the bus pulled away, spawning a new cloud of dust.

Montoya returned with the drinks, and emitted a low whistle as he handed a glass to Barclay. Barclay took the glass without looking, his eyes, like Montoya's, on the woman standing on the far side of the street.

The first thing that struck him was her xanthous, shoulder-length hair. After three decades in Tecimal, the sight of glistening golden hair was so unexpected that it produced an almost palpable shock. In

4

rapid sequence he noticed with increasing unease that she was young, tanned, slim and well-poured.

"Zunuva beech," said Montoya again, almost inaudibly.

"Daughter," corrected Barclay, his eyes still on the woman. "Daughter of a bitch. Hell! She's seen us. Don't you dare tell her my name, Montoya."

Barclay pulled the brim of his hat down so that it almost covered his eyes and let his body go limp, feigning slumber.

———

Her heart sank as the bus pulled away. She had guessed it was going to be bad when she had been unable to find Tecimal on any of the maps in the university library. But if she'd had any notion that it would be as bad as this....

The metropolis of Tecimal comprised, as far she could tell, a single wide unpaved street — the *Calle de Generalissimo Javier Felipe Duarte*, according to an unevenly lettered, hand-painted sign hanging crookedly on the corner opposite — lined with tiny stores, all of whose doors were closed for siesta. Branching off the *Calle* more or less at right angles was a series of unevenly-spaced narrow streets lined with shoddy houses, many of which remained upright in apparent defiance of the law of gravity.

She looked slowly up and down the *Calle*, but the only movement came from the receding dust-enveloped bus and a pair of slightly seedy-looking men on the far side of the street. One was standing beside an unoccupied rocking chair, the other appeared to be asleep.

She looked along the *Calle* again, hoping to spot a sign that might indicate a hotel or a guest house, but the only signs were advertisements for Coca-Cola ("*El Sabor de la Vida*", in what might once have been white, against a background that was, perhaps, twenty years ago, red), *Cerveza de Chiclahan* (there were several of these: garishly colored, showing a too-perfect Indian-Latino girl smiling with flawless, brilliant-white teeth), and the hand-lettered signs above the stores.

She looked more carefully at the two men as the sinking feeling in the pit of her stomach grew. The one who was standing stared at her with what she could interpret only as lascivious approval, which brought to mind disturbing thoughts of what could happen to an American college girl travelling alone in this part of the world. The other man seemed to be asleep in his chair, his face hidden by the wide brim of his hat. She pressed her shoulder bag slightly, comforting herself with the reassuring hard curvature of the can of Mace.

There was nothing for it. She picked up her holdall, hitched her shoulder bag more securely, and crossed the *Calle*.

"Good afternoon," she said in Spanish, infusing her voice with false cheeriness.

Montoya threw her a smile intended both to reassure and to disarm the defenses of any woman. The newcomer saw in the smile only thinly veiled lust. Barclay did not move; his face remained hidden from her gaze.

"Is there somewhere I could stay for a few days?" she asked.

"Of course, señorita," replied Montoya, bowing in an excess of gallantry. "Permit me to introduce myself. I am Diego Fernando Montoya, barber to the town of Tecimal. May I be the first to welcome you to our humble town. You will be staying with us a few days? You desire a guide? Someone to help you see the sights? Up in the hills there are interesting ruins, and I would be happy to escort you there myself. For a gracious lady such as yourself, there would of course be no charge. I do...."

Barclay emitted a loud grunt, cutting off the flow.

"I'm sorry," said Montoya. "I didn't mean to impose. The sight of a pretty señorita...." He left the rest of the sentence to her imagination.

"Please, you said there was somewhere I might stay for a day or two?"

"Of course. You see that house there? The green one with the small windows? It belongs to Señora Delgado. Tell the Señora that Diego Montoya sent you, and you will be assured of a heartfelt welcome."

"Señora Delgado," she repeated, fixing the name in her memory. "And you're sure she'll accept a visitor?"

"Oh, yes. We have few visitors here in Tecimal. But those who find their way here invariably stay at the house of Señora Delgado. Is there any other way I can help you? Carry your bag, perhaps?"

"No, no. It's all right. But wait a minute, yes, perhaps you can help me. I'm looking for a man named Barclay — Andrew Barclay. He's an Englishman. His publisher told me he lives here."

She cast her gaze dubiously along the *Calle de Generalissimo Javier Felipe Duarte*, her expression making it clear that, whatever Barclay's publisher had said, she found it difficult to believe that anyone would voluntarily live in such a run-down, pissant flea-pit.

6

Because her eyes were on the street, she did not see Montoya's reaction to her statement; had she done so, perhaps the entire subsequent course of her life would have been different. Instead, she continued to look forlornly at the empty street, wondering if perhaps there were two towns called Tecimal and she had somehow found her way to the wrong one.

As she watched, a lank, disreputable-looking yellow dog wandered out of a side street and began to cross the *Calle*. Halfway across, the dog halted, circled once, then lay down in the dust. The animal closed its eyes.

"Barclay?" Montoya repeated the name as his eyes bored into the crown of Barclay's still-lowered hat.

The question took the woman's attention from the dog. "Yes. Here, I have a picture."

She opened her shoulder bag and withdrew a hardbacked book, turning it so that its back cover faced Montoya. From the cover gazed a black and white photograph of a young man, his mouth smiling but his eyes glaring suspiciously at the world. In the background was a filled bookcase, the titles too blurred to be readable.

The man whom she had assumed to be asleep (she had mistaken his grunt for a kind of snore) suddenly extended his hand towards her, causing her to start.

"You want to see the book?" she asked.

"Please."

He tilted his head slightly, so that for the first time she could see his face. Most of it was in shadow, but she could see that he was quite old, perhaps in his sixties, possibly even older, with a long, crevassed, weathered face. A thin beard of gray hairs stuck to his chin. His mouth was open in what might have been a smile, although it could equally well have been a grimace. His teeth were yellow but even; his eyes were too deeply hidden in the umbra of his hat for her to see them clearly.

"Does Señor Barclay live in Tecimal?" she asked, surrendering the book temporarily as a *quid pro quo* for the question.

Barclay took the book wordlessly and turned it over to look at the front cover. The book was a novel, and its front cover was graced by a woman in a bikini and a bronze, muscular man, standing at the shore of what might have been a lake, with the sun almost touching a line of unnaturally verdant trees on the far shore. *The Condition of Love*, the

7

cover declared; underneath, in slightly smaller print: *The Bestselling First Novel by Andrew Barclay.*

Barclay stared at the cover for a few seconds, then turned the book over. He looked at the youthful figure gazing suspiciously at him for perhaps ten seconds.

"Do you know a Señor Barclay?" he asked Montoya.

"Um...."

"Your book, señorita," said Barclay. "The face looks familiar, but I am not certain the man you want is here. You should ask Señora Delgado. No, perhaps better, you should ask her daughter, Isabella. You will recognize Isabella immediately you see her. She paints herself like a whore."

"Th-thank you."

She took the book, wondering if she could possibly have either misheard or misunderstood what the man had said.

She began to move away, but was halted by Barclay calling after her.

"Señorita?"

She turned. "Yes?"

"Your name? You forgot to tell us your name."

"Donna," she replied. "I'm from the United States." Then, realizing from their knowing smiles that of course they had known all along that she was from the North, she turned and hurried away in the direction of the green house with the small windows.

Two Houses

Señora Delgado's house was no more than a hundred meters from the place where Donna had held her brief, inconclusive conversation with Diego Montoya and his companion, but it seemed much farther. She could feel the eyes of the two men, especially those of Diego Montoya, every step of the way.

It was hot — as hot as hell, much hotter than Los Angeles, which, God forbid, had been hot enough. By the time she was halfway to the house, sweat was dribbling down her brow, around the corners of her eyes, down her cheeks, into her mouth and trickling to the end of her chin, whence it fell, augmenting the slowly-growing damp splotch on the front of her blouse.

She swore at the two of them under her breath, knowing they would laugh at any sign of weakness, attributing it to her gender or her citizenship or both. So she kept walking, refusing to break stride, letting the sweat dribble down her face, her neck, between her breasts (*God! How can women bear to wear bras every day in this heat?*).

She halted in front of the house, putting her holdall down and turning slightly, trying to make it seem that she was simply looking up and down the street, instead of trying to see if they were still watching her.

They had gone. Where the men had been there were now just two empty rocking chairs. The door of the store behind the chairs was open. She turned away and felt in a pocket for a handkerchief.

She wiped the sweat from her face. Surreptitiously, hiding the gesture in the motion she used to replace the handkerchief in her

9

pocket, she pulled her bra forward and shook it slightly in an attempt to remove some of the moisture. *I hope they have running water. I'd give a hundred dollars for a good shower.* Then she stretched out her hand and lifted the heavy metal knocker.

The doorknocker was in the shape of some kind of animal: a dog, or possibly a pig. Whatever the animal was supposed to be, the knocker was poorly designed: even though she knocked as loudly as she could, the sound was almost inaudible, even to Donna.

She stood there, wondering how to extract more noise from the obdurate pig (or dog), when without warning the door was yanked open.

"Good afternoon, señorita."

Donna found herself looking at a rounded, smiling woman somewhere in her forties. She was surprisingly tall, almost as tall as Donna herself. Her eyes were crinkled, echoing and confirming the smile on her lips. She was well-dressed, in clothes that must have come from a large town, for it seemed unlikely that there would be anywhere to buy such habiliments in Tecimal. Her hair showed a trace of gray at the temples.

"Good afternoon. My name is Donna. I'm an American. I was told that perhaps you might be able to rent me a room for a couple of nights."

"From the North?" the woman yelped enthusiastically. "Los Angeles? Chicago? New York? I know about these places; I've seen the movies in Chiclahan. My daughter, you know, she's always going to Chiclahan and buying beautiful clothes. You think these clothes are beautiful, no? They were a gift from my daughter.

"Sometimes she says to me, 'Momma,...' She's a good girl, you know. Always calls me Momma. Never disrespectful. May the Good Lord grant you a daughter half so beautiful and half so mindful of her duties to her Momma.

"'Momma,' she says to me, 'today you are coming with me to Chiclahan and together we will see a movie about America.'

"*Beverly Hills Cop*, yes? And *ET*? It is a beautiful country. Yes. Beautiful."

She subsided, apparently engrossed in a beatific contemplation of America as portrayed by Hollywood.

"I'm from Los Angeles," said Donna, when she was sure that the flood of words had ceased. "I was wondering if you could rent me a room for a couple of nights."

"A room? Of course, of course. An American, in my house. Here, in Tecimal." The woman was speaking to herself, nodding slightly as if unable to fully believe the miracle.

Then, as if suddenly frightened that Donna might change her mind, the woman took a step backward and gestured for her guest to enter.

"Come in, come in. You honor us. My daughter will be so interested to meet you. Her name is Isabella. She...."

Doing her best to keep up with the flood of Spanish and smiling determinedly, Donna picked up her holdall and went inside.

The house was cooler than the street and Donna halted, appreciating the change in temperature. There was the slightly greasy scent of some kind of food, either left over from lunch or the harbinger of the evening meal.

Ten minutes passed before Donna was installed in her room, mostly because Señora Delgado insisted on showing Donna all the conveniences provided by her establishment, to the accompaniment of a veritable torrent of observations on how wonderful America was; how wonderful Harrison Ford was; how wonderful the president, the president's wife, the movies, the people and even the weather were.

Donna smiled through it all, doing nothing to encourage Señora Delgado except to offer an occasional nod.

Eventually, Señora Delgado ran out of steam. She said goodbye and closed the door, leaving Donna alone in her room. Donna let out a long phew! of relief, and sat heavily on the bed.

The room was better — much, much better — than she had feared. Not only was there running water, there was even a small *en suite* bathroom with a tiny shower in the corner, although the only way to reach it was by lowering and then clambering over the toilet seat.

The bedroom itself was clean, as were the sheets on the bed. There was neither telephone nor television, although there was an ancient radio on the bedside table.

The room was on the second (and topmost) floor of the house, and looked out over the *Calle de Generalissimo Javier Felipe Duarte*. Now that siesta was over, the *Calle* was no longer deserted. She could see half a dozen women on the street, darting into and out of the stores, carrying their shopping in bags and nodding and exchanging greetings. In the middle of the road the yellow dog still slept undisturbed.

Almost directly opposite the house was what appeared to be a bar, the words *El Presidente* scrawled above a door in an almost illegible script. In front of a massive sign for *Cerveza de Chiclahan*, whence a manic, white-toothed señorita offered a much-larger-than-life can of beer to all passersby, loitered six men, talking amongst themselves. Four of the men leaned against the sign; the other two sat on the bare ground facing the street. Each man held a can from which he took an occasional swig as the mood took him.

Donna switched on the light, locked the door, pulled the drapes closed, and began to run the water for a shower.

The water had an odd, slightly moldy odor, and after flowing for about half a minute it acquired a distinct brownish hue and slowed to little more than a trickle. Donna, naked now, eyed it skeptically.

When in Rome....

She clambered over the toilet seat and stepped into the shower.

Afterwards, Donna felt much better. She changed into clean clothes, stuffing the dirty ones into a drawer. Somewhere, even in Tecimal, there had to be either a laundromat or someone who would wash her clothes in exchange for payment.

Opening the drapes, she looked out and saw that the street was virtually unchanged. There were now seven men in front of *El Presidente*, and the dog was nowhere to be seen, but apart from those minor differences, the view was essentially identical.

Picking up the bag of dirty clothes, Donna went in search of Señora Delgado.

She found her quarry in the kitchen, pressing tortillas. The kitchen was unexpectedly modern, with several old but serviceable appliances. There was even an air conditioner rattling away in the window.

"Excuse me," began Donna, "but I was wondering if there's a...," she paused, trying to think of the Spanish for "laundromat." She gave up and started again. "I was wondering if there was somewhere in town where I could wash my clothes?"

"No need for that." Señora Delgado smiled cheerily. "Just leave them with me." She rubbed flour off her hands. "You would like some coffee? See, I have a Mr. Coffee. The only Mr. Coffee in all of Tecimal. You will join me? Please, sit down."

It would have been impolite to refuse, and Donna found herself seated at the kitchen table while Señora Delgado bustled around making

12

coffee, all the time talking and giving Donna no chance to ask whether the señora knew the English author she had come all this way to see.

"My Isabella, she's asleep right now. She always takes a long siesta, that girl." Señora Delgado arranged the filter in the Mr. Coffee. "My Isabella gets through clothes so quickly. I don't know how she does it. I'm always washing her things." She opened a cupboard door and removed a brightly colored jar of coffee. "Fortunately she bought me a washing machine. There are only three washing machines in all of Tecimal, can you imagine that? Everyone brings their clothes to me. My Isabella, she's a smart girl. She bought me a Maytag, so it never breaks down."

She laughed as she counted out six measures of coffee. Donna laughed too, partly to please her hostess and partly because the notion of the Maytag repairman waiting pointlessly in a store somewhere along the *Calle de Generalissimo Javier Felipe Duarte* was so preposterous.

"You know," the señora continued, running water into the flask, "when I became pregnant with Isabella, I thought it meant I would never have any of the things I wanted. I thought it was the end of all my dreams. Now look at me: I am the luckiest woman in Tecimal. There, that should do. Now we just have to wait. Ah, it's good to get the weight off my feet. Listen to what I tell you, señorita, always take good care of your legs. That's the first thing a real man looks at. But of course I'm being stupid: you know all about men, a beautiful girl like you."

Donna blushed. "Please," she began, seizing the opportunity to change the subject, "I came here to find someone. Do you know a man called Andrew Barclay? He's an English writer, and I have a letter from his publisher telling me he lives in Tecimal."

Señora Delgado clapped her hands in delight.

"Señor Barclay? You came here looking for Señor Barclay? Of course I know Señor Barclay. How could I live in Tecimal and not know Señor Barclay? Everyone knows Señor Barclay."

Donna refrained from observing that the two people she had asked on her arrival didn't seem to know him.

"We all love Señor Barclay," continued the Señora. "He adopted us, and we adopted him. He is our famous son. His book, you know, is in every house in Tecimal, even those where no one can read. Come with me, I'll show you my copy." She began to rise.

Donna shook her head. "No thank you, that's all right."

The señora looked momentarily disappointed, then relaxed back on to her stool. She continued, "He wrote a message in my book, just like he wrote a message to everyone. But mine is different. I looked after him before we knew he was famous. Before we knew he would stay." She sighed. "It was a long time ago now, of course."

The bitter smell of strong coffee began to fill the room.

"Then you know where he lives?" prompted Donna.

"Of course." Señora Delgado stood and conjured a pair of oddly formal china cups and saucers from a cupboard. As she poured the coffee she said, "He lives on the *Avenida La Guardia*. The third house. Pink with white shutters."

"Is he married?" Donna ventured, taking the cup that the señora offered and wrinkling her nose at the strength of the coffee's acrid aroma.

"Señor Barclay? Married? No." The señora gave Donna no opportunity to pursue the topic as she rattled on. "Señor Barclay could live anywhere, you know. He is a rich man. But he chooses to live here in Tecimal." The señora spoke proudly. "Tecimal," she repeated. "People from outside think there is nothing here, but we who live here know better. Señor Barclay, he knows better."

"Do you think he would be home now? I mean, he's not away or anything, is he? On a trip?"

"No, no, my dear. Apart from occasional visits to Chiclahan, the only place Señor Barclay ever goes is into the mountains, and he only goes there once a year. No, he's in town. I saw him myself this morning. And if he's not at home, you can always be sure of finding him at *El Presidente* in the evening."

"*El Presidente?* The bar across the street?"

Señora Delgado nodded. "Just ask the men outside for Señor Barclay. Everyone knows him. Do you want more coffee? I made enough."

"No. Really, I should be going. I've come all this way, and I feel like I'm so close now I should introduce myself to him as soon as I can."

Donna quickly stood and made her escape.

It was still hot outside. As Donna paused outside the front door to get her bearings, she became uncomfortably aware of the stares from the men lounging in front of *El Presidente*. Her appearance outside Señora

Delgado's had caused them to suspend their discussion, and now they were all gazing across the street at the gringa.

Flustered, Donna realized that she had forgotten to ask Señora Delgado for directions to the *Avenida La Guardia*. She turned to her left, and walked quickly along the *Calle*.

She was lucky. The *Avenida La Guardia* was the third cross-street she came to, and turning into it she immediately spotted the house she was looking for.

The faded pink house with the peeling white shutters looked little different from its neighbors. It looked just as seedy, just as poorly maintained; its windows were just as dusty, its paint just as faded. The only minor difference was of a negative kind: the diminutive yard that separated it from the street was simply an extension of the dusty, compacted dirt of the *Avenida La Guardia*, without even the attempt the neighbors had made to enhance it with flowers or a shrub or two. An erratic line of small ocher stones was the only division between street and front yard.

Next door two children played a noisy game with two sticks and a grubby object that looked like a weighted rag. They stopped their game as Donna halted outside the pink and white house. Donna smiled at them; they stared at her.

"Hello," she said.

They were girls, one about seven, the other a couple of years younger. The younger one tried to hide behind the older, who stood her ground with a defiant scowl.

"Who are you?" the older girl asked belligerently.

"My name is Donna," Donna said with a friendly smile. "Can you tell me, does Señor Barclay live here?"

"Why is your hair that color?" asked the child.

Donna masked her annoyance by smiling more widely. "It just grew that way. Does Señor Barclay live here?"

"It looks strange," said the older child emphatically; then she added, "Señor Barclay doesn't like us. He says we make too much noise."

"I expect he just finds it hard to work sometimes, that's all."

"Mama says Señor Barclay doesn't work at all. He just drinks."

Donna could think of nothing to say to that, and the conversation was abruptly brought to an end as the younger of the two children suddenly turned and ran crying into the house. After giving Donna's hair one last stare, her sibling followed.

Swallowing once, and trying to ignore the butterflies that had suddenly taken residence in her stomach, Donna stepped over the line of stones and walked up to the door of the pink and white house. There was neither doorbell nor knocker, and the door, which opened inwards, stood slightly ajar. She rapped her knuckles against it.

There was no response. After half a minute or so, she tried again.

Still no one came to the door. Pushing it farther open, she called, first in Spanish and then in English, "Hello! Anyone at home?"

No one replied, and for a while she hesitated on the threshold. At length she straightened her shoulders and walked inside.

There was a vaguely sour smell inside the hot, stuffy house. Donna was in a bare hallway, with no pictures on the walls to hide the grubby paint and nothing to soften the hardness of the bare concrete floor. A dusty dun poncho hung on a hook beside the door.

She called again, "Hello, is anyone home?"

Still there was no answer.

An empty doorway led to a room in which she could see a bookcase. Treading lightly, for the thought had just come to her that perhaps the writer was taking a late siesta, she poked her head inside the room.

It was a kind of office-cum-study. Book-filled shelves lined the walls; the librarious overflow was stacked in half a dozen foot-high piles in one corner. In the middle of the room was a desk, its surface almost completely covered with haphazard papers. In the center of the desk was an ancient typewriter, into which a sheet of paper was inserted. A glass stood beside the typewriter, an inch of colorless liquid covering the bottom. There was no one in the room.

Donna tiptoed to the desk. Bending down to smell the drink, she pulled a face at the sharp tang of undiluted tequila. She looked at the papers on the desk. They seemed to be a work in progress: most of them were typewritten, double spaced, with heavy annotations in red.

The disorganized papers were unnumbered, so that it was impossible to guess the order in which they were supposed to be read. Not daring to move them, she simply let her eye rove over them, trying to get an idea of the kind of book that Barclay was writing.

But the pages were so disordered and there were so many crossings out — sometimes entire pages were struck out with a single red line slashing like a wound through the text — that she could form no coherent picture of what it was supposed to be, except that it was obviously a novel of some kind.

The sheet in the typewriter had only a couple of sentences on it. She read:

```
Cornmarket lay desiccating in the hot sun as, in the distance
ten miles to the northeast, a rotating cloud began to reach an
exploratory finger towards the ground. The first person to see
it was Sheldon the driver of a tractor John Deere as it crested
the slight rise in the north field of the Hodgson farm.
```

It read like the beginning of a novel, but not a very good beginning.

There was a movement at the window, and Donna's head jerked up just in time to see a figure moving away from the glass. With a sinking feeling, she realized that someone had been watching her. It occurred to her that Barclay would probably not appreciate anyone coming into his study and looking over his rough drafts without his permission.

Without stopping to think, she rushed outside and ran around the house to the study window. She looked desperately around. The watcher had gone.

For a moment she wondered if it had all been her imagination.

"Hello," she called loudly. "I was just looking for Señor Barclay, that's all."

But the only answer was the sound of the children next door as they tumbled out the house and began to play again.

After a minute she turned and walked away, back towards the *Calle*.

El Presidente, and Afterwards

Tecimal had just one bar, *El Presidente*, which was located, like every business in Tecimal, on the *Calle de Generalissimo Javier Felipe Duarte*. *El Presidente* was almost opposite the house of Señora Delgado, perhaps not entirely by accident.

El Presidente closed its door only between the hours of midnight and four a.m., and not even then if Pedro Grande — a short, stout, smiling man with a neat moustache and overlarge ears — thought it worth his while to remain open.

During the day, often the only person inside *El Presidente* was the man behind the bar, usually either the owner himself or his fourteen-year-old son, Pedro Pequeño. Customers, of whom there was a brief flood at the beginning of siesta and a steady trickle throughout the rest of the day, would come in to buy a *Cerveza de Chiclahan*, and then take it outside to drink with the other men who were a perpetual feature of the street outside *El Presidente*.

Around eight o'clock, everything changed. Men dropped by for a beer on their way home; or, if there was no one waiting for them there, for a meal chosen from the menu of frozen TV dinners brought in from Chiclahan.

It was Barclay's habit to be in his customary place before the busy period started, sitting on his stool at the end of the counter, nursing a drink — sometimes beer, more often tequila — although whether it was his first drink of the evening or his fourth, no one except he and the barman knew.

18

Tonight, had any of the customers bothered to look closely, they would have observed that Barclay seemed more thoughtful and perhaps grimmer than usual. He downed his drinks speedily, so that by the time Diego Montoya appeared at his side, the Englishman had already lost count.

"Sorry I'm late," said Montoya, nodding at Pedro Grande and taking his place on the stool next to Barclay. Pedro Grande wordlessly pushed a tequila toward Montoya. Montoya explained: "Fernando Gonzalez came in just as I was about to close, and we got talking. You know how it is."

Barclay nodded distractedly; he glanced at his half-full glass, then knocked his head back and drained it. He gestured to Pedro Grande to replenish the drink.

"So, are you going to tell me what it's all about?" Montoya asked as he sipped his tequila.

Barclay looked at him with an unreadable expression.

"The gringa," Montoya elaborated. "She had your book and she was looking for you. So why didn't you tell her who you are? And you were expecting her, weren't you? That's why you made that bet about the bus stopping."

"You remember what I said this afternoon? About God being an English Catholic?"

Montoya nodded.

"The trouble is, so's the devil. The devil knows his own, maybe better than God does. And it's my experience...." His voice trailed off, his gaze on the glass in his hand.

"Yes?" prompted Montoya.

"It's my experience that whatever the devil wants, he usually gets. God may be all-powerful in heaven, but God knows Tecimal isn't heaven. Down here, it's the devil who usually gets his way." Barclay looked at Montoya. "Sorry. You mustn't mind me. I'm maudlin. It's the booze talking, that's all."

"What's the matter?"

Montoya was genuinely concerned for his friend. Everyone knew that a peculiar moodiness sometimes gripped the English writer, but it was a long time since Montoya had seen him looking so thoroughly defeated. "Who is she and what does she want?"

"She's a student."

Barclay rummaged in a pocket and withdrew an envelope, crumpled and streaked with dirt. He handed it to Montoya, and Montoya examined it while Barclay finished his drink and ordered another.

It was an airmail envelope, with stamps that bore the silhouette of a crowned woman but no country of origin. Opening the envelope, Montoya extracted a one-page letter and another envelope, this one with American stamps. He unfolded the letter.

"It's in English," he said.

"Sorry. Here, give them to me. I'll translate."

Barclay opened the letter and spread it out on the surface of the bar. Pedro Grande put a drink down next to it. Barclay fortified himself, then began to translate aloud.

> *Dear Andrew*
>
> *I do hope you will forgive this letter. The enclosed arrived at our offices last week, and through some abominable mix-up the young lady who wrote the letter was informed of your place of residence, although not your exact address. Please accept my heartfelt apologies for this incident; you can be sure that the person responsible for the breach has been duly reprimanded. You have my personal assurance that it will not happen again.*
>
> *As always, I trust that you are well. We await eagerly the drafts of your new work.*
>
> *Yours sincerely*
> *John Adams*
> *for Adams & Gilt, publishers.*

"The other letter, the one from her, is even worse," Barclay said. "She's a bloody student and she's got it into her head that I'm a suitable subject for a Ph.D. thesis. Can you imagine anything more ludicrous? What's she going to write? I can imagine the first sentence now: *I went to a pissant Latin American town nine tenths of the way to hell, and when I got there I found a washed-up inebriate who once wrote a bestseller but who can't write even the first paragraph of his second book after trying for more than a quarter of a century.*

"Bloody hell! She sent me a letter care of the post office to say she'd be arriving today. I was hoping she wouldn't show up. She types the confounded things on one of those electronic word processor abominations, and uses a typeface more suited to a newspaper column than a letter. What kind of idiot interposes a machine between herself and the recipient anyway? She should have written her damned letters by hand. Not that I would have answered anyway. I suppose...."

Barclay caught himself, realizing that he had strayed from the point. "But the damned fool showed up anyway. That's the trouble with Americans: they never can tell when they're not wanted. Now she's here, and I don't suppose she'll rest until she's hounded me down. What makes it worse is that she probably thinks my hiding from her just makes me all the more interesting." He lifted his glass and half-emptied it in a single gulp.

"So what are you going to do about her?"

"What does it look like I'm doing? I'm staying out of her way. I'll move in here. Even an American college student should have enough brains not to walk into a bar in a town in the middle of Central America. Oh, bloody hell."

This last was in response to the fact that *El Presidente*, for the first time in its existence, had without warning ceased to be a male preserve. Even Isabella, that most favored of women, had never tried to breach *El Presidente*. But now, standing in the doorway and peering into the dim interior, was the blonde gringa whose arrival had been the dominant subject of conversation in Tecimal since siesta.

Silence descended on the bar more quickly than the tropical night. All eyes swiveled to the gringa with the blonde hair and the walnut tan. All movement ceased.

The woman smiled uncertainly as she surveyed the interior of the bar. She descried Pedro Grande behind the counter, and crossed the room to stand opposite him.

"Excuse me," she said without the merest trace of shame, almost as if she were completely unaware of the enormity of her transgression. "I'm trying to find a man called Barclay. Señora Delgado told me I would find him here."

Pedro Grande arched an eyebrow. "Señora Delgado said you would find Señor Barclay here?"

"Yes. He's a writer. English. He wrote this book." From her bag she pulled a Spanish paperback of *The Condition of Love* and showed it to Pedro Grande.

He ignored the book and looked piercingly down the bar at Barclay.

Barclay mumbled, so quietly that only Montoya could make out the words, "The devil always gets his way in the end."

21

He slid off his stool. The gringa watched him shamble towards her.

Without a word, Barclay put an arm around her shoulder and propelled her in the direction of the door.

"I'm sorry, Pedro," he called over his shoulder. "It won't happen again. She's from the North."

Pedro nodded.

"Wait a minute, what the hell are you doing?" the gringa protested as Barclay unceremoniously pushed her through the doorway ahead of him.

Outside, a group of men who had been watching stepped back to make room for the unlikely pair. Barclay grabbed the gringa's wrist tightly and began to march her away down the street.

"What the hell do you think you're doing? Where are we going?" Her voice began to rise to a scream.

It was a nightmare. Here she was, in a tin-pot town in a third-world country, being dragged into the night by a drunken desperado — and everyone was just letting it happen.

"Shut up, you bloody idiot," snarled Barclay in English.

She was astonished into silence. Open-mouthed but no longer protesting, Donna let herself be led away down the street, then around the corner into the *Avenida La Guardia*, whence Barclay led her into the pink and white house. Once they were inside, he slammed the door behind them so loudly that the building shook. He turned to Donna furiously, but she got in the first word.

"What the hell do you think you're doing?" she repeated. She rubbed her wrist where he had manhandled her. "You're Barclay, aren't you? You can't treat me like this. And what the hell did you mean this afternoon by letting me make a fool of myself in front of that other man, asking for you when all the time you were sitting right there laughing at me. I mffmwh...."

He slammed a hand firmly across her mouth, but before he could say anything she bit down hard.

Too hard.

He screamed and snatched his hand away. "You bloody bitch. You've drawn blood."

"Good. Serves you right. Get the hell away from me. I'm going home."

"That's the best news I've heard all day. Go back where you came from. I never want to see you again. Ouch. That bloody well hurt."

Donna took an uncertain step toward the door. She was furious, but Barclay's hand was bleeding freely from a red crescent that disfigured the thenar webbing. The man was a pig, but even so she shouldn't have bitten him quite so hard. He sucked his hand, glaring at her as she hovered indecisively at the door.

"Look," she said. "I'm sorry. Really. I didn't mean to hurt you."

"Go away," he said, his words barely intelligible.

But she couldn't. She took a step towards him. "Here, let me look at it."

She pulled his hand from his mouth.

"That needs dressing," she declared as a drop of blood fell on the bare concrete floor. "Do you have a first aid kit anywhere?"

"In the bathroom, but if you think...."

"Oh, be quiet, will you? Which way is it? Never mind, I'll find it myself." And before he could stop her, she was off, looking in every room until she found the one she was looking for.

He rolled his eyes heavenwards and mumbled, *sotto voce*, "Bloody women," while she opened drawers in search of the elusive first aid kit.

She returned, frowning and holding something in her hand.

"Is this what you call a first aid kit?" She held up a small plastic box that prominently displayed a red cross on a white background.

"What's wrong with it?"

"You want a list? It's twenty years old, half the stuff's been used, and what's left is useless. Here, bring that hand into the bathroom. Let's run some water into the wound. What's the water here like? It looks filthy, but is it fit to drink?"

"How the hell should I know? What kind of idiot would drink filthy water instead of good tequila?"

She took his hand and led him into the bathroom, where she thrust his hand into the basin and turned on the lone faucet as far as it would allow. After a brief and impressive torrent, the water diminished to little more than a brownish trickle.

"Do you have any iodine in the house?"

"No. Why? Are you thirsty? If so, I recommend tequila over iodine."

"Oh, go to hell. Look, this is serious. Oh, God! I'm sorry. Let me think for a moment." She closed her eyes and put her hands to her temples.

"What is this? Some new mystic style of meditation? I'll make it easy for you. Go away. Do you want me to spell it for you? G-O, go; A-W-A-Y, away."

"Shut up, will you? There's a doctor here, right? Even a godforsaken hole like this must have a doctor. Here, dry your hand on this... this towel. This is a towel, right? Tell me, don't you ever do any laundry? This towel's a disgrace. With my luck, you'll pick up an infection from the towel."

She blotted the blood and water off his hand with the stained piece of cloth.

"To answer your questions in the order asked — one: yes, there is someone in Tecimal who claims to be a doctor. However, he has never been known to take a drink voluntarily, and therefore I regard his claim with studied skepticism.

"Two: yes, this is a towel. Spanish: *toalla*; French: *essuie-main*; German: *Handtuch*, and if you don't like the state of my belongings, there's the door.

"Three: yes, I do my laundry. Like most of Tecimal, I do it whenever the mood takes me, which it does on average about once every three or four months.

"Now, assuming you have finished quizzing me, please just go away and leave me alone. I'll live. Now what's the matter? Oh, hell. You're not going to cry, are you?"

She was standing, the dirty towel in her hands, looking at him. There was no mistaking the moist reflections in her eyes, and before either of them could do anything about it, she leaned her head forward against his chest and began to heave.

He wrapped an arm around her shoulder.

"Come on," he said, his voice unexpectedly gentle, "you didn't mean to hurt me, and it really doesn't matter. Listen, if it'll make you happier I promise I'll go to the doctor tomorrow and let him have a look at it. Please, now, stop crying. Just go. I'll be fine."

"I... I'm sorry," she sobbed. Producing a handkerchief from somewhere she dabbed her eyes and blew her nose. "I'm sorry," she repeated. "I don't know what's the matter with me. I never cry. I guess... I guess it's just that today has all been too much."

He nodded absentmindedly as he opened a drawer and reached into its depths. He withdrew a full bottle of tequila. "Here, unscrew this for me," he said.

She untwisted the cap, and he took the bottle and poured a liberal quantity of its contents into the wound, baring his teeth at the sharp sting. Then he put the bottle to his lips and took a large gulp.

"All right," he said. "Look, here's a dressing strip, just wind it around my hand. Yes, that's it."

She wrapped the dirty-white strip several times around the hand, securing it with a rusty safety pin. She looked at the result dubiously.

"It'll be perfect in a day or two," he assured her, then ruined everything by adding, "and now, if you've quite finished, will you please just go away?"

"You're still angry with me."

"If you go away I won't be angry any more."

"What's the matter with me? Why won't you talk to me? I said I'm sorry."

"Nothing's the matter with you. I won't talk to you because I won't talk to anyone. Don't take it personally. Just go back to Los Angeles and choose a more cooperative subject for your thesis. I assure you, it will be much better for both of us."

"Please."

"And don't waste your time simpering. Just go away."

Her temper snapped. She snarled, "Damn you! I came all the way down here because I happen to think that *The Condition of Love* is the best novel written in the last fifty years. I wanted to meet you because I thought I could learn something from you. Something important. Something about touching people with the written word. I already know how to drink."

He shook his head ruefully. "Robert Redford to Paul Newman, *The Sting*, 1969 or thereabouts. Redford, I have to say, was considerably more convincing than you."

"Go to hell."

She shoved him to one side and stormed out the house. It was not until she had turned the corner on to the *Calle de Generalissimo Javier Felipe Duarte* that she stopped in mid-stride and swore to herself.

"Damn! Stupid, stupid, stupid."

She took half a dozen deep breaths, holding each one while she counted to ten.

The exercise had the desired effect. Calmer now, she said to herself, "All right, Mr. Barclay, you won that round. But it's not over yet. I'm not going to let you get the better of me that easily."

Forcing herself to take measured steps, she strode away in the direction of Señora Delgado's.

The Doctor

In the normal course of events, Barclay never rose before ten o'clock. But on the day after the gringa came to town his throbbing hand woke him at eight.

"Bloody thing's infected," he mumbled as he pulled himself off the mattress, leaving a damp valley where his weight had been.

There were no drapes on his windows, so as he glanced outside he had a clear view of the American student walking down the *Avenida*, away from his house.

He vaguely recalled hearing a sound at the front door, and realized it was Donna's knocking rather than the pain in his hand that had woken him.

"Damn woman," he said under his breath.

He pulled on a pair of baggy underpants and went to the door. Stuck into the frame was an envelope. He ripped it open, wincing in pain.

He read:

Dear Mr. Barclay

I am sorry for hurting you yesterday. I am also sorry for invading the privacy of your home during the afternoon. That was you at the window, wasn't it? Anyway, it was wrong of me. I am truly sorry and I hope you'll forgive me.

I really do mean what I said yesterday about The Condition of Love. It is a beautiful book, probably the most underrated book of the last half century. But surely you recognize that in order to understand the book fully, I have to understand the author. And once I understand him, I want to use my thesis as a vehicle to communicate my understanding to others. Won't you please just talk to me? That's all I ask: a few hours of your time.

Please come to the Casa de Food tonight at nine o'clock. I will buy you dinner, and in return won't you please grant me an interview? Just one, that's all I'm asking. Is it really so much? I promise I'll stay out of your way until then.

Hoping very much to see you tonight.

Donna

"Is it really so much?" Barclay apostrophized the gringa. "Of course it's so bloody much. Stupid woman. Can't even tell when she's not wanted."

He crumpled the letter and envelope and tossed them into a struggling yucca in the yard next door. Two children who had been playing with dirty rag dolls stopped to watch him with wide eyes; he made a face at them, sending them scuttling inside, calling for their Momma.

He went back into the house and ate a desultory breakfast of fried tortillas and goat cheese, doing his best to ignore the pain in his hand.

After breakfast, it was his habit to retire to his study to work for a couple of hours before the heat became oppressive, at which point he would happily succumb to the first drink of the day and go in search of Montoya. But today his hand provided a ready-made excuse not to write, so as soon as breakfast was over he pulled on a pair of shorts and what passed in Tecimal for a clean shirt. Slipping cracked leather sandals on his feet, he went to see the doctor.

Doctor Enrique Pasquale had been raised in Tecimal, although he was born in Chiclahan. He had come to Tecimal when he was eighteen months old, to live with a desiccated woman who at that time was in her late forties and lived on the outskirts of town, making a living binding books for the library in Chiclahan.

Blanca Pasquale was an enigma to the other inhabitants of Tecimal. She had no true friends and lived alone until Enrique was thrust on her by a jocose Providence. She lived in a small, one-story house on the northern edge of town, with nothing but desert between her and the mountains. Blanca was one of the half-dozen people in Tecimal

28

who owned a car, although, unlike the others, no one ever dared ask Blanca for a ride in *her* vehicle.

Her car was a Chevrolet of uncertain vintage: massive, chromed, and endowed with pointless pointed fins. In the hot, dry climate of Tecimal rust was all but unknown, and there seemed no reason why a car should not run forever. Blanca Pasquale's Chevrolet was proof of this fact, since no one could remember Blanca ever calling on Luis, the town mechanic, for more than minor repairs.

Eighteen-month-old Enrique appeared in town without warning, squalling and carried by Blanca on her return from one of her periodic visits to Chiclahan to exchange a cargo of repaired books for several boxes of books in need of mending. The sudden arrival of the infant sent Tecimal into a frenzy of speculation. No one could guess why the confirmed spinster had brought home a toddler, and for more than a year speculation and ill-informed guesses abounded until the truth was finally established by the brief appearance of a lawyer from Chiclahan who explained that the child was her nephew, orphaned by a car crash that had killed his parents.

Enrique led a childhood unique in Tecimal. Alone of all the children he did not attend school, his aunt instead taking responsibility for his lessons. But the most unusual aspect of Enrique's childhood was that Blanca instilled in the child her own religion: for Blanca Pasquale was Tecimal's only avowed atheist.

When the bell rang for Sunday Mass, the only unresponsive home in all of Tecimal was that of Blanca and Enrique Pasquale. Even Barclay, the eccentric English author, responded to the bell. But the Pasquales were deaf to its call; Sunday was to them simply another day, distinguished only by the inconvenience of the closed stores along the *Calle de Generalissimo Javier Felipe Duarte.*

One day shortly after Enrique turned fifteen, his aunt bundled him into her massive Chevrolet along with an enormous suitcase that was almost as large as he. They drove away in the direction of Chiclahan. Late that evening, Blanca Pasquale returned alone. Enrique did not return for eight years.

When he did come back, it was no longer to live with Blanca Pasquale. Instead, he brought with him a visibly pregnant wife, and together they rented a small house near the north end of the *Calle.* Outside the house there promptly appeared a sign announcing that Doctor Enrique Pasquale was willing to treat patients at very reasonable rates.

For the first six months, Doctor Pasquale's practice was so slim as to be almost nonexistent. In his absence he had moved no closer to embracing Catholicism, and his wife shared his lack of enthusiasm for the faith, with the consequence that no one who succumbed to illness even considered the possibility of consulting the young doctor. Those who did fall sick were faced with the same choice as always: doing nothing; calling in the midwife; or, if truly desperate, cadging a ride to the hospital in Chiclahan.

The doctor was on the point of giving up and leaving Tecimal when Barclay changed everything.

From his rocking chair in front of Montoya's barber's shop, Barclay commanded a good view of the length of the *Calle de Generalissimo Javier Felipe Duarte*. He and Montoya were at siesta one afternoon about six months after Enrique Pasquale returned to town, when a movement at the south end of the *Calle* caused Barclay to turn his head.

It was the middle of February, the coolest month of the year. During the winter months in Tecimal, siesta was more a habit than a necessity; temperatures were balmy rather than oppressive, and many of the town's inhabitants, especially women with small children, idly wandered around Tecimal at this time of day simply to pass the time. On this particular afternoon, Señora Pasquale had evidently decided to go for such a walk with her three-month-old child strapped to her back.

Barclay watched as she made her way along the *Calle*, approaching the barber shop. Two women passed her on the opposite side of the street, but neither acknowledged the doctor's wife.

"What do you think?" Barclay asked Montoya, breaking the silence as the doctor's wife came closer.

Montoya was on the point of nodding off. Blinking himself awake he asked in confusion, "About what?"

"About Doctor Pasquale."

Montoya shrugged. "I don't think anything about him."

"But what would you do if you fell sick?"

"If I was sick? I suppose it depends how bad. If it was nothing serious, I'd probably go to the midwife, although her potions never seem to do much except give me the runs." He laughed quietly to himself. Almost the entire male population of Tecimal had had the

30

same experience. Most of them suspected her of harboring a secret hatred of men.

"But what if you were really sick?" persisted Barclay, his eyes still on the mother and the infant strapped to her back, no more than fifty meters away now.

"Then I'd go to Chiclahan, of course. Why?"

"Señora!" Barclay called.

The doctor's wife broke her stride and looked around in confusion. Barclay waved. "Here, Señora. Could you spare me a minute?"

She smiled, relieved perhaps that someone, even if it was only the Englishman, had at last acknowledged her existence. But when she reached the two men Barclay made no attempt to rise from his chair, so she was left standing awkwardly in front of him, her baby asleep in the carrier on her back, its head lolling to one side.

"My name is Barclay."

"Señora Pasquale," the doctor's wife bent a knee in greeting.

"And this is my friend Diego Montoya, the town barber."

The barber and the doctor's wife exchanged irresolute smiles.

"I'd like to ask you a couple of questions. Do you mind?"

She shrugged. Enrique had told her about the eccentric Englishman whom she saw sitting here at siesta every day. He was an author who had appeared in Tecimal many years ago. He had written one book, which at her husband's urging she had read; despite herself, she had been forced to concur that Señor Barclay was a brilliant writer. He was, so Enrique insisted, the only man in Tecimal who lived there by choice, a claim she did not take seriously since the same could be said of the doctor himself.

"How long have you been in Tecimal?" Barclay asked.

She shrugged. "Six months, señor."

"And in that time, how many patients has your husband seen?"

There was a pause. "One."

"Blanca Pasquale?" Barclay hazarded. "His aunt?"

She nodded.

"I see. And how much longer before your husband calls it a day?"

She shrugged again. "A month or two. Tecimal is not an expensive place to live, and we still have a little money left. But if something doesn't change soon we'll have to move to Chiclahan where there's work for my husband."

"If there's work for him there, why hasn't he gone already?"

31

A tinge of red appeared on her face, as if she were either embarrassed or angry. "Because, señor, these people need him. People here suffer unnecessarily. They don't seek treatment until a condition becomes too serious. And even then they are as likely to go to the midwife as they are to see a real doctor in Chiclahan."

"You're saying the midwife doesn't do a good job?"

She bit her lip and shook her head. "No, I didn't mean that. I'm sure she does a fine job of delivering babies. But she's simply unqualified to treat people who are seriously ill."

"I see."

Barclay pulled his hat down over his head, and the doctor's wife looked from Barclay to Montoya in confusion.

"Is that all?" she asked, befuddled.

Barclay grunted. Montoya smiled at her uncertainly but said nothing. After a few moments, the doctor's wife turned and walked angrily away.

That evening, Barclay vacated his seat at *El Presidente* early, and, in full view of the men gathered outside, walked the short distance to the doctor's house.

He knocked on the door.

The door was answered by the doctor himself. Enrique Pasquale was tall and lanky, and attired neatly in clothes that might have looked slightly shabby in Chiclahan, but which in Tecimal marked him as a prosperous man. He wore glasses that had a habit of slipping down his nose, which they promptly did when he saw the Englishman standing on the threshold. The doctor pushed the errant spectacles back into place.

"My name is Barclay. May I come in?"

The doctor smiled guardedly. "There is something wrong with you? You are ill?" He could note keep a note of hope from creeping into his voice.

"Not at all. But if you ever want to see anyone who is sick, I advise you to let me in."

Frowning, the doctor took a step backward to let Barclay enter. He closed the door behind the Englishman. "You want to come into my living room or into my office?"

"Neither, thank you. I'll come straight to the point. Your wife tells me you can stay only another month or two before you'll have to leave."

"My wife has no business discussing such matters with strangers."

"But you don't deny it?"

The doctor shook his head, causing his spectacles to slip down his nose. He took them off and held them in his hand. "Of course not. How can I? Apart from Mama, no one has come to see me in all the time I've been here. It's not as if they aren't sick. I see them when I go with my wife to the stores: red eyes, limps, people walking slowly, holding their stomachs, hands trembling. But I can't force myself on them, can I? What is it, Señor Barclay? Why won't they come to me?"

"You mean you really don't know?"

"Of course I don't."

"I'm surprised. I would have thought it was obvious, especially to a man trained in the art of logical deduction. It's because of Mass, Doctor Pasquale. You're the only man in town who doesn't go to Mass. Your wife, apart from Blanca, is the only woman. How can the people trust a man who doesn't attend Mass?"

The doctor looked incredulous. "But that's ridiculous...," he began.

Barclay interrupted. "I didn't say it was sensible, or intelligent. But that's the way it is. If you were to go to Mass this Sunday, I guarantee that within a week you'd be seeing half a dozen patients a day."

"But I can't do that."

"Why not?"

"It would be dishonest. It would go against everything I believe."

Barclay smiled a kind of half-secret smile, as if he were sharing a joke with himself. "And what exactly do you believe, Doctor Pasquale?"

The doctor drew himself up to his full, and not inconsiderable, height. "I believe in the dignity of mankind, Señor Barclay. I cannot believe in a God who permits the evil and suffering that pervades this Earth. And since there is no God to relieve that suffering, then the job falls on human shoulders."

"Such as yours?"

"Such as mine."

"Then if there is no God, whom would you offend by attending Mass?"

A flash of irritation crossed the doctor's face. "You try to trick me, señor. To attend Mass would be a lie and the act of a coward. I will not pretend to worship a God in whom I do not believe. It would be disingenuous to show my face at Mass; it would be no better than a confidence trick."

33

"Then you won't do it, even if it means you have to leave Tecimal?"
The doctor shook his head. "No."

"Pride, doctor, is a terrible thing. It has killed more people than greed, envy and lust combined. Think on that next time someone in Tecimal dies. Say to yourself, 'I could have saved that man, if only I had not been too proud to go to Mass.'"

The doctor looked at Barclay, bereft of words. He'd never thought of it that way.

"You see, doctor, things are not as simple as you think. You men of science are all the same. You like everything to be compartmentalized. Black and white. Good and evil. Right and wrong. But such decisions are too easy for the likes of men. That's why God gives us this kind of life. In this mortal life there is no black and there is no white. Decisions are never easy, and whichever way we choose to resolve a dilemma, we know that someone will get hurt.

"If you choose to go to Mass, you will hurt yourself. You will feel guilt, and you will have to live with the knowledge that you've acted out a lie. If you choose not to go to Mass, you will hurt the people of Tecimal.

"No, doctor. I can see in your face what you're going to do. You're going to go to Mass after all. I know what you're thinking: better to hurt myself than the people who need me. But that's no solution either. Don't you see — no, perhaps you don't, because you're still young — don't you see that if you compromise your beliefs by doing this, you will undermine the foundation of your entire being? Your beliefs are wrong, I have no doubt, but it's not for me to try to convince you of that. If you stay in Tecimal long enough, you will see that for yourself eventually.

"So I'll take the choice away from you. Come with me. Let's go for a drink."

"But I don't drink."

Barclay laughed delightedly and grabbed the doctor's arm.

"All the better. Maybe we can solve your problem a different way. Tonight, Doctor Pasquale, for the good of the people of Tecimal, who need you more than they can guess, you will drink. And you will drink. And you will drink. You'll drink so much that tomorrow you will regret this night as you have regretted no other night in your life. And tomorrow, the people of Tecimal will begin to allow you to help them."

34

And so it was.

The people who had refused to share their weaknesses with Doctor Pasquale, the straitlaced atheist from Chiclahan, those same people were more than ready to bare their very souls before Doctor Pasquale, the feisty, grinning toper who had finally slid to the floor of *El Presidente* unconscious at three o'clock in the morning.

Enrique Pasquale was now a valued member of the community, even though he and his family still did not attend Mass and he had never visited *El Presidente* a second time. He was regarded as an eccentric, but no longer as an outsider.

The doctor's consulting room was in his home, and, unlike doctors in more civilized parts of the world, he had never embraced the notion that sick people should choose the times of their ills to coincide with hours that suited him, so the front door of his house was always unlocked, ready to admit anyone in need of his help.

Barclay rang the doorbell. Enrique himself answered it, and his face broke into a ready smile when he saw who was standing on the threshold.

"Come in, come in," he waved Barclay inside, out of the waxing heat of the day.

He led his patient into the consulting room, and quickly set about examining Barclay's hand.

The room was a comfortable size, and boasted every modern medical convenience that Doctor Pasquale could buy, beg or borrow. Every visible surface was scrubbed clean. The windows were some of the few in the town that boasted screens. Doors had been installed horizontally at waist height around three walls to serve as counters. At the back of two of the makeshift counters was a collection of old plastic soda bottles, each with the top third removed and replaced by a linen cover kept in place by an elastic band. Every bottle was neatly labeled by hand: popsicle sticks; small dressings; needles; sutures — the paraphernalia of the medical profession neatly lined up, standing to attention as if for inspection.

The third counter was Doctor Enrique's pharmacopœia. The surface was divided into twenty or more small compartments, inside each of which was a collection of pill-bottles or tubes of ointment.

There was no ornamentation in the room; the only furniture was a table that the doctor used for writing notes and a trio of utilitarian chairs, arranged two-on-one. On one wall hung a clock, loudly ticking away the seconds.

"Good job you brought it in straight away," the doctor said as he cleaned out the wound and redressed it with a bandage taken from one of the soda bottles. "If you'd left it another day it might have become quite nasty. As it is, just rub some of this on it a couple of times a day for the next day or two and that should take care of it." He handed Barclay a small tube of ointment taken from his pharmacy. "The gringa has quite a bite, then?" he asked with a smile as he pushed his spectacles back into place.

"The gringa is a fool if she thinks she's going to get anything out of me," said Barclay. "Do you know what she's had the gall to do? She's invited me to dinner."

"Perhaps you should go. Dinner with a beautiful young woman? Not many men would turn down such a treat."

"And have my life dissected by a busy-body stranger? I'm happy the way I am, thank you, and the last thing I want or need is to have my routine disturbed."

Enrique looked at him skeptically. "Are you really? Are you really happy the way you are?"

"Of course I'm happy. I'm my own man, and how many people my age can say that? I have no wife to nag me, no children to tire me. I have my work, which keeps my mornings occupied; I have my friends and my books, which pass the afternoon and evening. And I have Isabella." He threw the doctor a rakish smile. "What is there not to be happy about? I don't have to get up in the morning if I don't want to. I don't owe anyone money. No one bothers me. Of course I'm happy."

Enrique emitted a wordless grunt, which might have been acquiescence, or might just as easily have been an expression of skepticism. "And there's always tequila," he suggested.

"And what's wrong with that?" Barclay stood to leave and pulled a small leather pouch from his pocket.

"Not yet," said Enrique. "I'm not finished. Tell me, Señor Barclay, do you still drink as much?"

"As much as what?" Barclay selected two bills and pressed them into the doctor's hand.

"You know what I mean. I've told you many times, Señor Barclay, what drinking will do to you. Do you intend to drink yourself to death?"

"I'm fine. As fit as I ever was, except for a touch of indigestion now and then."

"And your food? Do you eat regularly? Good meals?"

"I eat," Barclay shrugged. "You know how it is in summer. It's too hot. Now, if you've quite finished your interrogation, I'll be going. Thanks for fixing the hand."

"It's not the hand I worry about, Señor Barclay; it's you."

"I'll see myself out."

The doctor heard the sound of the front door closing behind his patient. For a long while he stared vacantly into space, until the sound of the clock striking nine woke him from his reverie.

An Appointment Unkept

Just as Tecimal boasted only one doctor, one barber and one bar, it had only one restaurant.

The *Casa de Food* was known by everyone in Tecimal simply as *José's*, after the man who owned it (although it was José's wife who did all the cooking and much of the washing up, and José's nubile seventeen-year-old daughter who generally waited on the tables). *José's* was hardly a restaurant of the type found in more-developed countries. It boasted no particular menu; neither was there any promise, either stated or implied, that food would be delivered within any fixed period of time after an order was placed. It was more a kind of place-to-eat-at-home-without-having-to-cook than a restaurant in any formal sense of the word.

Donna, however, had no way of knowing this. When she asked Señora Delgado if there was anywhere to eat in Tecimal, she was told simply *"José's."* On continued interrogation, Señora Delgado informed her that by *"José's,"* she actually meant the *Casa de Food*, and that the food there was always good. On the strength of this recommendation Donna had suggested the restaurant as a suitably neutral meeting place for Barclay and herself.

In her note, Donna had promised to stay out of Barclay's way all day, and this she accomplished by the simple expedient of staying in her room and alternating between rereading much of *The Condition of Love* and writing in her notebook her impressions — hardly, it has to be said, complimentary — of Barclay and the place in which he had chosen to live.

She ate lunch with Señora Delgado, who proved as irrepressible as always on any subject that she thought would be of interest to her exotic guest. By this means, Donna learned involuntarily of the doctor's lack of faith (which she silently admired), the saintliness of the town's priest (which she silently doubted), the laziness of the town's men (which she gladly affirmed) and the hardships of a woman's life in Tecimal (which she could all too easily believe).

The two women were interrupted halfway through lunch by the arrival of the señora's daughter. She was tall, young (nineteen or so, Donna guessed) and undeniably beautiful. She wore her hair long, so long that it almost reached her waist, and it was of the blackest jet that Donna had ever seen. Her lips were painted bright red, and there was a delicate touch of shadow around her eyes. Donna could not decide whether her long lashes were real. Her face was perfectly formed, and her body, whether seen in profile or from the front, had the shape that nine hundred and ninety nine girls out of a thousand lust after, but only one in a thousand possesses.

"Isabella," announced Señora Delgado, rising from the table to embrace her daughter and kiss her on the cheek.

"Hello, Momma."

Isabella flashed Donna a broad smile with teeth almost as white as those of the girl on the poster for *Cerveza de Chiclahan*.

Señora Delgado introduced Donna, and the two younger women embraced briefly. Isabella constructed a tortilla salad from fixings on the counter, then joined her mother and Donna at the table.

"I was just telling the señorita about life here in Tecimal," said Señora Delgado.

"Oh, that's boring," said Isabella. "Please, señorita, tell us about life in the United States. Is it true what they say, that everyone in America has a car and a telephone and a television?"

"It's true, more or less," said Donna, and before she quite knew how it had happened she found herself fielding a barrage of questions from Isabella about her homeland.

Afterwards, she stayed behind to help Señora Delgado wash the dishes while Isabella retired to her room "to rest", even though she had apparently only just woken.

When the dishes were finished, Donna returned to her room, where she remained for the rest of the afternoon alternately napping and reading.

39

She arrived at *José's* ten minutes before the appointed time. She had gone to considerable trouble to make herself look simultaneously businesslike and feminine. She wore the one dress she had brought to Tecimal: a thin sleeveless cotton print with a design of intertwined pastel-hued flowers on an eggshell background. Hanging from her shoulder was a leather purse, inside which was a Dictaphone with two spare tapes, as well as a small notebook and two pencils.

The only thing that distinguished *José's* from any other house was the faded sign above the door: *Casa de Food* in peeling, uneven letters. Donna hesitated, wondering whether she should knock before entering. Deciding against it, she pushed the door open and walked inside.

She was in a small room with five tables, around each of which were grouped five chairs. There was barely room to walk between the tables. An oscillating fan stood on a ledge in front of a window, moving from side to side in a stately manner and causing a barely perceptible draught to brush the fine golden hairs on Donna's arms every few seconds. There was no one in the room.

"Hello," Donna called.

There was a noise somewhere, and after a brief interval a door at the far end of the room opened and a girl, no more than ten years old, poked her head into the room. She stared at Donna with wide eyes, then called back into the depths of the house, in a voice filled with surprise, "Mama, it's the gringa."

The girl turned to regard Donna once more, and she continued to stare until she was brushed aside by a middle-aged, rounded woman.

"Señorita, you do us an honor," the woman said. "Please, take a seat," she gestured expansively, indicating that Donna had her choice of places.

Donna chose the table nearest the far corner. The woman hovered nearby, and the young girl held on to her mother's skirt, not taking her eyes off Donna.

"What would you like?" the woman asked.

Donna looked in vain for a menu. "I think I'll just have a glass of water to start. I'm waiting for someone. I'll order when he gets here."

The woman raised an eyebrow; then she bustled away, chivvying her child back into the depths of the house.

She returned a minute or two later, carrying a glass of water which, as Donna realized as soon as she tasted it, must have come directly from a faucet, for it was at room temperature and tasted brackish. She smiled politely in thanks, and the woman disappeared once more.

Donna waited patiently for nearly half an hour, every now and then summoning up the courage to take a sip of the water and then immediately regretting it. Every few minutes, someone — the child, her mother, or a pert young woman in her late teens — briefly opened the door at the far end of the room and peered momentarily at Donna before withdrawing once more.

At first, Donna was merely annoyed at Barclay. Then, as time passed and there was still no sign of him, she began to feel angry. It seemed unbelievable, but it gradually became all too obvious that Barclay had stood her up.

The front door opened, and a man walked in with his wife. They were well dressed: the woman wore a long dress patterned in geometrical black and red; the man wore a tie and slacks. Both smiled at Donna before seating themselves at the most distant of the tables.

The teenager reappeared, and the man and his wife promptly ordered a meal of beans, rice and pork stew without asking to see a menu. The girl looked at Donna inquisitively. Donna signaled that she was now ready to place her order.

"I'll have the same," Donna said, "and a glass of rosé if you have it."

The young waitress disappeared, to be replaced a few moments later by the woman, who, after greeting the couple at the other table, eased her way past the chairs to Donna's table.

"Excuse me," the woman said, "but you said you were expecting someone?"

"Yes, I was."

"Please, señorita, if you tell me who it is, I would be happy to tell Olivia to go around to his house and see if he's at home. I assume it is a man?"

"Yes, but no thank you. It's all right. I wouldn't want you to go to any trouble."

"It's no trouble. Tell me, is it Señor Barclay?"

So everyone knew.

Donna supposed she should hardly be surprised after the scene yesterday at *El Presidente*. She wondered what kinds of rumors were floating around Tecimal. She tried to explain.

"I'm a student and I'm trying to write a kind of biography of him for my thesis. I was hoping he'd come and let me interview him over dinner...." Her voice trailed off, unsure what else to say. Even to her it sounded distinctly thin.

The woman looked at her with ill-concealed skepticism. "Señor Barclay is usually at *El Presidente* by this time. I'll send Olivia with a message to remind him you're here."

Donna shook her head firmly. "No, thank you. If he's there, he'll be drinking. I want to talk to him when he's sober. Just get me my meal, please. I'll eat without him."

The woman went away, but after a few moments the man at the other table approached.

"May I join you for a moment?"

Donna shrugged. Her mind was occupied by Barclay. It was obvious that he was simply not going to have anything to do with her. She had wasted her time making the journey to Tecimal. She might as well give up and leave on the next bus.

The man sat at her table. He was in his late thirties, and obviously more well-to-do than most of the people she had seen in Tecimal. Now that she could observe him more closely, though, she saw that his clothes were far from new, as if he had once had more money than was now the case, or perhaps he had purchased his clothes second-hand. He wore glasses that slid down his nose as he sat. He stabbed at them with a forefinger and tilted his head backward slightly, to keep them from immediately repeating their short journey.

"I apologize for interrupting, but perhaps I can help. My name is Enrique Pasquale. I'm the local doctor." He smiled and extended a hand.

She shook it wordlessly, her mind on the wasted months of planning that had gone into this trip. She would have to begin her thesis from scratch, choosing a less interesting but altogether more accommodating subject. Her advisor's skepticism about Barclay as a thesis topic had been well founded.

The doctor interrupted her train of thought. "Señor Barclay came to see me today. You have quite a bite when you are angry, señorita."

His words forced her to pay attention. She looked at him properly for the first time. He returned her gaze evenly, still smiling.

She said, "I know I shouldn't have done it. I told him I was sorry. But I'm glad he came to see you. And surprised, too. I didn't think he would."

"He told me a little about you, but he didn't tell me your name...."

"Donna. I'm a graduate student in English literature at UCLA. Los Angeles. I wanted to write my thesis on Señor Barclay. He wrote a brilliant novel once, you know."

She paused, waiting for either agreement or dispute, not knowing which to expect, nor which she would prefer.

He nodded. "*The Condition of Love.* Yes, I know. My Mama... that is to say, the woman who brought me up — my own parents died when I was a child — anyway, my Mama made me read his book when I was a teenager. She told me, 'All of life is in this book. If you read only one novel in your entire life, this should be it.' She used to say that Tecimal is home to the most gifted writer in the world, but everyone else was too stupid to know it. You know the saying, señorita? The one about a prophet being without honor in his own country? Well, that's how my Mama always spoke of Señor Barclay. But he isn't just a great writer; he's also a truly great man. If it weren't for Señor Barclay, I would have been forced to leave Tecimal long ago."

"How so?" she asked, interested in spite of herself.

The doctor told her how Barclay had saved his almost stillborn practice. At the close of the story, Donna said dubiously, "That doesn't sound much like the Barclay I've met. He must have changed. Nowadays I don't think he'd go out of his way to help his own mother unless there was a drink in it for him.

"Anyway, I'm going to have to go home and find a more willing subject for my thesis. The man's impossible."

The doctor shook his head emphatically, sending his spectacles to the end of his nose once more.

"You misjudge him, señorita. And I'm afraid you give up much too easily. If you will forgive me my boldness, I have a suggestion. If I were you, I would eat my meal here, then go back to his house and wait for him there. When he comes home after his evening at *El Presidente*, tell him you won't leave until he agrees to talk to you. Tell him I told you to do this."

She shook her head. "He'd throw me out. Anyway, he's already caught me snooping around his house once. I don't think I'd dare do it again."

The doctor, whose smile had until now been firmly fixed in place, suddenly dissolved. He pushed his glasses back up his nose and leant forward, causing them instantly to slide down his nose again. He took them off and held them in his hand for the remainder of the conversation.

"May I share a confidence with you?" he asked in a low voice, although the only other person within earshot was his wife, watching from her table.

"Sure."

"Señor Barclay is not a well man. He drinks too much, far too much. Drink will kill him if he doesn't change his habits. I've been arguing with him for more than a year, but nothing I say seems to have any effect."

"I know the feeling."

"Anyway, Señor Barclay has fallen into a rut, and he is incapable of pulling himself out of it. He needs a distraction, something that will force him to stop and take stock of his situation. Only then is there a chance he'll realize where he's heading. I think you, señorita, might be that distraction. Señorita, if you leave Tecimal now, not only will you have to choose a new subject for your thesis, but you may be signing the death warrant of a great, but also a very lonely, man."

"You can't be serious."

"I am a doctor, señorita. I never joke about life and death. Unless Señor Barclay changes his ways, he will kill himself. You are his first, and probably his last, real hope. Señorita, Señor Barclay needs you. Please, won't you try to help him?"

She looked at Doctor Pasquale helplessly. He had placed her in an impossible position. She was more than half sure that the doctor was exaggerating the precariousness of Barclay's health for some unknown purpose of his own. But how could she refuse? Whatever she thought of the arrogant manner in which Barclay had treated her, she couldn't simply ignore what the doctor had said. If she were to leave now and it chanced that the doctor was right, she would never forgive herself.

"Of course," she heard herself saying.

The doctor nodded quickly several times, his face wreathed in smiles. "Good, good," he said, replacing his spectacles. This time, miraculously, they remained in place. "I thank you, señorita, from the bottom of my heart. Just go to his house and do not leave until he agrees to talk with you."

"All right. I won't. You talked me into it."

The doctor returned to his table, leaving Donna alone with her jumbled thoughts.

When she left *José's* an hour later, she turned without hesitation in the direction of the *Avenida La Guardia*.

She halted briefly outside Barclay's house. The sun had long since set, and the house was in darkness. From the house next door came the raised voices of an argument. She tried to ignore the quarrel and to concentrate instead on maintaining her fading resolve.

I have no choice, she told herself. *I gave my word.*

She knocked quietly, although she was sure no one was at home.

After waiting a decent interval, she pushed the door open and tiptoed inside. She called Barclay's name, quietly at first, but then more loudly. There was no response. Ignoring a pang of guilt, she entered Barclay's study and flicked the light switch.

The window became an impenetrable black rectangle, and it occurred to her that if Barclay were to come home now he would be able to see her from the street while she would have no warning of his arrival.

The room had not changed: the same papers were strewn over the desk; the same sheet was in the typewriter, its two altered sentences staring back at her; the same rows of books filled the bookcases.

She crossed to the shelves and began to read the spines. Almost all the books were fiction, mostly in English: modern, mainstream novels, most of them hardbacks. The books were arranged in alphabetical order of the author's last name, beginning with Richard Adams and concluding with Emile Zola. Some authors were represented by a single work, others by their entire corpus.

She pulled out a volume at random: Colleen McCullough's *The First Man in Rome*, which Donna had read a couple of summers earlier. Opening it to the first page, she was surprised to see the margins heavily packed with cramped annotations in red ink.

She flicked through the book. Almost no page was unscathed. In the text itself, words were crossed out and rearranged, punctuation altered. Here and there a word or phrase was circled and marked with an exclamation mark, and almost every page contained multiple annotations in the margins. Comments like "Impossible," or "but see page 276" abounded. Every now and then a phrase or even an entire paragraph was marked with a vertical line in the margin, alongside which might be written "Good," "V. good," or, as on a couple of pages, "Brilliant!"

She replaced the volume thoughtfully and withdrew another book: *Therapy*, by David Lodge. This book had been marked in exactly the same way. She selected two more volumes at random. They, too, were similarly marked.

Taking a step back, she did a quick calculation and arrived at the astonishing conclusion that the room contained more than two and a half thousand books; and apparently every one of them had been read and meticulously annotated by someone whose life gave every appearance of being rudderless and without purpose.

Her eyes fell on a copy of *The Condition of Love*, filed between *The Coral Island* and *The Wonderful Wizard of Oz*. Had Barclay, she wondered, annotated his own work?

She took down Barclay's book and opened it. There was an inscription on the flyleaf. In handwriting that she recognized from the annotations in the other books, she read:

> *To myself the reader,*
> *From myself the author.*

Underneath was a signature, the letters of Barclay's name carefully formed as if to ensure that there could be no mistake that it was truly Barclay who had signed it. After the signature came a date, more than thirty years before, shortly after publication.

She turned to the first page and was astonished at what she saw.

The first paragraph, the one that had entranced her when she had first read it as a senior in high school, so that she knew even before she reached its end that she was reading the words of a master, was crossed through by a series of deep parallel red lines. "Crap!" was scrawled savagely across the paragraph, so deeply that the paper was scored.

Every word in the second paragraph was either deleted, or rearranged, or replaced by some other word, making it all but impossible to read. She turned the page. The marks continued, but halfway down the second page, Barclay had scrawled, "This is the worst book I've ever read. I can't go on." The third page had no marks. She turned the page. Then again. She flicked through the entire book. The rest of the book was unmarked.

Slowly, a glimmering of understanding began to steal over her.

The First Book

It was past four o'clock in the morning when Donna finally lost the battle to keep her eyes open.

She had taken Barclay's copy of *The Condition of Love* from the shelves and ensconced herself in an armchair beside a reading light in the corner of the study.

Even though she had read the book at least a dozen times, and parts of it she could quote by heart, reading Barclay's own copy of the book in his own study was an epiphany to the twenty-three-year-old student.

She looked at the obliterated opening paragraph, then closed her eyes and recited the offending words from memory:

It was summer, and I was twenty one: a tall, gangly no-longer-a-youth, not-yet-a-man, silently desperate to find a way to return to the security of childhood; terrified that it had been stolen from me by an enemy whose attacks would never cease, until one day, tomorrow or the day after, I would awake to find myself old, weak and helpless, pleading with Time to summon his colleague Death to end the pointlessness of my existence.

Donna looked at the marks on the page and wondered exactly why Barclay had felt so strongly about his own words. What was signified by the damning "Crap!"? Was the observation directed at the words themselves, or at the pessimistic sentiment the words expressed — a sentiment that was so ably refuted by the four hundred and thirty pages that followed?

She moved to the next paragraph, which existed in two versions: the printed one, the published work of Barclay the author, and the one into which the printed version had been transformed by Barclay the reader. She compared the two versions and concluded that there was nothing to choose between them. They both said what needed to be said. They both hinted at the masterpiece to come.

She pressed on, and quickly reached the end of the annotations. None of them, in her judgement, made any difference to the impact of the first couple of pages. Leaving the red ink behind, she was soon absorbed in the story, so that she became oblivious to the passing of the hours until, around four o'clock and roughly a third of the way through the book, her eyelids began to droop.

She placed the book on a small table beside the chair, covering several dozen bleached rings left by the slopped contents of as many drinks; then she turned off all the lights, made herself as comfortable as possible, and went to sleep.

She was woken by the slam of a door.

Light was coming in at the window. She looked blearily at the doorway to the hall just in time to see Barclay shuffling past without looking into the study. He moved slowly, like an old man, and her momentary view of the vacant, pained look on his face suggested a hangover of depressing magnitude.

Her watch said ten past six. A soft groan escaped her lips.

From somewhere at the back of the house came the sounds of movement. Every instinct warned her to sneak out of the house without letting Barclay know she had been there. But then she remembered her conversation with the doctor. She had promised. She couldn't leave without talking to Barclay.

But, she argued with herself, she was in no fit state to talk to anyone. And neither, to judge from his brief appearance in the doorway, was Barclay. Much better to leave now and come back later. There was no reason why Barclay need ever know she had stayed the night.

Making no sound, she picked up Barclay's book and tip-toed to the bookcase. She was in the act of pushing the book back into its place when a voice grated from the doorway.

"What the hell do you think you're doing?"

She span around, a guilty flush on her face.

Barclay stepped into the room. He looked dreadful. In his tremulous hand he clasped a glass of transparent liquid. There were dark arcs under his eyes. His hair looked like it had not been combed for several days. His face was colorless and sere, the lines about his eyes, cheeks and lips exaggerated into trenches. He lifted the glass and emptied it.

He repeated his question.

"What the hell do you think you're doing?"

"I... I'm sorry." Her mind raced, trying desperately to think of something that would defuse the situation and put her less in the wrong.

"I didn't ask for an apology. I asked what the hell you think you're doing."

"Then I'm putting your book back where it belongs."

"Don't bother. It's sophomoric crap. Take it with you with my blessing. Now get the hell out of here."

Perhaps it was simply because she was tired and not thinking very clearly. Perhaps it was that she was fed up of Barclay and his assumption that he could order her around as he wished. Perhaps it was that some part of her was warning that if she acquiesced and did as Barclay suggested she would lose all chance of ever getting anything from him. Whatever the reason, something snapped. Donna pushed the book back into the bookcase, then turned to face him. Her eyes flared angrily.

"I will not. In the first place, it's not crap. In the second, you stood me up. In the third, I'm not leaving." Inspiration handed her an offensive weapon. "And in the fourth, where the hell were you all night?"

Barclay looked taken aback, a man who had prodded a worm and discovered a snake. He frowned into his glass.

"Get out," he said, not looking at her.

"No."

"I'll throw you out."

"In your state the only thing you could throw is up."

His frown deepened for a moment as he struggled to parse her words. A brief almost-smile flitted across his features before he rearranged them quickly into a mask of anger.

"We're not talking about me," he said. "This is my house and my study, and I didn't give you permission to be here."

"You're in no state to know whether you gave me permission or not."

"Will you stop changing the subject? Are you going to leave?"

"Yes."

He looked startled, as if he had leant against a door that had unexpectedly swung open.

"Yes, I'll leave," she continued, "just as soon as I've got what I came for."

"What the hell did you come for anyway? I wrote a book thirty years ago. It was excruciatingly bad. But the critics, in their myopic, ovine manner, couldn't rush to praise it quickly enough. In disgust I decided to turn my back on what passes for civilization and spend the rest of my life doing what I want to do. End of story. If you can make a thesis out of that, good luck to you. There's nothing more, so don't even bother to ask. Now, if you'll excuse me, I'm going back to *my* kitchen and pour myself a well-deserved drink. Incidentally and for what it's worth, you've ruined any chance of my getting any work done today; which makes two days in a row. Congratulations. Now goodbye, señorita. I trust you know that a bus leaves Tecimal in about four hours. I strongly suggest you be on it."

She glared at him, but said nothing.

"Are you just going to stand there?" he asked.

"No."

"Good. Don't slam the door on the way out."

"I'm going to go into the kitchen, where I shall determine whether by some miracle it contains anything edible. If so, I'll make us both breakfast."

"Like hell you...."

"And while I'm doing that, you're going to stay here and think about what you're going to tell me so I can use it in my thesis. For your information, Mister Barclay, I spent most of last night sitting here waiting for you to come back from wherever you were hiding yourself. Since I had nothing else to do, I started to read. You have over two thousand books in here, but guess which one I chose."

She took *The Condition of Love* from the bookcase, looked at the cover disparagingly for a moment, then threw it at Barclay.

Barclay made no effort to catch it and the book landed on the floor, open and face down. He looked at it stupidly.

"That's the book I chose, Barclay, and do you know why?"

A young, bland, too-perfect woman smiled up at Barclay from the cover of his book. He shook his head wordlessly.

"Because it's the best god-damned book in the room. Shit! You made me swear, and I only swear when I'm very, very angry. Out of my way, Barclay. I'm going to make us breakfast."

She swept past him and strode away toward the rear of the house.

She expected him to do something: run after her, scream at her, stalk angrily out of the house. She waited for whatever it was to happen; but instead, as she halted in the doorway of the kitchen, she heard only silence.

The state of the kitchen caused her to feel a despair as great as anything she had felt so far. The room was filthy. Dark, desiccated, unidentifiable scraps of what presumably had once been food littered the floor around the periphery of the room. The walls were a kind of greasy yellow; the smell of cooking oil hung heavily in the air. A pile of plates and dishes filled the sink and overflowed on to the countertop. Two flies, almost the first she had seen in Tecimal, were disturbed by her arrival and began to buzz noisily near a bowl of what appeared to be blackened fruit. She wrinkled her nose in disgust; then she set her face defiantly and got to work.

She opened all the cupboards, and found only cans of vegetables, spaghetti in tomato sauce and corned beef, augmented by half a dozen bottles of tequila in various degrees of emptiness. It was not until she opened the refrigerator that at last she felt a surge of hope. Inside were a dozen eggs, a block of cheese with only a veneer of mold, most of a bottle of milk, and even some vegetables that, although past their prime, could be rendered edible by the simple expedient of excising the bad parts and thoroughly cooking the remainder.

Donna was not a good cook, and when she finished even she knew that what she had produced was more like a mixture of scrambled eggs with corned beef and vegetables than the Spanish omelet she had intended. Still, the mixture was edible and that was the main thing. She divided the food evenly on to two plates she had rescued from the sink and washed.

She carried the breakfasts to the study.

Barclay was seated in the chair in which she had spent the night. He looked up as her shadow darkened the doorway. He was reading *The Condition of Love.*

"Breakfast," Donna said emphatically. "Do you want it here, or would you rather eat in the kitchen?"

Barclay closed the book and put it down on the table beside the chair. Getting up and crossing to Donna, he relieved her wordlessly of a plate and gestured for her to sit in the chair he had vacated.

She sat. For several seconds he looked at her with an unreadable expression; then, without saying a word, he sat at his desk, pushing the typewriter to one side to make room for the plate. Then he began to eat.

They ate without speaking. For a while after they had finished the silence continued, becoming increasingly awkward. Donna realized that Barclay was staring at her, and she tried to find somewhere else to look, but every few seconds she glanced back at him and saw that he was still watching her.

She waited, determined not to be the first to speak. The ungrateful pig had not even thanked her for breakfast.

He cleared his throat. She looked at him expectantly.

"Thank you," he said. "That was very good."

"You're welcome," she replied icily.

Silence fell once more, but only briefly. "You're wrong, you know," he said.

"What about?"

"*The Condition of Love*. It's not a great book. But...." He halted, as if he hoped that she would interrupt him. She remained silent, and after a few seconds he was forced to continue. "But I was wrong too. It's not that bad either. You know, I haven't even looked at it for twenty five years. I could never get that first paragraph out of my mind. It was so bad. I kept asking myself, how could I have written something so truly awful?"

"It's not bad. Without it the book wouldn't be the same."

Barclay shrugged. "It can't be changed now. Tell me, do you really want to write a thesis about me?"

"Yes."

She smiled, and for the first time she saw a reflection of her smile on Barclay's face.

She said, "I think *The Condition of Love* is the best book written in the past half century. I wanted to try to understand the man who could write something so powerful. But more than that, I wanted to try to understand why you've never written anything else. If a man can write so powerfully in his first novel, can you imagine what his second, or his fifth, or his tenth might be like?"

"Maybe he said everything he had to say in his first book."

She shook her head firmly. "No. Not Andrew Barclay. Not the man who wrote *The Condition of Love*. Not you." She pointed at the typewriter. "I'm right, aren't I? You've started a second book."

Barclay sighed, so wearily it was almost a groan. He gestured to the papers strewn around the desk. "You see these? These papers are six months' work." He gathered them into an untidy pile about an inch thick, then dropped them with a thud into the trash can.

Donna sucked in her breath through her teeth; but she said nothing.

"There is another book in me. I know that," said Barclay. "Although God knows I've despaired of finding it often enough. For more than twenty five years I've sat in this room almost every day, trying to find it. I'm not any closer now than I was when I started. Here, let me show you something."

He crossed to the bookcases. His finger ran along the spines until he reached the book he was looking for. He pulled it out and opened it to the first page. Handing it to Donna, he said, "Read the first paragraph." He regained his seat at the desk.

She glanced at the title: *The Heart of the Matter*, by Graham Greene. The paper of the first page was stained yellow with exposure. There was a single annotation in the margin: an exclamation mark running the height of the first paragraph. Flicking through the rest of the book, she saw that only the first page was yellowed, as if the book had been left open at that page for a long time. She noticed something else: only a few pages were marked with Barclay's annotations.

She began to read out loud, and as she did so, Barclay joined in, reciting the words from memory, just as she had recited Barclay's opening paragraph the night before.

"Wilson sat on the balcony of the Bedford Hotel," they began. Donna fell silent, and her eyes followed the words on the page as Barclay continued. "...with his bald pink knees thrust against the ironwork. It was Sunday and the Cathedral bell clanged for matins. On the other side of Bond Street, in the windows of the High School, sat the young Negresses in dark blue gym smocks engaged on the interminable task of trying to wave their wirespring hair. Wilson stroked his young moustache and dreamed, waiting for his gin-and-bitters."

Barclay stopped speaking and Donna looked up. On Barclay's face was a look of awe, as if he were a priest who had just recited the Institution.

He blinked, and seemed to remember where he was.

"It's the best opening paragraph ever written," he said matter-of-factly. "Greene once said that writing the beginning of a story was far harder, and much more important, than writing the end. He's absolutely right. The first paragraph sets the scene for everything that follows. That was what was wrong with *The Condition of Love*. That's what's been wrong with everything I've tried to write for the past twenty years. One day, though... one day I'll find the paragraph I've been searching for all this time. And once I've found it, the rest of the book will write itself."

He paused for a moment, then asked. "Are you going to catch that bus?"

She wondered what answer he expected, what answer he hoped for. She shook her head.

"No."

"Then tomorrow morning be here at nine o'clock sharp. Bring some warm clothes."

"Why? It'll be as hot tomorrow as it is today."

"You want to understand me? Then you must learn not to ask questions; just do as I say. I think you'd better leave now."

Donna opened her mouth to protest. Barely an hour ago she had almost given up hope of ever making progress with the pigheaded author, and now he seemed on the verge of opening up to her. She did not want to leave; she wanted to stay and ask him her questions before he could change his mind.

Instead she closed her mouth again and nodded obediently.

"Nine o'clock tomorrow morning. Warm clothes."

She got up to leave. He did not move from his seat behind the desk.

"I'll see you tomorrow, then," she said. He replied with a grunt.

Wondering if she would ever understand him, she left.

For a long time after she had gone, Barclay did not move. Then he leant forward and read the words on the paper in the typewriter. He pulled it out of the machine, crumpled it into a ball, and threw it on top of the other discards in the trash can.

Barclay

Donna decided that she was finally getting somewhere. Since arriving in Tecimal she had vacillated: sometimes she was optimistic that, having come this far, she was likely to achieve her objective; at other times it seemed that the whole venture was turning out to be nothing but a waste of time.

Until now, Barclay's actions had seemed to support the pessimistic outlook. Indeed, it seemed that he had gone out of his way to be as deliberately obstructionist as possible. But as Donna walked away from the faded pink house with the peeling shutters she felt a surge of hope that the hardest part was over, that Barclay at last realized that she was here simply to understand, and she had no intention of intruding. Tired though she was, her step was more sprightly than at any time since she had arrived in Tecimal.

She halted at the corner of the *Avenida La Guardia* and the *Calle de Generalissimo Javier Felipe Duarte*. Instead of immediately turning toward Señora Delgado's, she decided that this was a good opportunity to get to know Tecimal better. It would make good background for her thesis; and perhaps she might catch a glimmering of what had drawn Barclay to such a remote and backward place.

The *Calle* was almost deserted. It stretched the length of the town, perhaps half a mile, fading at both ends into the unpaved track that crossed the desert towards the mountains and Chiclahan in the north and the town of Mesada del Sul in the south. The *Avenida La Guardia* was on the eastern side of the *Calle*, somewhat north of the midway point. Ranged along the central portion of the *Calle* were Tecimal's stores. From the place where she was standing, Donna could see the faded façades of the hardware store, a combination post office and general store, a soda fountain, a tiny service station, and two clothing stores.

On her own side of the street was a small pharmacy that also sold candy and cigarettes, the barber's (with its two rocking chairs outside, now empty), a butcher and another general store. More distant was *El Presidente*, with its massive smiling señorita, permanently on the verge of drinking her oversized *Cerveza de Chiclahan*.

Despite the early hour, it was already hot. In another hour or two, the heat would be unbearable.

A woman came out of one of the clothing stores. She carried a small bag in one hand; with the other she clasped the hand of a small girl who was chattering animatedly and whose gait was a mixture of a jog and a skip as she hurried to keep up with her mother. Donna was too far away to hear what the girl was saying; her mother's distracted air was that of someone who was mentally running through a shopping list instead of listening to her daughter's observations. The young girl noticed Donna, and pointed excitedly. Donna could tell from the look on her face that she was telling her mother to look at the strange woman with the golden hair. The woman said something to the child and the pair disappeared into one of the general stores. As they did so, the child looked over her shoulder at Donna as if she were an odd and exotic species of never-before-seen animal.

A lanky yellow dog, perhaps the one Donna had seen soon after her arrival, padded along the far side of the *Calle*. It halted beside the clapboard façade of the post office and relieved itself, creating a dark patch of dampness and then moving away. Its head bounced metrically with its loping gait; as it passed, Donna could see the creature's ribs through its thin, matted fur.

She turned away and began to explore the rest of the town.

Apart from the concentration of stores at the mid point of the *Calle*, Tecimal comprised a collection of wooden and tin houses that became more and more rundown the farther they were from the stores. The only exception was the church, which stood near the southern edge of town in the center of a vacant halo of arid, dusty ground, as if the houses themselves were unclean and recognized that they must not approach such a sacred object.

The church was adobe, spotlessly whitewashed; its doors and windows were highlighted with geometrical designs painted in unfaded mazarine and sienna. The bell tower was the highest structure in Tecimal, perhaps forty five feet high, the bell inside glistening brightly. Apart from the tower, the church was squat; at some point in its history it had been inexpertly extended to include a manse: the only residence in Tecimal to sport a real garden, a splash of green that contrasted with the dusty ocher of the yards of the tin shacks on the other side of the dirt annulus.

Donna was looking at the church and the adjoining manse, luxurious by the standards of the rest of the town, thinking dark thoughts about the hypocrisy represented by the vacant land that separated the sacred buildings from the village they purported to serve, when a short, stout, dark-clad figure wearing a wide-brimmed hat stepped out of the manse. The figure made its way through the greenery and stepped into the bare halo of desert that protected the buildings from worldly contamination.

The priest (for that was who the figure undoubtedly was) spotted Donna and adjusted his course to pass close by. He carried a shopping bag; his gait was that of a man rather past his prime, and as he drew near she guessed that he was somewhere in his early sixties.

"Good morning, señorita."

He spoke in an oddly high register. Smiling widely, he exposed a row of teeth whiter than any she had seen since arriving in Tecimal — always excepting the smile of the woman on the *Cerveza de Chiclahan* poster outside *El Presidente*.

He doffed his hat, momentarily revealing a bald head and narrow crescent of white hair that reached from ear to ear around the back of his head. His face was pale and puffy. His words, despite the peculiar whininess of his voice, were slow and clear, either because he was a man used to speaking in public or perhaps because he was uncertain of Donna's Spanish.

She returned the priest's smile without enthusiasm. "Good morning, father."

"I hope you're enjoying your visit to Tecimal. If you will forgive me saying so, we don't get many visitors, so you are doubly welcome. Would you like to see inside the church? I was about to go shopping, but if you want to see inside, I'd be happy to postpone my chore and show you around."

Donna shook her head. "No, thank you. Perhaps some other time." Or perhaps not. "I was just out for a walk, that's all."

"You are in Tecimal to see Señor Barclay?"

Good grief; even the priest knew why she was here. "Yes."

"He is a good man." The priest said this in an oddly emphatic manner, as if challenging her to deny it.

She gave a slight shrug. "He certainly wrote a good book."

She began to edge away, trying to give the impression without actually saying so that she was late for an appointment.

"That was a long time ago, before he found himself. Now, if you will forgive me, I should do my shopping before it gets too hot."

The priest doffed his hat a second time; then he strode away, the swish of his soutane fading as he walked around the corner of a tin house and disappeared from view.

For some time Donna gazed at the place where he had disappeared, as she pondered the priest's odd statement. What did he mean by implying that Barclay had "found himself." As far as she could tell, Barclay was simply a defeated drunkard, trying desperately to recover some shred of the greatness that had once lain within him. Barclay certainly exhibited none of the peace she associated with the idea of "finding oneself."

A trickle of sweat tickled down her cleavage, interrupting her thoughts. With a shrug she turned and headed back to Señora Delgado's. On her arrival she was surprised to discover that a visitor was waiting for her. She had barely closed the door and felt with new appreciation the first sweet wave of conditioned air when Señora Delgado appeared in the hallway with Doctor Pasquale hovering behind her.

"Señorita," the señora said, "I'm glad you're back; the doctor has been waiting to talk with you." After this uncharacteristically brief speech, Señora Delgado slipped silently away, offering the doctor a deferential nod as she went.

Donna looked around uncertainly, wondering if they were supposed to talk here in the hallway where Señora Delgado would be able to overhear everything they said or whether she was supposed to take her visitor upstairs to her room. Before she could decide, the doctor spoke.

"Forgive me, señorita, but I wanted to talk with you again. I will take only a minute or two of your time."

"What is it? Is something the matter?"

"Not at all, señorita. I'm merely curious, that's all. When last we spoke, you promised to try to help Señor Barclay. I'm told you went to his house as we agreed. I'm curious to know what happened, that's all. Please understand, I'm not trying to pry. I just want to help him."

Donna exhaled loudly, drawing out a long sigh. Was it impossible to do anything in Tecimal without it being instantly known throughout the whole town? She wondered what the doctor had been told. That she had spent the night at Barclay's house? Was that what the priest thought as well?

"I don't know that there's anything I can do for him," she said coolly. "It's true: I went to see him last night. But he didn't come home until after sunrise. God only knows where he spent the night. Wherever it was, he was probably in a drunken stupor. He looked like hell when he came in, and as soon as he saw me he tried to throw me out."

The doctor sagged visibly. "So you are giving up," he said quietly, apparently speaking as much to himself as to Donna.

"Not yet."

The doctor straightened and a hopeful look appeared on his face as Donna continued, "The man's impossible. But I wouldn't let him throw me out without a fight. In the end he agreed to help me. He told me to be at his house tomorrow morning. He said to bring warm clothes, although I can't imagine why he thinks I'll need them: this place is hotter than LA. Do you have any idea what he might be planning?"

The doctor considered the question, then shook his head. "Not really. Unless he's planning to take you into the mountains."

The doctor shrugged. "Sorry. Anyway, I'm glad he's beginning to cooperate. I know how annoying he can be. He's the most stubborn man I've ever met. But remember, he's also very sick and you mustn't let him convince you otherwise. There's nothing I can do for him any more. He won't listen to me. But perhaps you'll be able to get through where I've failed."

"I don't know. But I'll try."

"That's all I can ask. I'll stop by and see you later in the week. Saturday, maybe. Thank you again."

The doctor let himself out. Donna turned and saw Señora Delgado standing in the doorway to the kitchen, where she must have overheard the entire conversation. She looked serious.

"Señorita, do you have a few minutes? Would you like something to drink? Iced tea, perhaps? I know how Americans like iced tea."

There was a pleading look in her eye and, although Donna was exhausted and not at all sure she was up to the demands of a conversation with the loquacious señora, she drew her features into a smile and followed her hostess into the kitchen.

Señora Delgado busied herself with the tea, keeping up a stream of chatter all the while as if she were afraid that, were she to cease talking, Donna would sneak out and escape upstairs.

Donna ignored the torrent, contributing an occasional nod and making sporadic grunts of encouragement while she pondered the events of the morning....

She realized that Señora Delgado had fallen silent. The señora was now seated opposite her, looking at her expectantly, apparently waiting for an answer. A glass of iced tea was in front of Donna, and a plate of small cookies sat in the middle of the table. The steady drone of the air conditioner, which she had not noticed while the señora had been speaking, seemed to fill the kitchen. A fly, its buzzing smothered by the sound of the air conditioner, alighted momentarily on one of the cookies. It took a couple of exploratory steps, then took to the air once more, zigzagging its way across the room and out the doorway that led to the rest of the house.

"I'm sorry," said Donna. "I was thinking of something else. Did you ask me a question?"

"I asked what you thought of Doctor Pasquale."

Donna was noncommittal. "He seems like a nice man. Concerned about Barclay." She sipped her tea; it was dark and strong and tasted uncharacteristically bitter. Señora Delgado, she noticed, was drinking coffee.

"Do you like the tea?" the señora asked. "I make it that way for Isabella."

"Yes, yes. It's good." Donna smiled and took another sip, trying to ignore the sharp taste of tannin at the back of her tongue.

"Help yourself to more. There's the pitcher." The señora pushed a ewer towards Donna, who dutifully topped up her glass.

"Doctor Pasquale is a good doctor," said the señora, "but he would make a poor priest, even if he did believe. Which, of course he does not. Perhaps a man can be a doctor or a priest, but not both; I do not know. Anyway, that's the way of things with Doctor Pasquale. He looks at Señor Barclay and sees only a man who drinks too much. He tells Señor Barclay to stop drinking, and is at a loss when his patient ignores him. I could not help overhearing; now he has tried to enlist your help in this misguided attempt of his. You realize, of course that the doctor is quite wrong?"

Donna tried to think of a polite way of disagreeing with the señora, but before she could think of what to say, she was astonished as the señora burst into laughter. It was quite some time before the middle-aged woman recovered herself. To mask her confusion, Donna took refuge in gulping down what remained in her glass, then she stood to leave.

"No, no! Stay, señorita. Please. I'm sorry. You must think me foolish, perhaps even a little *loco*, no?"

"I'm sorry. I'm tired. I'd like to go upstairs and rest for a while. Thank you for the tea."

"Please, señorita. This is important." All trace of laughter was gone. "You came to Tecimal to learn about Señor Barclay. Look at me a moment. I am more than forty, and in all my life I have known only one true friend. I would do anything for that friend. If I thought it would help him, I would long ago have told him to stop drinking. But it would do no good. The doctor means well, but he never stops to wonder *why* Señor Barclay drinks."

"So why does he drink?"

"Because he is a writer who cannot write. It's simple: he drinks because he is frustrated. Señorita, I am not an educated woman. I am not like you. The only thing I ever learned was how to please a man. I know that I talk too much. I realize that I'm not important. I was born in Tecimal, and I shall die here. I will never travel farther than Chiclahan. I can read only simple words, and I know there is much in this world that I will never understand. I don't understand why Señor Barclay wants to write another book, nor why he's unable to do so, but I do know it's his frustration that makes him drink."

The señora paused, then added with an odd certainty, "But Doctor Pasquale is quite wrong; the drink will not kill Señor Barclay. At least, that's what Señor Barclay believes."

"How can you be sure?"

Señora Delgado opened her mouth to speak, but then seemed to think better of it. She shook her head. "He has his reasons, and it's not for me to talk about them. He's sure, that's all."

"But how can he possibly know something like that? Doctor Pasquale says that Señor Barclay's liver is diseased. He says that unless Barclay stops drinking, it won't be long before his liver shuts down altogether."

The señora refused to be drawn. "I shouldn't have said anything. Maybe you'll find out for yourself tomorrow."

"Do you know where he's going to take me?"

"I've said too much. I mustn't say any more. But I do want to tell you something about Señor Barclay." The señora paused, gathering her thoughts. She popped a cookie into her mouth, washing it down with the last of her coffee. Donna took a cookie too. It was sweet and chewy, and tasted faintly of coconut. The señora indicated the pitcher, still half full of iced tea, and, too polite to refuse, Donna refilled her glass.

Donna cast her eyes around the kitchen while she waited for the señora to continue. The contrast between Señora's kitchen and Barclay's could not have been more stark. There was barely a speck of dirt to be seen. The walls gleamed with recent whitewash, and the only dishes and plates to be seen were stacked on the counter, either waiting to be put away in one of the cupboards or in readiness for the next meal. It was no wonder that the fly that had wandered in by accident a few minutes earlier had found no cause to remain.

Señora Delgado began abruptly. "When I discovered I was pregnant with Isabella, I thought it was the end of the world."

Barclay reread the paragraph he had just typed, marking the paper twice with a red pen, once to correct a spelling mistake and once to replace the word "revoke" with "rescind." He read it again and, satisfied, turned the platen to begin the next paragraph.

He reached out across his desk without looking, lifted his glass and put it to his lips. He looked at it in surprise when the merest dribble trickled into his mouth.

Outside it was hot. The word was too weak — perhaps "torrid" would have been better, A Spanish word came to him. *Infierno.* Inferno. August in Tecimal was a terrestrial hell. An inferno. Thirty one days of searing heat. Whole hours would pass when the only movement on the *Calle de Generalissimo Javier Felipe Duarte* was a stray animal crossing from one side to the other in search of shade. Even the normally incessant screams of children at play along the side streets was, for a few hours at the hottest part of the day, forcibly punctuated by siesta.

Now it was mid afternoon, and siesta was nearly over. The first of the men were returning to their stores. Any moment now the children would begin to leave their homes to take up their interrupted games of *fútbol* and tag.

Barclay pushed back his chair and stood; a trickle of sweat dribbled from his right armpit, slithered ticklingly down his bare torso, settling momentarily at the waistband of his shorts before being absorbed by the fabric. He crossed the room and closed the window. It would make the room even hotter, but it would keep the noise of the children out, allowing him to concentrate on his writing.

It was going well today for a change. He had been working for more than two hours, and in that time he had produced five paragraphs. Sometimes he wrote less than that in an entire week. With progress so rapid, he would keep going as long as he could today. He had foolishly promised his publisher that the second book would be finished three months ago. How could he have foreseen how bad the book would turn out to be? His first book had taken barely four months from start to finish; the second had taken eight years. Eight years! What was wrong with him?

He thought he had been finished nine months ago. But when he sat down to read what he had written, a fit of disappointed rage had seized him and he had burned the whole thing, telling John Adams that his only copy of the manuscript had been destroyed in a fire (leaving his publisher to reach the conclusion that the destruction was accidental). Adams had expressed his understanding and condolences, and willingly gave Barclay another six months to rewrite the book as best he could.

But things were going no better this time. The book Barclay was writing bore only a passing resemblance to the one he had wanted to write; the characters kept getting away from him, refusing to follow the outlines he had drawn for them. He stared blindly out the window, his thoughts far away; the disturbing possibility edged around a corner of his mind that perhaps there were no more books in him.

Two boys wearing cut-offs came racing around a corner in pursuit of a plastic soccer ball; the movement interrupted his musing. His train of thought broken, Barclay turned from the window and headed for the kitchen to refill his glass of water. The thought of something stronger stole into his mind, only to be suppressed. It was much too early for a drink, and in any case he knew better than to try to write after drinking.

Someone knocked on the front door, the sound barely audible over the water running into his glass. Turning the faucet off, he listened. The knocking came again, and Barclay wondered who his visitor could be. It was an odd time for someone to call unexpectedly, just after siesta on a Thursday afternoon.

Barclay was no less surprised when he saw the person standing on the threshold. Father Emilio greeted him with a smile that did little to disguise the anxiety that Barclay had seen written on the priest's face in the moment after he had opened the door and before his visitor had had time to adjust his features.

The two men had few physical characteristics in common. The priest was a decade older than Barclay, and while the writer still retained much of the leanness and vigor of youth in his wiry frame and carried only a few gray hairs in his abundant thatch, the priest was short and tended to embonpoint, and as he removed his wide-brimmed black hat he exposed a head surmounted by a narrow, backward-facing tiara of white hair.

"May I come in?" the priest asked in his reedy voice.

Barclay ushered Father Emilio to his study, where the priest settled into the armchair that Barclay used for reading in the evening. Barclay went briefly to the kitchen and returned with a glass of water for his visitor.

"I'll not waste any time," the priest said after taking the edge off his thirst while Barclay regained his seat behind the typewriter. "I'm worried about Consuela."

There were half a dozen Consuelas in Tecimal, but the priest did not need to elaborate; they both knew which Consuela he meant.

Barclay said nothing. After a few moments, the priest continued, his voice flat and unemotional, as if he were giving a rehearsed speech. "She came to me for confession this morning."

A frisson of guilt pricked Barclay. He had not been to confession for months now. He looked at Father Emilio, trying to discern whether he was expecting Barclay to provide an explanation of his absence, but the priest was looking at the bookshelves and he continued talking as if he had not realized that his mention of confession might disturb Barclay.

"Naturally, I must be circumspect about what was said. You understand that when I act as confessor, as in all my priestly duties, I cease to be a man and instead become a representative of God himself."

The priest turned to look at Barclay for confirmation, and Barclay dutifully inclined his head. That Christ's biquiddity — Man and Deity — was mirrored, however weakly, in the stout Father currently occupying his favorite chair was one of the lesser mysteries of the Church's teaching, and one Barclay found considerably easier to accept than some others.

Father Emilio scrutinized Barclay for several seconds as if, now that the moment was here, he needed a visual assurance that he was not making a mistake. Apparently he saw whatever he was looking for, for he continued, "You promise me before God that what I am about to say will go no further?"

Barclay raised a sardonic eyebrow. "You wish me to make a promise that you yourself are unable to keep?"

The priest's face broke into a wide smile. "Not for the first time, you convince me that you have missed your true calling, Señor Barclay. You should have been a priest. You see errors in my thinking that even I do not see."

"Perhaps, Father, but the question is a serious one. Consuela's predicament is apparently quite grave. So I need to be certain there's no misunderstanding between us."

"Consuela's predicament, as you call it, is sufficiently grave that I am unable to keep my promise not to break the seal of the confessional. It is because I am a man, and not only the representative of God, that my humanity must manifest itself by reaching out to help her. But you are quite right: it is unfair to ask you to bind yourself with a promise I am too weak to keep. Then let the responsibility rest on my shoulders, where it belongs. You are free to act as you wish once I have placed the situation before you. But first, I must ask you a question."

The priest paused, trying to think of some way of phrasing what he had to say without causing embarrassment to his host. He concluded that it was impossible. He said, "I trust you will believe me when I say that your answer to the question I am about to ask will go no further?"

"I can guess your question, Father. In reply I can tell you only that the child is probably not mine. However, I cannot be certain. If, when it is born, it is a healthy Caucasian pink and covered with fine, light hairs, I think we may safely conclude that I am mistaken. The probabilities, however, are against it."

"I am sorry, Señor Barclay; I had to know."

Barclay said nothing. Before Consuela had become pregnant, he had been a faithful visitor to Father Emilio's dark, overwarm confessional. The priest must have noticed his absence, and he could hardly be blamed for linking the two events. If there was a connection, however, it was more tenuous than simple cause and effect.

Father Emilio said, "You are her friend, though?"

Barclay thought about this for a while. "I'm not sure she would describe me as such. But if you are asking whether I can be relied on not to desert her, then yes, I suppose I am her friend."

"Good. Then I have come to the right man. Señor Barclay, I am worried about what Consuela might do. Last week she visited Chiclahan. It is the first time she has ever travelled so far. I am not at liberty to say what transpired there, but I can say that I'm afraid that in her desperation to rid herself of the child she may do harm to both the child and to herself."

"I'm sorry, Father; when you say 'harm' what exactly do you mean? As I said, I want there to be no possibility of misunderstanding."

"I mean I am afraid that in her current state of mind, she is liable to kill herself, Andrew."

Barclay's Christian name hung in the air as a testament to the seriousness of the priest's words. Priest and writer had known each other for five years, and this was the first time Father Emilio had used Barclay's Christian name.

"What do you want me to do?" asked Barclay.

"I want you to show her you are her friend. I want you to talk to her as only a friend could or would. I cannot talk to her in such a way, and even if I could she would not listen. She knows that to take her life would be to condemn her soul, but I would be a fool to believe that spiritual matters carry the same weight as the practical realities of daily life. Fear of damnation might cause her to pause before going through with it, but ultimately it would not be enough to deter her. People are not saved by fear, Señor Barclay, but by love. You understand what I'm asking you? I'm asking you to love her. I want you to give her a reason for carrying on."

The priest's words died away, and for a long time neither of them spoke. The priest watched Barclay as he wrestled with his thoughts, his eyes locked, unfocussed and unseeing, on the keys of the typewriter before him. Eventually, Barclay exhaled a deep, sonorous sigh.

"What exactly are you asking me to do, Father? To move in with her? To marry her? I couldn't do either of those things. I don't love her enough. Don't misunderstand me: I like her. I think Consuela is one of the most likeable people I've ever met. But...." Barclay's voice trailed off. How could he say what he wanted to say without sounding selfish?

"I'm not asking you to do anything in particular. I'm simply asking you to do what you can for her. Don't distance yourself from her as others are doing. Remember that she, like all of us, is simply a weak, purblind person struggling with a reality that threatens to overwhelm her, and she is in grave danger of making a deadly mistake with eternal consequences. Just be a friend to her, Señor Barclay, that's all I'm asking; just be a friend."

"*Greater love hath no man than this: that he lay down his life for his friends.* Friendship can be a terrible burden, Father; sometimes even a fatal one."

"Does that mean you refuse?"

Barclay shook his head slowly. "No, Father. I cannot promise to love, and I think you're mistaken if you believe that friendship can be manufactured. But I recognize that when the Creator filled me with the spark of life, he also settled on me a responsibility to others. I will do what I can to comfort Consuela, not because I want to, but because I must. You've handed me a bitter cup, but I have no right to push it away untasted. Our Lord took away that right when he stumbled through the streets laboring under the weight of the instrument of his death."

"I shall be praying for you, my son."

"Pray for Consuela, Father, not for me."

A smile creased the priest's face. "And that, Señor Barclay, convinces me more than ever that I've done the right thing by coming to see you." He pushed himself to his feet. "I shall see myself out."

As the priest was leaving the room, Barclay called out to him, causing him to halt momentarily in the doorway. "Father, I would like to confess. Would tomorrow at ten be all right?"

Father Emilio smiled widely. "Of course. I look forward to seeing you then."

The priest left the house. In the study, Barclay laid his fingers on the keys of the typewriter. But it was a long time before any words came.

Into the Mountains

Donna left Señora Delgado's house next morning at a quarter to nine. In her hand she carried the holdall that had accompanied her to Tecimal. The bag was lighter now, containing only a thin sweater (the only warm clothing she had brought with her) and a pair of jeans. As she turned left and began to walk down the *Calle* toward the *Avenida La Guardia*, her mouth was a taut line.

It was all Isabella's fault.

If Isabella had not arrived, uncharacteristically, to share breakfast with Donna and Señora Delgado, Donna would have gone to her appointment with a light, expectant heart, wondering what Barclay had planned. But since Isabella's revelation she could feel only a desperate disappointment in Barclay, a disappointment that more than offset the warmth engendered by Señora Delgado's story of how Barclay had helped her through her pregnancy.

If it weren't for her thesis, Donna would have stood him up. And if there had been a bus to Chiclahan today, she would surely have been on it. But there was no bus, and there was a thesis, so she compressed her lips more tightly and strode grimly down the *Calle*.

It was already hot. A black, large-eared mongrel lying on the opposite side of the *Calle* lifted its head from its forelegs to watch Donna's progress. Another dog, perhaps the same yellow, emaciated specimen she had seen before, trotted across the street fifty yards ahead and, without deigning so much as to glance in her direction, disappeared into the alley between two stores. From the tin roofs, heat ripples were already rising. Somewhere not far away a door slammed. A distant engine, which Donna had not noticed, suddenly stopped.

She halted at the corner of the *Avenida La Guardia*, summoning her strength for the ordeal to come. As her eyes wandered down the side road, ignoring the strays, the ruts, the discarded cans of Coca-Cola and *Cerveza de Chiclahan*, they were arrested by the sight of a Land Rover parked outside Barclay's house.

She approached the vehicle tentatively. It was old — although it was impossible to guess exactly how old, since cars did not rust in the dry air of Tecimal. The Land Rover was more than casually dented, and the passenger's window — on the left side of the car — which she thought at first was simply rolled down, proved on closer inspection to be completely absent. A crack ran across the center of the windshield on the driver's side. The entire vehicle was covered by a thin layer of ocher dust.

She walked around the vehicle, inspecting it. It had no license plates. There was a key in the ignition. On the rear seat was a small bag; in the back, she could see what looked like camping equipment. A horrible possibility occurred to her.

"Good morning," a voice called cheerily from the house, and she looked up to see Barclay striding towards her. Disconcerted, it was a moment before she realized why he looked different: he was smiling. "Got some warm clothes? Sling them in the back or stuff them behind your seat."

He got in and looked at her through the gap where the passenger window should have been. "Are you coming?"

She opened the door and jammed her holdall into the narrow space behind the passenger seat.

"The seat belts don't work. Don't even bother trying," said Barclay.

The moment she was seated, even before she had closed the door, Barclay turned the key in the ignition; the motor came to life instantly. He depressed the throttle a couple of times, and the roar of the racing engine filled the car.

He rolled down his window and rested his elbow on the sill.

"All set?" He was still smiling.

"Aren't you even going to close the door?" Donna indicated Barclay's house, whose door stood slightly ajar.

"Why?" he asked with apparently genuine puzzlement; then, when she did not reply, he said, "All right, then; here we go."

He put the car in gear and, briefly touching the horn to clear the strays from his path, he made a U-turn and drove in a cloud of dust to the end of the street. He turned right on the *Calle*.

Donna, even though she could think of at least half a dozen things she wanted to say, bit her lip. Less than a minute later they passed the last of the shacks that marked the northern end of Tecimal. Barclay looked across at her, opened his mouth to speak, then apparently thought better of it. He shrugged to himself and attended to his driving.

None of the car's instruments worked. The odometer remained as stubbornly fixed on 51206 as the speedometer did on zero miles per hour. The gas gauge indicated that the tank was a little less than empty. The tachometer insisted that the motor was not running.

They drove northward, leaving a trail of dust that would have obscured the view in the mirrors had the Land Rover possessed any.

The road was bumpy, and the springs in Donna's seat seemed designed to accentuate every jolt. She wondered if Barclay was driving so quickly on purpose. She nearly asked him if he could slow down, or at least be a little more careful to avoid the largest bumps and potholes. But then she decided that that was probably exactly what he was waiting for, so she clamped her mouth even more tightly shut and vowed to herself that she would not be the first to break the silence.

After about half an hour, they reached a fork in the road. The main road continued to the right, whither, some hundred or so kilometers distant, lay Chiclahan. To the left was a narrow track, wide enough for only a single vehicle, although, since the road was merely a somewhat smoother portion of the surrounding desert, that hardly mattered. Barclay dropped down through two gears, wrenched the steering wheel to the left, and accelerated into top gear once more.

Ahead of them were the mountains that could be seen from Tecimal, *Las Montañas del Cielo*. Although they were called mountains, they were more like large hills: hills that were covered with a mantle of greenery that gave them an oddly ominous look from the scorching plain below. Most afternoons, clouds gathered around the mountains. Sometimes in the evening it was possible to see lightning playing around the upper slopes. Now it was mid morning, and the first faint wisps of cloud were just beginning to appear above them.

Still Barclay drove on in silence.

70

The road narrowed even more, and gradually they began to climb. The barren desert landscape of rocks and cactus began to be supplemented with occasional bushes. Soon these were joined by stunted trees. For the first time, the road became an obvious track, a brown swath where little vegetation grew. The air was noticeably cooler.

They rounded a corner and without warning Barclay braked. The Land Rover skidded to a halt. A cloud of dust briefly enveloped the car, coming in through the open windows. Donna coughed. When she recovered (Barclay did nothing to help) she saw that they had stopped perhaps a quarter of the way up the side of one of the mountains. The ground fell away steeply, giving Donna a spectacular view of the lower slopes of the mountain and the desert through which they had been driving. In the distance, shimmering through the heat haze, lay the reddish-gray cluster that was Tecimal.

She looked interrogatively at Barclay.

"Lunch time," he said, the first words either of them had spoken since leaving Tecimal.

He got out and removed a paper bag from the rear of the Land Rover. From this he extracted a sandwich, which he began to munch while he looked out over the desert toward Tecimal.

"What about me? You didn't tell me to bring anything to eat," said Donna accusingly.

He tipped the open bag toward her, allowing her to see inside.

"I made some for you as well. And I brought beer if you want it."

She got out of the car, making no attempt to hide her displeasure, and took the remaining sandwich from the bag.

The "sandwich" was simply a thick layer of meat stuck between a pair of even thicker slices of dark bread. She looked at the meat suspiciously.

"What is it?" she asked.

"The butcher called it beef."

Donna made a dubious moue.

"Take it or leave it," Barclay said. "I recommend that you take it."

She bit off a small piece of meat and chewed it cautiously. It was unlike any beef she had ever tasted.

"I'll get the beers," said Barclay, finishing off his sandwich with apparent relish. "It'll help take the taste away. Go sit over there; I'll be with you in a minute."

"You're sure this is beef?"

71

"Like I said, that's what the butcher said."

Nibbling thoughtfully, she made her way to the place Barclay had indicated. It was a small grassy area with short evergreens on both sides overlooking the desert in the direction of Tecimal. Donna sat with her back against a tree. A cooling breeze wafted gently up the slopes, and a hawk rode the currents above her head. Apart from the soft sussuration of the trees, the silence was complete.

Looking at the distant, heat-hazed town, Donna was surprised by a sudden feeling that, despite the ill-mannered company and the maybe-beef sandwich, the moment was one that would remain with her forever.

Barclay walked across from the Land Rover and deftly opened two cans of *Cerveza de Chiclahan*. He handed one to her.

She took a hesitant swig and grimaced at the taste of the warm, sweet liquid, which tasted like a diabolically inspired cross between Coca Cola and Bud Lite.

Barclay downed half his beer with apparent enjoyment, then took a hard boiled egg from the bag that had held the sandwiches and began to peel it.

"There's an egg for you as well," he said. A minute later he added, "I brought enough food for two days. We won't be getting back to Tecimal until tomorrow evening."

He said it as if it were a matter of no import. Donna was about to bite into her egg, but she stopped and looked at him in horror.

"You don't mean we're going to be away overnight?"

The meaning of the gear in the back of the Land Rover was now abundantly clear. She had been right to worry.

Barclay looked at distant Tecimal as he replied. "Unless you can think of some way of leaving today and getting back tomorrow evening without being away overnight, yes, that's exactly what I mean."

Donna scrambled to her feet and stared at him. Her face was flushed with anger. She stabbed in the air, pointing at the distant town with the hand in which she still grasped the egg.

"This has gone far enough, and it stops right now. I don't know what you think you're doing, but we're not going any farther. You're going to take me back to Tecimal. You had no business dragging me out here without telling me we would be away overnight. If you think I'm going to... well, if you think I'm that kind of woman you can just think again. We're not all Isabellas, you know."

He arched an eyebrow at her and unconcernedly finished his egg in silence. When the last of it had disappeared, he took a long draft of beer. Then he contemplated the can, rotating it in his hand.

"You know," he said, addressing the can, "you're a real pain in the neck. Are all American women as much trouble as you?" He lifted his face to look at her; she searched his steel-gray eyes for some sign that he was joking. She found none.

"Sit down," he said. "I won't bite."

She didn't move.

"Sit down, or do you intend to walk all the way back to Tecimal?"

She sat down.

"Let's get a couple of things straight," he said. "In the first place, you may be the prettiest package I've seen for a decade, but I wouldn't sleep with you if you were the last woman in the world."

"Why, you arrogant...."

"And in the second, I brought you up here for a very good reason that has nothing whatsoever to do with sex. I thought you wanted to understand me."

"I do, but...."

"Then stop jumping to conclusions and give me the benefit of the doubt. We came up here to see someone. We'll talk to her tomorrow, and after you've met her I think a lot of things will be clearer. In the meantime, I certainly don't plan to ravish you. Speaking of which, what the hell did you mean with your crack about Isabella? What exactly do you think you know about her?"

"Nothing. I shouldn't have said anything."

"Your delicate sense of morals is offended, is that it?"

She shrugged. "It's none of my business."

He smiled. "Quite right. I'm glad you've at least got enough sense to understand that much."

Donna opened her mouth, then closed it again. What was the point? The man was impossible.

Barclay's gaze floated out over the desert. Donna waited for him to say something more, but he seemed to think the matter closed. Finally, she could stand it no longer. "Is that it? You're just going to let the subject drop?"

He arched his eyebrows in surprise. "What subject? You mean Isabella? I thought we just agreed it was none of your business?"

"But... she's a... she's a *whore*. She told me so this morning. And you...."

His expression did not change. "She's a whore and I take advantage of her services?"

"You don't even bother to deny it." She sounded incredulous. "You use her."

"Why deny the truth?" He frowned. "I don't understand you. So Isabella is a whore and I sleep with her. I'd hardly call that *using* her. It's a mutually acceptable arrangement. And in any case, why should you care?"

She glowered back at him, then got up angrily. "I'm going back to the car. I'll wait for you there. You can finish my beer."

She stalked away in the direction of the Land Rover, her progress followed by Barclay's eyes, his face still creased in a frown.

He finished his own beer, then leisurely drank hers. He put the empties into the paper bag, then sat for a while, hugging his knees, looking out over the desert, enjoying the tranquility. For a while he watched the hawk ride the thermals. At length he stretched out on his back, his hands behind his head. He closed his eyes.

The sound of a car door slamming woke him with a start. Turning his head, he opened one eye. Donna was striding toward him, her fury obvious.

"No bloody peace," he said to himself, just loud enough for her to hear. Opening the other eye, he wearily raised himself, supporting his weight on one arm.

"What is it now?" he asked equably.

"Are you just going to lie there and sleep all afternoon?"

"No," he declared, adding *sotto voce*, "it doesn't seem like you're going to give me the chance."

He dragged himself to his feet and dusted himself off.

A shadow crossed them and they both looked up to see that the sky was now more than half covered with an expanding mass of dark clouds. The afternoon's rainstorm would begin before long.

"Time to be moving," Barclay said.

He strode quickly away towards the Land Rover. Seething, Donna followed.

They had been driving for about half an hour when the rain began. Barclay rolled up his window, leaving only a crack, but Donna was quickly soaked by the rain that came in through the missing window on her side of the car. She complained to Barclay, who was having a difficult time peering through the cracked glass of the windshield (the windshield wipers were no more functional than the instrument panel) and trying to navigate the rivulets and potholes in the road.

"Can't you stop and find something to cover this window?" asked Donna. "I'm getting soaked."

Barclay glanced at her, and the right wheel of the Land Rover landed with a heavy splash in a pothole, nearly spinning the steering wheel out of his hand. He regained control and said, keeping his eyes firmly on the road. "If I stop, we'll get stuck in the mud and we won't get out till morning. If you were any other woman of my acquaintance, I'd tell you to take off your blouse and use that to cover the window. But since that would doubtless offend your delicate American sensibilities, I have no advice to offer."

Donna harrumphed in disgust, but she could think of no reply. After they had gone another half mile or so, they turned a corner and the rain began to come straight in through the missing window, striking Donna on the side of her face. She looked helplessly at Barclay, then grimly began to unbutton her blouse.

"Don't you dare look."

"In case you haven't noticed," he said, his eyes never wavering from the road, "I've got other things to occupy me."

She finished removing her blouse, and contrived to wedge it so that it covered the window. She leaned back in the seat, her hands folded across her breasts, wishing that she had chosen something other than the skimpy pink bra she had put on without thought that morning.

"You look at me and I'll never talk to you again," she said.

"Is that a promise?" Barclay said, eyes still on the road.

"Just drive, and don't you dare look at me."

"No, ma'am. The thought never crossed my mind." A smile creased Barclay's face, but his eyes remained locked on the road ahead.

The storm did not last long. After about three quarters of an hour, the sky lightened, and the rain eased. Donna removed her blouse from the window, but it was so sodden that she immediately reconsidered her intention to put it on again. "Can you stop now?" she asked. "I'd like to get my sweater out of my bag."

"In a minute," Barclay replied, and after they had gone another half mile or so, he brought the vehicle to a halt.

"I suppose you want me to close my eyes?" he said with a smile, looking directly ahead.

"If it wouldn't be too much trouble."

He shrugged, and ostentatiously closed his eyes before turning toward her. "You realize, of course, that if I were to write this scene into my book, the publisher would want me to remove it on the grounds of implausibility."

Without dignifying his observation with a reply, she clambered into the back of the vehicle and retrieved her bag, from which she extracted her sweater and quickly put it on.

"All right now. You can look."

He opened his eyes. "You know, señorita, this may come as a shock to you, but I have seen a woman's breasts before."

"I'm not one of your whores."

The smile disappeared from Barclay's face. "May I say something?"

"Sure. What?"

He spoke softly, although it was obvious he was angry. "You're making a mistake. Two mistakes. You think I'm something the cat brought in because I sleep with Isabella, and you think she's something even worse because she's a whore. No, wait, don't interrupt. I won't try to defend myself, not because I can't but simply because it's not worth the effort. But I have to say something on Isabella's behalf.

"You obviously think there's something indecent, maybe even something subversive, about Isabella being a prostitute. But you're not in the United bloody States now. You're not even in Chiclahan. Tecimal couldn't survive without a few women like Isabella. She provides a service, not just to the men of the town, but to the women as well. What do you think the men are supposed to do when their wives tire of sex, or are not as compliant as they might be?

"It's no good looking shocked. Isabella earns a good living by the standards of Tecimal. And so she should. She's good at what she does. She's a professional. Just as much a professional as was her mother. Oh, don't look so surprised. Don't tell me you hadn't worked that out. You don't see any sign of a Señor Delgado around the house, do you? Señora Delgado was plain Consuela when I first came to Tecimal, and she was almost as good at her job as is Isabella."

Donna covered her ears. "Don't tell me. I don't want to know." She raised her voice to drown out Barclay's words..

Barclay gently pried her hands from her ears. "All right, I won't say much more. But please, don't look down on us because we're different here. Tecimal isn't Los Angeles. Tecimal is Tecimal: an impoverished town, most of whose inhabitants live barely above subsistence level. The only ways of escape for most of the men are in *El Presidente* and the arms of Isabella and others like her. For women, *El Presidente* and Isabella provide respite, places where their men can go and place demands on others instead of their wives for a while. By all means come and stay with us. Observe us. Write about us if you must. But don't judge us. Instead try to understand us. Please."

She looked into his slate eyes. "You mean that, don't you? You really care about these people. You think of yourself as one of them, don't you?"

He shook his head. "No. I say 'we' and 'us', but I don't really mean it. I can't. They were born to this life. They know no other, and realistically they have no way of escaping if they want to. I choose to live in Tecimal, but the truth is that I could leave in a moment if I ever wanted to. I live cheaply and try to blend in, but I'm far, far richer than any of them will ever be. I will never have to worry about my next meal. Or," he added with a smile, "my next drink."

"But why? What made you choose a place like Tecimal? Surely you could have chosen to live almost anywhere?"

"True. But then I wouldn't have understood."

"Understood what? What it's like to be poor?"

"No. What it's like to be human. Don't you go to church?"

The question took her by surprise and she shook her head uncertainly.

He seemed to find her answer as unexpected as she had found the question. "Then perhaps you should. You might learn something that surprises you. When God chose to walk the Earth, He could have done so as a king, or a governor, or a general, or an emperor. After all, He's God, right? He can do whatever He wants. But He chose to come as a poor man, the son of a carpenter. And as He travelled the countryside, with blistered feet and tired limbs, who were His chosen companions? Not princes; not kings; not rich and powerful men — although they sometimes came to Him and often went away shaking their heads in dismay at His message.

"No. He chose for His friends tax collectors and prostitutes. Most of His disciples were impoverished fishermen. Why do you think He chose to come in such a fashion, Donna?"

Uncomfortable at the sudden religious turn in the conversation, Donna said, "I don't know. I've never really thought about it. I'm not even sure any of it's true."

"As for its truth, it's not my job to convince you of that. Just assume it for the benefit of argument.... I think He came as a poor, wandering Jew because it was important for Him to truly experience life as a man. And that meant He had to spend time with the downtrodden and the powerless, the ones whom civilized society looked down on. That was the only way He could truly understand. Don't you think there's a message there for all of us?"

"But surely, after thirty years here, you...."

"I understand enough? Perhaps. Perhaps not. In any case, I couldn't leave Tecimal now. This is where my friends are. And I'm not a well man, Donna. Doctor Pasquale tells me my liver is deteriorating. One day it'll decide it's taken enough punishment."

"Yes, he told me."

Barclay smiled. "I thought so. He's told everyone else, and perhaps he thought a pretty young gringa student might succeed where everyone else has failed."

"Then you know how worried he is about you. He says your drinking is killing you. Perhaps if you were to stop drinking so much...?"

"If, if, if. Yes, if I were to stop drinking, maybe I would live a little longer. But I'm not God. I'm just a man, Donna. And men are weak. I can't stop drinking. Even if I could, perhaps it's too late; the damage has probably been done."

"But if it's as bad as that, you could have a liver transplant."

"In Tecimal?" He smiled wryly.

"No, of course not. But in the States. Or back home in Britain...."

He shook his head. "No, Donna, you still don't understand. I couldn't possibly do that, because no one else in Tecimal could hope for a liver transplant if they were in my condition. And in any case what's the point? Why should I expect the world to give a new liver to a man who has spent half his life willfully destroying his own? Give it instead to someone young, someone who has done nothing to deserve his fate."

"I'm sorry," she said. "Is it really that bad?"

He shrugged. "Who knows? I may have ten years left. Anyway, as you'll discover tomorrow, I know my time isn't up yet."

"How so?"

"You'll find out tomorrow."

"You can't be sure. Doctor Pasquale doesn't seem to think you'll live...." Her voice tailed off. She couldn't finish the sentence.

"I can be sure."

"I don't understand."

"Tomorrow. You'll see."

And Barclay refused to discuss the matter further.

He started the car, and they set off down the track. They were silent, as they had been all day, but now the silence had a different quality. Instead of simmering with anger, Donna was wondering if she had misjudged the man seated beside her. He was certainly much more complicated than she had imagined. And how could he be so certain about his future? How could anyone be that certain?

She wondered if she would really learn the answer tomorrow.

Xloxratl

The Land Rover bumped to a halt as the sun fell quickly toward the horizon. The headlights, as Barclay diffidently explained, did not work.

They had driven through a pass and were now on the far side of the mountains, out of sight of Tecimal. On this side, the trees grew taller and thicker. It was difficult to see much of the desert through the close-packed boskage. In the distance, it was just possible to make out the grayish smudge that marked Chiclahan.

Barclay pitched the tent on a flat, grassy area. As he worked, Donna's doubts began to resurface: there was no sign of a second tent. But she said nothing and was glad she had kept her thoughts to herself when Barclay pulled a sleeping bag from the back of the Land Rover and handed it to her saying, "Here. This is for you. I'm sorry it's not very clean. Don't use it if you don't want to. Anyway, the tent's yours."

"But what about you?"

"It doesn't usually get too cold at this time of year. I'll sleep in the open. If it gets too chilly, I'll get into the car."

"You're sure?"

"I'm sure."

"All right. Thank you."

With a smile he said, "You may decide that your thanks were premature after you've had a good look at that sleeping bag. I'll make the fire now."

While she arranged herself in the tent — the sleeping bag was not as bad as he'd implied, although it could have done with a wash

— he went in search of firewood. He proved adept at starting the fire and it was not long before they were eating a supper of canned beans and sweet potatoes, washed down with the ubiquitous *Cerveza de Chiclahan*.

After the meal they doused the fire, and Donna retreated to the tent. For a long while she lay in her underwear inside the sleeping bag, listening to the sounds outside the tent, thinking about the puzzle that was her companion. Gradually, her breathing became shallow. She slept.

She woke with the dawn. In the trees, birds greeted the new day with an ill-tuned chorus of twitterings, chirps and songs. She heard Barclay walking past, and smiled to herself at the sound of a stream of liquid spattering against the trunk of a tree. The sharp *zzzwp* of a zipper, then more footsteps. She waited a decent interval, then noisily extracted herself from the sleeping bag. She paused, sniffing the air inside the tent, and then herself; she wrinkled her nose at the smell that was coming from her body.

"We'd better get moving," called Barclay from somewhere over near the Land Rover, "otherwise we won't get back before dark."

"Coming," she called, quickly pulling on her spare pair of jeans and the wrinkled blouse that had protected her from the rain the day before.

Barclay was waiting outside. "Here's some breakfast." He thrust a paper bag at her. "You eat and I'll strike the tent."

She looked inside the bag. It contained a sandwich, a hard-boiled egg, and a bottle of *Cerveza de Chiclahan*. Culinary imagination was obviously not Barclay's strong point. She pulled a face, but Barclay was too busy pulling stakes out of the ground to notice.

She managed to eat the sandwich (though she was more certain than ever that the "beef" came from no cow) and the egg, but she could not face the beer so early in the day. Barclay gladly took it from her and drained the bottle, then indicated that they should get into the Land Rover.

"Where are we going?" Donna asked, without any real hope that he would tell her.

"You'll see when we get there. Shouldn't be long. Luckily the trip back down should be much faster. We should be able to stay an hour or two and still get back before dark."

She had to be satisfied with that, for Barclay refused to say any more.

Like yesterday, they drove in silence, although there was no longer the tension between them that there had been. Donna's head was full of questions, but she restrained herself. There would be plenty of time for questions on the journey back to Tecimal, when perhaps her companion would be more forthcoming.

They drove for another hour. The track became increasingly over-grown and pitted and the ride became bumpier. By the time Barclay finally turned off the track and on to a wide path that was all but invisible among the trees, Donna was in danger of regurgitating her breakfast.

The path petered out after a hundred yards or so, debouching into a grassy clearing that hugged a denuded cliff. Barclay stopped the engine.

The clearing was perhaps a hundred feet across, but had evidently once been much larger, for the trees around the edge were noticeably shorter than those of the forest that surrounded them. A tin hut stood against the cliff, near the black entrance of a cave that was perhaps twice as high as a man and half again as wide. Here and there amongst the young trees were evidences of other huts, fallen down now, uninhabitable ruins.

But the one hut that remained was not uninhabited, for it boasted a cylindrical metal chimney from which a gray ribbon of smoke ventured into the still morning air.

Next to the hut, on the opposite side from the cave, was a well-tended vegetable garden. Donna saw corn, beans, potato and tomato plants, along with others that she did not recognize.

A goat was tethered to a post on the far side of the clearing. The goat was munching on grass in front of the cave, ignoring the presence of half a dozen chickens that pecked assiduously at the ground while issuing desultory clucks.

Donna turned to look at Barclay, who was regarding the clearing. A slight smile played around his mouth.

"Where are we?" she asked.

"Originally it was called *La Mina del Cielo*; then someone added *y de la Esperanza* to the name. So in English it's the Mine of the Sky and Hope. Or, perhaps more reasonably, Heaven and Hope. Rather a pretentious name I always think, although, to give it its due, it was, for a brief time around the turn of the century, the most prolific silver mine in the world. Unfortunately, the veins, although rich, were not numerous. In less than five years the mine was played out. Everyone left."

"So who lives here now?" She pointed at the hut.

"The person we've come to see."

He got out and removed a heavy-looking canvas bag from the trunk. Grunting with effort, he slung it over his shoulder as Donna disembarked.

"Follow me," he said, and began to walk across the clearing towards the tin hut.

The goat stopped eating and regarded them. It made a bleating sound, more like a sheep than a goat. Donna observed a second goat, which had been dozing some distance away and which now woke and got clumsily to its feet.

A burst of clucking came from the chickens, but it lasted only a moment before they returned to their pecking in front of the tunnel.

Approaching the hut, Donna saw that it had no door: there was simply a rectangular gap where the door should have been. The one window too was as empty as the passenger window of Barclay's Land Rover. She saw a movement in the shadows inside. A moment later, someone stepped out into the sunlight.

Donna could not tell whether the person was male or female. He, or she, was dressed in shapeless androgynous clothes that gave no clue to the sex of their wearer. On his — Donna tentatively assigned the figure the male sex — on his upper half, he wore a woolen jersey of a color somewhere between burgundy and filthy brown. The jersey was too large for him, but he wore the sleeves turned back so they would be out of the way of his hands. On his lower half he wore jeans, presumably once blue but now a color hardly any different from that of the sweater. He wore no shoes.

As they approached, Donna realized that he was a very small man — she wondered if the figure might really be female — standing no more than five feet high. All the exposed parts of his body were stained a deep walnut, almost the same color as his clothing. His hair was gray, and straggled down his shoulders without benefit of barrette or holder. He smiled, exposing a wide grin that featured only half a dozen randomly spaced brown teeth.

"Barclay," he said. His voice was scratchy and deep: a man's voice.

Barclay unlimbered the bag from his shoulders and let it fall to the ground with a thud. He opened it, and Donna saw that it was full of boxes and bags. Barclay began to lift them out one at a time for the tatterdemalion to see.

"Salt, and flour. A little sugar. Rice. There's a can of gasoline in the car, and some matches, of course."

"You are too kind, Barclay," the man croaked.

Barclay shrugged. It seemed to Donna that he was oddly embarrassed. "I'm sorry I'm a little early this year."

"I was expecting you."

Barclay smiled. "Of course. I should have known. But were you expecting...." He gestured towards Donna.

"I knew she would come one year."

The man turned to look at Donna. For a long moment, Donna looked directly into his face, and she felt a sudden unnerving nakedness — not just of her body, but of her very being. It was as if he were reading her entire life, even her most intimate thoughts.

The moment passed, and Donna was merely looking into the face of a very old man.

"Wizened" was the only word that Donna could think of to describe the impression given by the myriad lines that crevassed the man's face. Even his nose was covered with parallel wrinkles. She found herself wondering if the man's face were entirely the result of the natural aging process, or whether the lines were somehow self-inflicted. His lips were almost invisible, no more than thin accentuations of the walnut brown of his skin. His nose was large and flat, almost negroid. But most arresting of all were the man's eyes.

Donna had never seen such eyes before: the right eye was yellow, the left green. But such a yellow, and such a green. They looked like a cat's eyes, as if they would glow in the night with a preternatural light all their own. But this was not all. There was something stranger yet: his eyes moved independently of one another. The green eye looked at her face, unmoving, while the yellow eye roved up and down her body, as if it were assessing her according to some criteria entirely its own.

For a moment she thought that the green eye was unmoving because it was blind, but the thought had no sooner crossed her mind than it too began to move, darting around her face, its motions completely uncorrelated with those of its other-colored mate.

Donna realized that she was staring at the man; she looked away, embarrassed.

"What's your name?" the man asked.

"Donna."

"Barclay did not tell you about me." It was a statement rather than a question. He turned to Barclay. "You thought to shock her." Another statement.

His accent was difficult for her to understand, and if he had spoken any more quickly it would have been impossible. But he spoke slowly, as if he were unused to speaking his thoughts out loud and needed the time to remember how to form the words.

"Perhaps 'surprise' would be a better word," Barclay suggested, but the man shook his head and smiled his half-toothed smile.

"Kinder, perhaps, but not better; and certainly not as accurate. But I am forgetting my manners. Thank you for the provisions, Señor Barclay. They are sufficient. Please, bring them inside. Donna, you come as well. And do not mind me. Say and do whatever you wish. Barclay will confirm that I am a very difficult woman to shock."

A woman! Donna tried to make the mental adjustment, and discovered that it was surprisingly difficult. The woman turned and walked ahead of them into the tin hut. She even walked like a man.

"What's her name?" Donna asked in an urgent whisper, walking beside Barclay.

His reply was unhelpful: "She'll tell you when she wants you to know."

Donna halted in the doorway of the hut, her nostrils assaulted by a stinging acridity. For a moment she thought she was going to gag; but she managed to control the reflex, swallowing half a dozen times without breathing, then taking several quick, shallow breaths, barely inhaling.

The stink — which the old woman evidently did not notice — was a combination of smells: surely no one single scent could be so bad. Sweat and body odor combined with other, less identifiable scents to produce a farrago that threatened to bring tears to Donna's eyes.

Following the old woman, she noticed that even Barclay halted for a moment in the doorway to gain control of himself before dumping the sack of supplies in a corner.

The interior of the hut was a single room, perhaps twelve feet square. At the far end was a fire, the source of the smoke she had observed outside. The chimney was grossly inefficient: as much smoke seemed to hang inside the hut as went up the cylindrical tin chimney. The smoke added its own foul scent to the miasma; Donna wondered what the woman used for fuel: not just wood, that was certain.

Near the fire a paltry collection of pots and pans stood on the bare floor. Next to these were several small piles of fruit and vegetables, as well as perhaps two dozen small heaps of what looked like dried grasses and flowers. An assortment of ancient gardening tools leant against the wall near the door. Several piles of what looked like enormous clumps of animal fat were gathered in one corner. There was no sign of running water.

"You are not staying long?" the woman said to Barclay. This time she was asking a question.

"I want to get back before dark. The headlights on the car don't work."

The woman nodded. "You will give me a little time to prepare?"

"Of course. Do you want us to leave while you're working?"

"No; please stay."

"You're sure?"

"I'm always sure."

Throughout this obscure exchange, Donna observed that one of the woman's eyes was fixed on Barclay while the other wandered over the small piles of dried herbage near the fire. Now the woman moved to the drystuff and began a process of selecting from the piles, sometimes the tiniest of pinches, sometimes a handful, and adding them to one of the pots on the floor. After a couple of minutes, she handed the pot to Barclay.

Barclay waited, holding the pot, while she went through the same motions a second time, although this time Donna noticed that the woman was less careful with her measurements, and she chose, for the most part, from different piles, placing the herbs in a second pot.

"You know where the water is," the woman said as she handed this pot too to Barclay. "Enough for two in the first one, enough for one in the other."

Barclay turned to leave.

"I'm coming too," said Donna, partly because she had many questions she wanted to ask him, and partly because, as she freely admitted to herself, she was more than a little frightened at the prospect of being left alone with the old woman.

"Stay!" the woman barked, causing Donna to jump. "You go," she commanded Barclay, "and you stay."

It was impossible to argue with the woman. Barclay threw Donna an encouraging smile, then left. The woman brought both her eyes to bear on Donna. Donna swallowed nervously.

"Sit down," the woman commanded. Donna sat.

The woman seated herself, crossing her legs underneath her meager torso. One eye remained on Donna, the other fixed itself on the fire. In the firelight they became disturbingly chatoyant, changing colors from moment to moment as the flames flickered — but in such a way that the two eyes were never the same color.

Donna's discomfort must have been obvious. "Don't be anxious," the woman said. "I am merely an old woman; I can do you no harm even if I were to wish it, which I assure you I do not. In any case, you will not be here long."

Donna did not know what to say — so she said nothing.

The woman picked up a couple of grass stalks from the floor. She held them, one in each hand, in front of her face, an eye looking at each. "I am called Xloxratl," she said.

"Xloxratl," Donna repeated, trying to get her tongue around the strange name with its peculiar double click.

"It's an Indian name, given to me when I first became a woman. Before that I was known by another name, which I forgot long ago. Few know of my existence. Fewer still visit me. And only one gringo, your lover, Señor Barclay."

The old woman paused, giving Donna, either by accident or design, the opportunity to set her straight.

"I'm not his lover," she protested. "I can understand why you might assume that, but that's not the way it is. I'm trying to write a thesis on Señor Barclay. He wrote a great book once, and I'm trying to understand more about him."

"No person knows himself, so how can one person know another?"

Xloxratl carefully placed the two grasses on the ground in front of her, making an eleven on the ground.

Donna tried to think of a way to explain. "There's so much about Señor Barclay that's... different from other people. Most people, after they've written one great book, would immediately set out to write another. But Barclay's never produced anything else. At least," she amended, remembering the papers Barclay had stuffed into the trash can in his study, "he's never written anything else he wanted to have published." She paused. "You do know what a book is?"

87

While Donna was talking, Xloxratl had been manipulating the two grasses on the ground before her. She started by twining them around one another at their midpoint, so that they made a rough X. Then she snapped off one of the stalks, so that the X became a Y. She lifted her construction and held it in front of her face for several seconds. She turned it upside down. Ignoring Donna's question, she offered her the grass ⅄.

Uncertainly, Donna accepted it.

"Keep it; one day you will understand," said Xloxratl.

Donna looked at the peculiar object for several seconds before absentmindedly thanking Xloxratl and then awkwardly putting the odd gift in a pocket.

"He will write again," Xloxratl said.

"He will?"

"Of course. He has just been waiting for you. Ah, he is back. Señor Barclay, put them here, in the fire, then take a seat. They will not take long to boil."

Barclay did as he was bidden, placing the pots in the fire, then taking a seat on the floor next to Donna.

"Be quiet, now. Do not speak. Let your thoughts wander where they will," said Xloxratl in a voice that was suddenly quiet and soothing. Donna's eyes searched out Barclay's, but Barclay was staring at the floor, his eyes unfocussed, almost as if he were in a kind of trance.

Donna felt more and more uncomfortable and she began to wonder if the old woman was a shaman of some kind. She knew that if she were back in LA, she would laugh at the idea of being scared of such a person. But here, in the old woman's gloomy hut, with Barclay meekly doing as he was told and the woman looking at Donna with those oddly mismatched eyes, the atmosphere seemed to be filled with something strange and other-worldly.

After a while Xloxratl got to her feet and began to move around the hut, selecting a trio of small tin cups from the collection of pots and pans. She placed one on the ground in front of each of her visitors. The third she placed in front of where she had been sitting.

Donna was finding it extraordinarily difficult to keep her eyes open. The water in the pots was beginning to boil, and a sweet, heavy scent reminiscent of ether filled the air. She blinked several times, trying to stay awake. At her side, Barclay's head was nodding; his eyes were almost closed.

Somehow, Xloxratl managed to fill the cups without Donna noticing, for suddenly the woman was seated on the ground in front of her visitors, cradling a full cup in her hands.

"Drink," she said, suiting the action to the word.

Barclay's hands extended and lifted his cup. His actions were slow and automatic. His eyes, although open, were glazed. He put the cup to his lips and began to drink.

"Drink," the woman repeated, and Donna found herself echoing Barclay's movements. She placed her cup against her lips, tilted her head back, and opened her mouth to receive the liquid.

The tisane was sharp, bitter and hot. It attacked her mouth viciously, burning the back of her throat as it slid down her gullet; but she was no more capable of stopping drinking than she was of standing up and walking out of the hut. Whatever spell the shaman had cast held her completely in its grip. "Drink," Xloxratl had said, so Donna drank, not stopping until the cup was empty.

She lowered the cup and observed with a kind of detached surprise that her arms no longer obeyed her will. She tried to turn the empty cup upside down, but her hand refused to obey. As if in a dream, she watched as her hand (but was it really her hand? her hand had never behaved like this: her hand had never grown larger and smaller as she watched it) her hand gently lowered the cup to the ground and released it.

An hallucinogen and a sedative, she thought to herself. *That's the only magic shamans know: the magic of drugs.* She closed her eyes; but on the canvas of her eyelids there appeared a grotesque parody of Barclay, all head and no legs. He grinned maniacally at her. He was shouting something, but even though the shout was so loud that it hurt her ears, she could not understand what he was trying to tell her. She opened her eyes to banish the image.

Barclay was still seated on the ground next to her. He had drawn his knees up and wrapped his arms around them, and he was rocking slightly from side to side, moaning with his eyes closed. Donna tried to concentrate on Barclay's motion, trying to decide whether it was real or an illusion. Perhaps it was her head that was moving.

She became aware that someone was speaking to her. She looked around for the source of the sound and eventually her gaze settled on the old woman — who looked, she decided, more like a man than ever. Xloxratl had moved and was now seated no more than an arm's length away. Donna stared at the unpaired catlike eyes, which gazed back at her without blinking. They were open unnaturally wide, so that the yellowish-white of her rheumy eyeballs was visible all the way around the irises. The pupils were enormously dilated. Donna struggled without success to remember what that meant.

The woman spoke again. Donna concentrated, trying to understand what she was saying. Something had changed, but it took Donna a few moments to realize what it was: the woman was speaking English.

"You admire Barclay," the woman said.

Donna heard her own voice answering "Yes" without volition. Her voice sounded weak and distant, the way it sounded when she heard it played back on a tape recorder.

"He is a great writer," Xloxratl said.

"Yes. I think he may be the best writer alive."

"You came here to study him."

"Yes."

"And to learn from him?"

"Yes." But she hadn't told anyone that. That was her secret. Why was she admitting it to this strange woman whose eyes would not let her go?

"Because you are a writer as well." It was not a question.

"I try, but I'm not very good. I thought I might learn something from him."

"He will write another book." The woman's voice was flat and as unfocussed as her eyes. "But he needs your help."

"My help," Donna echoed, partly affirming that she had heard the old woman, partly asking what kind of help she could possibly give Barclay.

"He will give you a gift, the greatest gift he has to offer. It is up to you to use that gift wisely. It will be hard for you, but it is the only way. True greatness builds only on a foundation of failure, defeat and above all sadness. That is the way the gods have ordered this life."

Donna tried to frown to show her lack of understanding, but her muscles refused to obey. She continued to stare at the woman, but Xloxratl said no more. It seemed like a long time passed, many minutes, while the two of them sat motionless, looking at one another. The woman's unmatched eyes became Donna's universe, on which were superimposed other images, as if she were dreaming with her eyes open. As in a dream, the images were disjointed and made little sense.

But sometimes an image recurred that did make sense: Barclay in his study, gathering his papers and dropping them in his trash can.

At length, Donna became aware that she was cold and hungry. Even more slowly she realized that she was no longer sitting up, but was lying on the dirt floor of the hut. She blinked and tried to speak, but the most she could manage was a feeble groan. The groan was echoed, more strongly and in a cracked bass register, somewhere nearby.

After a while Barclay said, "Something to drink, please."

"There is a cup by your head," said Xloxratl. "Yours as well, señorita."

Donna blinked several times, and Barclay came slowly into focus. He had raised himself on one arm, and grasped a tin cup in his free hand. He downed the contents in a single gulp.

"There's more if you want it," the woman offered.

Donna saw a cup near her own head, and with infinite care, for her head was pounding as if from a severe hangover, she lifted it and sipped. The liquid inside tasted faintly of fruit, and was surprisingly refreshing. She discovered that she had emptied the cup.

"Here," the woman said, refilling Donna's cup from a large bowl.

Donna drank again. She and Barclay drained their cups several times before their thirsts were slaked. Whatever the liquid was, it did the trick. Donna felt much stronger now, and her headache had almost gone.

"It is time for you to leave," said Xloxratl. "Can you stand?"

Donna struggled to her feet. Her legs wobbled beneath her, but after a couple of uncertain moments they agreed to support her weight. She felt stronger with every second that passed.

Barclay too had risen to his feet. He seemed subdued, almost embarrassed as he said to Xloxratl, "Thank you. This is the last time I shall see you, then?"

The old woman gestured toward the bag of provisions that Barclay had brought. "Thank you for thinking of me, Señor Barclay. It was a kindness. And now I think your young friend has the beginning of understanding. I can do no more for her. The rest is up to you. Now you must go if you intend to reach Tecimal before nightfall."

Their goodbyes were subdued. Donna was trying to understand why Barclay had brought her to see the old shaman; Barclay was quiet and looked unusually grave, as if he had just visited a doctor who had given him only a short time to live.

Xloxratl did not see them off. Donna glanced back at the clearing as the Land Rover bounced away, and it looked no different from the way it had appeared when they had arrived: one goat nibbled at the grass in front of the mine entrance, the other was somewhere out of sight; the chickens pecked at the ground as enthusiastically as ever. The only difference she could see was that no smoke now escaped the chimney of the little hut. She frowned, realizing suddenly that the hut had seemed strangely cold as they left, as if the fire had gone out long ago.

The One Who Tells the Truth

Barclay drove as quickly as he dared. He was frowning, although whether from the concentration needed to drive or because of something to do with their visit to Xloxratl Donna could not decide.

Donna's emotions were confused and confusing. The more she thought about what had happened, the more angry she became. Barclay had wasted two entire days simply to show her a dessicated, reclusive shaman who had polluted their bodies with mind-altering drugs. As if drugs and the distortions they brought were the answer to anything.

Was Barclay nothing more than he seemed? Was he simply a washed-out has-been? A man who had just one great book in him, doomed to spend the rest of his life in search of inspiration that would never come? She tried to reject this conclusion, but it was the only explanation that fit the facts.

They had been driving for more than an hour before Donna broke the silence.

"So? What was that all about? Am I supposed to learn something about you from the fact that you apparently seek out the company of an androgynous shaman who slips you hallucinogenic liquids. Other, that is, than drawing the obvious conclusion that your grip on reality is not all it could be?"

"We'll talk about it when we get back to Tecimal. I can't explain and drive at the same time."

93

"What's to explain? That you've had writer's block for a quarter of a century and you think that that woman's drug-induced pseudo-magic might break it?"

Barclay took his eyes off the road momentarily to look at her. "Is that really what you think?"

"What else should I think? It's the truth, isn't it?"

"You're a stubborn daughter of a bitch, aren't you?"

"At least I know reality when I see it."

Barclay shook his head. "I'm not going to let you draw me into an argument now. We've got to get back before dark, and I don't have time to stop and defend myself even if I wanted to, which I'm not sure I do. If you're remotely interested, I'll explain when we get back to Tecimal."

Donna shrugged meaningfully, trying to indicate that she didn't care, but Barclay's eyes were no longer on her. She said, "All right," and lapsed back into silence.

They exchanged no more than a couple of dozen words the rest of the journey. The last hour was a race to reach Tecimal before darkness fell. The sun set while they were still nearly sixty kilometers from their destination, and Barclay drove the last half hour.with his foot alternately pressing the accelerator and the brake, the Land Rover spewing an enormous cloud of dust that trailed in their wake all the way back to the town.

They arrived just as twilight gave way to night. Barclay parked outside his house. The front door was slightly open, exactly as he had left it. He leaned back in his seat, wiped his brow with the back of his hand, and stretched his legs in front of him.

"Want a drink?" He looked at Donna for only the second time since they had left Xloxratl.

"Is there any point?"

"Only if you want an explanation. If you're happy with the conclusions you've jumped to, you're welcome to leave now."

"Of course I'm not happy."

"Then my offer of a drink stands."

"What kind of drink?"

"Whatever you want. Beer, tequila, even what passes for water here if you insist, although I advise strongly against it."

"I'll take the water anyway."

"Ever suspicious. You needn't think my plans include getting you drunk so I can seduce you."

"Go to hell, Barclay."

"Can hell be worse than what I've gone through these past thirty years? I really don't know. The church preaches fire and brimstone, but sometimes I wonder if life isn't the real hell. Perhaps this is all some kind of perverse punishment for sins committed in another existence." He stopped abruptly. "But now you've got me philosophizing, which is always a grave mistake without a drink in one's hand. Come in, and I'll see if I can't change your mind about Xloxratl."

They went inside. Donna gravitated automatically to the study, where she examined the book-filled shelves while Barclay supplied them both with drinks from the kitchen. He handed her a glass of translucent brown-tinged water in which floated a couple of rapidly-dissolving ice cubes as well as flakes of some unknown contaminant. His own glass, perhaps half the size of hers, contained a transparent liquid from which emanated the characteristic scent of tequila.

He raised his glass. "Cheerio."

Donna said nothing, but sipped tentatively at her water. She pulled a face. It was every bit as bad as she had feared.

"Have a seat." He gestured toward the armchair.

She settled herself into the chair while he seated himself behind the typewriter.

Barclay looked thoughtfully at his drink for several seconds before he asked, "So, what did you make of our visit with Xloxratl?"

"I thought I'd made that pretty clear. I suppose that at least I understand you better now."

"Meaning?"

"Meaning that, as far as I can see, I just went through the kind of experience that's readily accessible to most college undergraduates back home — although somehow I managed to graduate without ever becoming stoned out of my mind. Presumably you go to see her for the same reason you drink too much: to try to avoid the painful reality that there'll never be a second book."

"Ah! On that point I know you're wrong."

"That there won't be another book?"

"Yes."

"So you've had an idea, then?"

He shook his head. "No."

95

"Explain. How can you be so sure?"

"Because Xloxratl said there's going to be one. Didn't she tell you? I thought she would."

Donna looked at him incredulously. "And that's enough? Barclay, don't you see? Don't you get it? She's just an old woman who dabbles in drugs. Nothing that happened up there was real. It was all in your mind. Her only magic is the magic of drug-induced dreams. And if you're going to let those rule your life, you're in even worse shape than I ever guessed."

"She didn't explain, then? I thought perhaps she might tell you about herself. Who she is.."

"Explain? What is there to explain?"

"Her name is Xloxratl." He pronounced it the way the old woman had done, his tongue having no trouble with the odd clicking sounds. "In her language, 'Xloxratl' means 'One who tells the Truth.' It is a revered name, one that carries a greater weight than any other in her tribe." He paused. "I should start at the beginning. Do you want any more water? No? All right."

And Barclay told her the tale of Xloxratl, the One who tells the Truth.

She's a pure-bred Chiclahan Indian (Barclay said). No one knows how long the Chiclahan have lived in this area, but conquistadores found them when they first arrived more than four hundred years ago, and there was every indication that they had lived here for many hundreds, and perhaps thousands, of years before that. The Chiclahan were a settled tribe; they had discovered agriculture and constructed a large permanent settlement alongside the Tibrilcil River, in a place that's now occupied by the northern suburbs of the modern city of Chiclahan.

When the conquistadores came, they arrived with two thoughts on their mind: treasure, principally gold, and converting the heathen Indians to the One True Faith. The Chiclahan, without intending to, stymied them in both endeavors.

The Chiclahan had no use for gold. It was all but unknown in their culture, and what little they did possess they apparently showed willingly to the conquering troops and were perfectly happy to have them cart it away.

All the gold the Chiclahan possessed had come from other tribes which valued the metal more than the Chiclahan. Most of it had been acquired by trading, in exchange for the right to take Chiclahan brides, for the Chiclahan were recognized as one of the most beautiful tribes in all of what later became central America.

A fraction of the gold was war booty, but not much, for the Chiclahan were essentially peaceful farmers. Unlike other tribes they had no interest in expanding their territory, and few other tribes bothered them, since Chiclahan land was recognized as being of little use, being mostly desert. The few wars they did fight they won, probably because the invading army was already half-defeated by the journey across the desert even before the first blow was struck.

But while the Chiclahan could defeat the other indigenous tribes, they stood no chance against the diseases and the encroachments of the Europeans. Half of them were killed by the diseases the conquistadores brought; most of the remainder were slowly assimilated, until now their tribe numbers only about two hundred and fifty, and they confine themselves to a small area to the northwest of Chiclahan. You should go there sometime, and ponder what modern man is capable of in the name of civilizing natives.

Anyway, the Spanish did not find much in the way of treasure, but they seemed to have more success spreading their religion, although actually they were much less successful than they supposed.

The Chiclahan, you see, believed in the One God. They called him Javí, which a Jesuit priest instantly pounced on as a local form of the word Yahweh, the unspeakable Name of the One True God in the Old Testament.

The priest was further pleased to discover that the Chiclahan had a myth centering on a person called Xloxratl, meaning One who tells the Truth. As the priest understood the tale, Xloxratl once visited the Chiclahan and was hounded to death because none of the ruling elders would believe his message, although what that message actually was had been lost in the intervening years. The Jesuit happily seized on this story and took great delight in showing how it paralleled the story of Jesus. The Chiclahan, of course, accepted the story told them by the priest as being a kind of reflection of their own story of Xloxratl. The

97

priest went away, convinced that he had converted an entire tribe to Christianity; similarly, the conquistadores moved on equally convinced that they were taking with them what little treasure the Chiclahan possessed.

Neither could have been more wrong.

What the conquistadores had failed to understand was that it was not gold that the Chiclahan treasured but silver, and that within Chiclahan territory was one of the richest deposits of that metal in the world. To the Chiclahan, silver was a holy substance, not to be profaned by the eyes of outsiders. Every last scrap of their silver was kept safely in the Temple of Javí, built far away, near the place where the silver was found, on the slopes of what we know as *Las Montañas del Cielo*.

Where the Jesuit priest made his mistake was in thinking that the story of Xloxratl was no more than a myth from long ago. It never crossed his mind that when the Chiclahan told him about Xloxratl, they were simply telling him of the first of many Xloxratl. He never realized that the first Xloxratl was followed by many others who bore the same title and who possessed, to a greater or lesser degree, the same gift as the first one of that name.

The Xloxratl do not form an unbroken line; many generations of Chiclahan have produced no claimant. Before the one you've met, two full generations passed without a Xloxratl. In those two generations, civilization came to many of the Chiclahan, so that now there are few left, and the number who believe in the power of the Xloxratl is smaller still.

You must understand that Xloxratl does not live in the mountains by choice. The Chiclahan believe that one with her powers is chosen by Javí to be a mouthpiece to the world of humans. Therefore, she must live close to God, and God, as evidenced by the silver that used to lie exposed on the mountainside, lives in the *Montañas del Cielo*.

Men came and took all the silver, and in so doing perhaps they further eroded the myth of Xloxratl. But after they had gone, a young child, who until that time had been no different from her peers, became a woman in the town of Chiclahan; and when she did so she began to prophesy and to see things that no one else could see. The remaining elders of the tribe came together and discussed her case. Eventually, after testing the accuracy of the girl's visions, they were forced to conclude that the God Javí had chosen a new Xloxratl to live in their generation.

Following the Chiclahan tradition, she was outcast, to symbolize the killing of the first Xloxratl. She travelled to the *Montañas del Cielo*, and made her home at the place where men had come and ravaged the abode of God. That was more than eighty years ago.

Barclay stopped, letting his words hang in the air as if they were enough to explain everything.

Donna looked at him skeptically. "You aren't trying to tell me you really believe that that old woman actually has some sort of magical power? She's a con artist, that's all. Back home in the States she'd be a used car saleswoman, or a politician, or a Scientologist, or something equally dubious."

"Is that really what you think?" asked Barclay quietly. "That there's nothing more to Xloxratl than simple trickery?"

"Of course that's all there is." Donna sighed heavily. "I don't understand you, Barclay. You're an intelligent man. I can't believe you've fallen for such an obvious ploy. All she did was to give us a drink that was doped with some sort of hallucinogenic drug. Everyone knows that most Native American Indian tribes used hallucinogens in their religious ceremonies. Their shamans used them to help them go into trances and interpret the will of the gods. You don't mean to say that you believe in this Javí character? I thought you were a Catholic. As I understand it, the Christian God doesn't take kindly to lesser deities, does He?"

Barclay looked disappointed and tired; his face, already long and thin, seemed to sag. "I think you'd better leave," he said.

"I'm sorry. I really am. I thought there'd be more to you, I really did."

Barclay shook his head. "No, I'm the one who's sorry. I've done everything I can. If you don't understand even now, there's nothing more I can do. I'm going to *El Presidente*. I won't be back until morning."

He heaved himself out of his chair and shambled out of the house. She followed him as far as the front door, where she stood in the doorway, watching him until he had turned the corner. Then, shaking her head sadly, she headed for Señora Delgado's.

A Day Lost

Señora Delgado was seated at the kitchen table, finishing her supper, when she heard the front door open and close. A few moments later, the blonde gringa looked in at the doorway. Señora Delgado thought she looked sick. The gringa was pale and her cheeks were hollow. She placed her bag on the ground.

"Excuse me, señora," Donna said, producing a man's wallet from the pocket of her jeans, "if it's all right with you, I'd like to pay you now. I'll be leaving on the bus in the morning."

"I'm sorry, señorita, but there is no bus tomorrow. The next bus is not until Monday."

Donna frowned. "I thought there were buses to Chiclahan on Mondays, Wednesdays and Saturdays."

Señora Delgado nodded. "That's right. Monday, Wednesday and Saturday. The next bus is on Monday."

"But tomorrow is Saturday."

The señora shook her head vigorously. "No, señorita. Today is Saturday. Tomorrow is Sunday."

Donna quickly recalculated how long she had been in Tecimal. "No," she said emphatically. "Today's Friday."

The señora shrugged. "Go ask one of the men across the road. You left on Thursday morning to go into the mountains with Señor Barclay. You were away two days. Now it is Saturday. Tomorrow is Sunday."

Donna opened her mouth to protest, but a sudden, awful suspicion began to grow. She remembered the burnt-out fire, and shivered.

100

Without saying another word she stalked out of the room. Señora Delgado looked at the doorway with a faint glint of amusement in her eye.

Garish signs advertising *Cerveza de Chiclahan* lit the exterior of *El Presidente*. In their unnatural light, more than a dozen men loitered near the entrance of the bar, leaning against the building and seated cross-legged on the ground in threes and fours, playing cards and talking loudly. As soon as Donna appeared, all activity ceased. Uncomfortably aware of the men's gaze, she stepped selfconsciously into the street and crossed the road towards them.

"Excuse me," she said, smiling and doing her best to ignore the leers, "Could you tell me what day it is?"

"Saturday, señorita," they replied in unison.

"Señor Barclay is inside," one of them volunteered. "Would you like me to get him for you?" He scrambled to his feet.

She shook her head and answered automatically, her thoughts elsewhere, "No, don't bother; I'm fine."

But she felt anything but fine as she walked back across the street. The men watched appreciatively, their eyes glued to the movement of her hips and the sway of her hair in the light from the signs.

Donna climbed the stairs to her room, where she sat on the bed and looked vacantly at the wall, trying to make sense of everything that had happened since she had left the house on Thursday morning.

There could be no doubt that two days, not one, had passed while she had been absent from Tecimal. There was also no doubt about where she must have lost the day: the only possible place was in the shaman's hut, under the influence of the old woman's drugs. Did Barclay know they had been gone so long? She tried to remember everything Barclay had said since they had left the hut; she could think of nothing to suggest that he knew about the missing day.

What did Barclay see in Xloxratl? Barclay seemed to be a strangely religious man in an oddly inconsistent sort of way, and perhaps that was the answer. Where Donna naturally inclined toward skepticism and disbelief, Barclay seemed to be of a quite different — and altogether more gullible — temperament.

She tried to remember all that had happened in Xloxratl's hut, but most of it was lost in a vague, drug-induced haze. Even what she seemed to remember was unreliable, for she knew that the mind could not be trusted when under the influence of chemicals. Even her few hazy memories might be inaccurate, conjured up by her mind like a dream. She was fairly sure of only two things: Xloxratl had mistakenly assumed that Donna and Barclay were lovers — which was as good a reason as any to disbelieve her purported powers — and she had insisted that Donna was going to help Barclay write a second book.

"Damned if I will," said Donna out loud, striking the bed angrily with her fist.

A wave of fatigue brought home how tired she was. It had been a long day, and her body was still fighting the after-effects of Xloxratl's drugs. What she needed was a shower and then a good night's sleep. Tomorrow... tomorrow was another day, and she would postpone thinking about what she was going to do until then. If the worst came to the worst, well, it wasn't long until Monday.

She headed for the shower. Ten minutes later she lay down between the sheets and fell instantly asleep.

She was back in LA, talking to her thesis advisor. Through some strange set of circumstances which were not entirely clear, she had managed to complete her thesis on Barclay, and she handed the thick wad of paper to her advisor for her to review it. Her advisor had barely started to read when suddenly the door of the room was thrown open, and in walked Xloxratl, accompanied by the distinctive aroma of her tin hut.

Ignoring Donna, Xloxratl said to her adviser, "They are lovers, you know."

Her advisor registered horror, turned to Donna, and asked with exaggerated menace, "Is this true? If it is, you know it will invalidate everything you've written."

Before Donna could deny the shaman's claim, her advisor threw the thesis at her and shouted, "Take it away, take it away. I never want to see you again."

Somewhere a bell clanged.

Donna turned to look at Xloxratl, but the woman had gone, her place taken by Barclay. "I told you no one would understand," Barclay said, not moving to help her pick up the sheets of paper that were strewn over the floor.

The bell clanged again. Its high-pitched dissonance was jarring.

"Help me pick these up," said Donna desperately, on her hands and knees now, struggling to pick up the papers which seemed to slip through her fingers as if they were alive.

She looked up at Barclay and saw that he was reading a page from her thesis.

"Don't read that," she shouted. She dropped the pages she had collected as she scrambled to her feet, clawing the air, desperate to stop him from reading what she had written.

He looked up from the paper and laughed. "Did you write this?"

"No, no."

Both of them knew she was lying.

The bell clanged a third time, and she woke to find herself shouting in English, her body tense and her heart thudding, adrenalin surging through her system. She fell back in bed, panting, trying to convince herself that it had been nothing more than a dream.

There was a knock on her door, smothered momentarily by another stroke from the bell.

From the other side of the door a voice asked, "Are you all right, señorita? Is something the matter?"

It was Isabella. *The whore*, thought Donna automatically as she fought to calm herself.

"Yes. No. I'm all right."

The door opened. Isabella, wearing a long, drab dress, was framed by the doorway. Behind her, looking over her shoulder into the room, stood Barclay, his brow knitted into a series of parallel lines.

For a moment Donna stared at the two of them before she realized that she was naked and the sheet had fallen to her waist.

"Go away!" she shouted, grabbing the sheet and pulling it to cover herself.

"I'm sorry, señorita," said Isabella unconcernedly and making no attempt to leave. "We were worried about you. You were shouting Señor Barclay's name, and we thought you wanted to see him."

"No. Go away. I never want to see him again."

Isabella and Barclay exchanged shrugs.

Isabella said, "Mass is in less than twenty minutes, señorita. You must hurry if you want to be in time."

Before Donna could think of a suitable reply, Isabella closed the door. The last thing Donna saw was Barclay, his eyes looking at her and sparkling with silent amusement.

"Bastard!" she said to herself as she lay there, sheet pulled tightly under her chin, listening to the sound of their footsteps moving away down the passageway. As soon as she judged it safe, she got out of bed, dashed to the door and turned the key in the lock. "Bastard," she repeated. She made her way to the bathroom.

In the kitchen, Isabella, Barclay and Señora Delgado gathered around the table.

"She's a strange one, Barclay," said Isabella matter-of-factly. "Are you sure she's not slightly *loco*?"

"Oh, I'm certain she's more than slightly *loco*," said Barclay. "Who else but a crazy woman would come all this way just to see me?"

The two women agreed that this was a good point.

"Why don't you two go ahead?" continued Barclay. "I'll bring her with me."

Isabella protested: "But what will everyone think? Now everyone merely suspects, but if you go to Mass together, everyone will be sure it's true."

"It's inevitable," said Barclay, as if he were talking about an unalterable law of nature: the downhill flow of water, or the cyclical advance of the seasons.

"But last night you told me you haven't slept with her," argued Isabella.

Señora Delgado was uncharacteristically silent, but it was obvious from the way she was holding herself perfectly still, leaning slightly towards the others, that she was taking a keen interest in the conversation.

"Xloxratl said we will be lovers," replied Barclay quietly.

After a moment, Isabella nodded.

"Then of course you will be lovers. If only because you believe her." She sighed. "Did Xloxratl say whether you would come back to me?"

"Are you jealous, dear Isabella?"

"Of course not," she declared petulantly. "I just want to know where I stand. I can fill my bed every night of the week without you, Señor Barclay."

Barclay shot a smile at Isabella's mother. "Is she always this difficult early in the morning?"

"You know who she gets it from," Señora Delgado said, laughing.

Barclay's face crinkled in a boyish grin. "Get out of here, you two. My lover-to-be and I will be along shortly, scandalizing the women and making the men envious."

Isabella stood, and Señora Delgado slapped her daughter playfully on the bottom. "Come on, Isabella. We mustn't keep God waiting.

He might send a curse on us. Señor Barclay might decide to move in permanently."

Laughing, the two women left the room. A few moments later, Barclay heard the front door open and close.

Upstairs, he could hear water running: Donna was having a shower. His face became serious and he took a deep breath, as if preparing himself for a distasteful task that could no longer be avoided. He began to climb the stairs.

Donna luxuriated in the shower, insofar as that was possible given the cramped bathroom and the brown, odorous water. But after only a couple of minutes, the plumbing seemed to decide that it had done its duty and the flow became a trickle, even with the faucet turned fully open. Knowing from her brief experience with the house's plumbing that it was futile to hope that the flow would be restored, Donna turned off the water and stepped out of the shower. Picking up a towel, she clambered over the toilet and walked into the bedroom, drying herself as she went.

She stopped in mid stride, horrified. Barclay smiled at her from the bed.

"Good morning," he said.

"What the hell are you doing here?" Clasping the towel in front of her — but knowing the damage was already done — she shouted angrily, "Get out. Get out of here."

Barclay made no move to obey. "I think we need to talk." He spoke calmly.

"We're done with the talking. Get the hell out of here. And how did you get in, anyway? I locked the door."

"Possibly you turned the key. That, I'm afraid, is not the same thing at all. You forget: this is Tecimal, not Los Angeles."

Donna looked around the room for something good and heavy that she could either throw at Barclay, or which might make a useful cudgel. It was obvious that he wasn't going to move unless encouraged by something more substantial than mere words.

The only thing she could see was a gaudy Virgin Mary, perhaps a foot tall, standing on the table beside the bed. She would reimburse Señora Delgado the cost of a new one. She grasped it firmly; it was comfortingly heavy. She approached Barclay, hefting it threateningly in her hand. She was afraid that if she threw it, she might miss.

Barclay eyed the statue uncertainly. "Xloxratl said you're a writer," he said, not taking his eyes from the statue.

She stopped, remembering that Xloxratl had said the same thing to her. She had thought it was while Barclay was out of hearing, getting the water for the drugged tisane, but it must have been later. Donna must have told the old woman her secret after drinking the cocktail of drugs: how else could the old shaman have known? And what else had Donna told her while under the influence? What other secrets might she have babbled without knowing?

Barclay continued, "If it's true — and I don't doubt it for a moment, because only a writer would be crazy enough to come here looking for me — I'd like to look at what you've brought. You did bring something for me to look at, didn't you?"

Donna stopped advancing. Suddenly she was torn. For a few seconds she vacillated. Then she said, "You'll only laugh." Her expression challenged him to deny it.

Barclay shook his head. "I won't. If I don't like it, I'll say so. But I'd never laugh. I know too well the agony that's expended on every word ever to find humor in either the act or the fruit of writing."

Donna looked at him, trying to decide whether he was pulling her leg. She remembered the papers he had discarded in the trash can. Slowly she lowered the statue.

"I'll bring it to you later. Now please leave, I want to get dressed."

"I'll go outside and wait for you. Don't put on anything too gaudy. And for goodness' sake don't wear jeans."

"Why not?"

"Because if you do, no one in Tecimal will ever speak to either of us again."

"What are you talking about?"

"It would be interpreted as disrespectful to go to Mass dressed improperly"

"But I'm not going to Mass."

"Yes you are. Consider it the price of my professional evaluation of your work."

He rose from the bed and walked to the door.

"I'll be waiting outside. Don't be long. Mass starts in ten minutes, and it'll take us five minutes to get there even if we hurry."

He went outside, closing the door behind him. Donna stared at it for ten long seconds before, with an "ooohh" of frustration, she let go of the towel and began to look through her meager wardrobe for something that would not send the people of Tecimal into fits of horror.

When she opened the door, Barclay, who was leaning against the opposite wall, instantly straightened. Eyeing her uncertainly he said, "Well, if you're sure that's the best you can do, we'd better be going. Come on."

And before she could respond, he was leading the way downstairs, taking the stairs two at a time. She bit her lip and hurried after him.

They were the last to arrive. The church was almost full, and the service was already under way as they found a couple of spaces near the back of the sanctuary.

Donna's experience of church was limited to half a dozen ill-remembered Christmas services from her childhood, a memorial service for a classmate killed in a car accident at high school and, more recently, two weddings. None of these was adequate preparation for Sunday Mass in Tecimal.

Barclay, like everyone else, knew the service by heart, and although he tried to guide her through the missal as the service jumped seemingly without reason from page to page, Donna soon whispered in Barclay's ear that she was hopelessly confused. Her confusion was multiplied by the fact that Father Emilio was all but inaudible at the back of the church, his thin, reedy voice greedily absorbed by the adobe walls. In the end, she had to content herself with standing when the others stood, kneeling when the others knelt, and generally trying not to act like the embarrassed gringa know-nothing that she felt.

When it came time to take the Host, she was too embarrassed to remain seated, and rose and lined up along with everyone else. She saw Barclay darkling, but she shrugged, as if to say, "What else can I do?" and knelt dutifully at the rail when her turn came, following the example of everyone else.

The wafer, which reminded her of rice paper, melted quickly on her tongue, adding a sweetness to her saliva. She swallowed and something caught at the back of her throat. She began to cough: not a discreet, ladylike wheeze, but a hacking violence that simply would not stop. No one came to her assistance; instead they all looked away in embarrassment, trying to ignore her paroxysm.

She walked, still coughing, back to the pew at the rear of the church. Barclay thumped her several times on the back and whispered, "Serves you right" in English. She was powerless to reply as, fuming, she regained her seat.

After Mass, people formed knots in the space surrounding the church, chatting and exchanging gossip. She saw heads swivel to regard herself and Barclay, but although a few of the men nodded to Barclay, no one spoke to either of them. Only Señora Delgado waved. At her side stood Isabella, unlipsticked and wearing her shapeless dun dress, as if anyone could forget what she looked like on other days. Isabella seemed to be glaring at them, although Donna could not decide whether the glare was targeted at Barclay or herself.

Donna opened the handbag she had brought with her, extracted a sheaf of papers, and made to hand it to Barclay.

He shook his head. "Bring it with you. You're having lunch with me."

Her patience finally snapped.

"Says who? I'm not your slave, you know." She spoke more loudly than she had intended, halting half a dozen nearby conversations.

Barclay sighed, rolling his eyes heavenward.

"I'm sorry, I keep forgetting to handle you with velvet gloves. Would you do me the honor of joining me for lunch, señorita?"

"And if I say no?"

"You won't."

"Damn you, Barclay. If it weren't for my thesis...."

"If it weren't for your thesis, you wouldn't have come to Tecimal. Which means you wouldn't have met me, and you'd still think I was a great writer instead of a second-rate hack who happened to get lucky once a long time ago."

"Damn you again. You don't really think I believe that, do you?"

"That's certainly the impression you left me with yesterday."

"That was yesterday. I wasn't myself."

He shrugged. "In that case, you think I have great potential but I ruin it by drinking it too much. There are few more damning words than 'great potential' when applied to a man my age. And not only do I drink too much but I'm also known to sleep with a whore."

"Which raises a damn good point...."

"What was I doing at Señora Delgado's early this morning? I'll let your imagination supply the answer. Now, are you coming to lunch? It's too hot to stand out here bickering."

"All right. I'll come. But I still don't understand how you can sleep with a woman like that. And then you both come to church on Sunday. You know what that makes you, don't you? You're hypocrites."

108

She had meant the barb to hurt, and it was immediately obvious that she had struck home.

Barclay's eyes flared angrily. "Don't you *ever* use that word to describe me again. Nor Isabella. She is the most unhypocritical woman I've ever known, with the possible exception of her mother. And as for myself, I admit that I may be many things, among them lazy, good-for-nothing, and too fond of a drink. But one thing I am, Miss Butter-Wouldn't-Melt-In-Your-Mouth American student, is honest.

"I don't carry around a half-finished manuscript in the hope that an established writer will agree to criticize it. Neither do I fool myself. I know that I have none of the answers. I'm not even sure I know the questions. But I do know that once in my life I wrote a book that people seem to think is halfway decent, and with your help I'm going to do so again. So will you stop being such a pain in the neck and act like an ordinary human being for once? Say what's on your mind instead of trying to be devious all the time and letting it dribble out in bits."

It was Donna's turn to flush scarlet with anger. "You want to know what's on my mind?" Her voice rose to a shout; she ignored the looks from the townspeople. "All right, I'll tell you. I came to this god-forsaken place because when I was in high school I read a book that made me see things in a way I'd never thought of before. I thought then, and I think now, despite all the evidence to the contrary, that that book has been vastly underrated and ignored for far too long. I thought that maybe I could help redress that balance if I could discover what happened to the author and why he'd never written a second book.

"No one seemed to know where the author lived, and all the biographies were hopelessly vague about what had happened to him. Eventually, I went to his publisher, who finally told me where to find him. And what do I discover? The man who wrote the greatest novel of the past half century has become a recluse and lives in a god-forsaken filthy hole in the middle of a desert in Central America.

"Being naïve, and perhaps too adventuresome for my own good, I wrote and told the author I was coming to see him because I want to write a thesis about him. The author, I might add, never even had the grace to reply.

"And what did I find when I got here? No, don't interrupt; let me finish. I'll tell you what I found. A man who immediately embarrasses me by not bothering to introduce himself, letting me prattle on about the man I'm looking for in his presence. Even so, I manage somehow to swallow my pride and seek him out in a bar with every man in the place ogling me and imagining himself in my bed. This gallant writer then proceeds to stand me up for dinner, and when he shows up next morning it's obvious he's spent the night drinking. Then, against my better judgement, I let him persuade me to go on a ridiculous trip into the mountains to visit a senile old woman who feeds us both some sort of drug-filled concoction that leaves me missing an entire day of my life.

"And finally, as if all that's not enough, I let him drag me off to a religious ceremony where I can hear nothing and understand even less, only to have everyone in the town staring at us when we leave because we're obviously having it off together. Even that bitch Isabella thinks so, or didn't you notice the look she gave us?

"So, *Mister* Barclay, why don't you just leave me alone until tomorrow? Go get drunk somewhere; you're good at that. When you wake up, I'll be gone."

She glared at the object of her wrath, her chest heaving. Around them no one moved. Everyone was staring at the couple, aghast that anyone could conduct a row in such a public place on a Sunday. More than one of the women turned to her husband and said, "I told you she was nothing but trouble," to underscore a previously expressed opinion that no good would come of associating with the pretty blonde gringa.

Barclay said quietly, "You're right. When I wake up, you'll be gone. And you'll spend the rest of your life wondering what would have happened if you'd stayed. You'll go back to Los Angeles, find some other, much less interesting, subject for your thesis, and churn out some drivel that no one will remember on some bland subject like the relationship between television and the novel. You'll have a couple of brief and unsatisfying relationships, and at some point about five years from now, out of sheer desperation, you'll marry someone and regret the deed even before the honeymoon is over. A few years later, probably after having one or more kids in the mistaken assumption that that will fix everything, you'll get divorced. You'll probably wind up as a secretary somewhere simply because you can spell and know how to type.

"*You* be honest now. Is that what you really want? Oh, don't bother to answer. I don't care. But at least be honest with yourself.

You owe yourself that much. Go on, there's the *Calle*. Señora Delgado's house is no more than half a kilometer away. Go there; I'm not going to stop you. I won't get drunk, but I'll make damn sure you don't see me again before you catch the bus. All you've got to do is put one foot in front of the other and keep on going. It's the easiest thing in the world."

Donna looked at him for a long time. She did not move.

Barclay too stood his ground, his calm exterior betraying none of the anguish and upheaval he was feeling. Xloxratl had it made it clear that the only chance he had of writing again was with this petulant, incomprehensible, egotistical, immature female as a partner, and he had just offered her the escape for which she had been looking ever since she had arrived in Tecimal. If she took it, his writing days would be over. He knew what his future would be: he would simply drink himself into oblivion, and Doctor Pasquale's prognosis would come true sooner rather than later. He waited for her answer.

"Damn you a thousand times, Andrew Barclay," she said, and he knew that the battle was over. He could, for a while a least, go on living. She was going to stay.

He said equably, "If you don't believe in God, then I don't see how you can believe in damnation. If there is no God, there is, one assumes, no heaven. And without heaven, what is the point of hell, unless it is simply the final resting place of us all?"

"Shut up, can't you? Oh, hell." This last was in response to the tears that had begun to dribble down her cheeks. Barclay took a step closer, his hand moving to his pocket for a handkerchief.

"Don't you dare touch me. You come one step closer and I promise you I'll walk away and I'll never think of this place again."

She opened her handbag and extracted a handkerchief: an unexpectedly delicate, feminine affair imprinted with pink flowers that was too small for the job demanded of it.

Barclay did his best to hide his amusement while she dabbed at her face with the increasingly soggy ball of cotton. Eventually, she blinked the tears away and said accusingly, "You're laughing at me."

"No." Then, despite his best effort, he chuckled. "I'm sorry, I couldn't help it. You're so desperate not to accept my help."

He was right, of course. His sardonic amusement should have angered her even more, but instead it had exactly the opposite effect.

It dawned on her how ridiculous she must look. Belatedly, she realized that everyone was watching them.

"Come on," she said. "Let's get away from here. Everyone's staring at us. You said something about lunch."

"My place?"

"Not if you're going to cook."

"I'll take that as an offer that you'll do the honors. It's a deal."

Barclay looked for a moment as if he intended to link his arm with hers, but a frown from her was enough to quash that idea before he could act on it. They walked away, side by side but with a definite space between them.

Slowly the people outside the church came to life once more.

Turning Point

Diego Montoya, his wife at his side, watched the argument between his friend and the zunuvabeech gringa. Both of them, the barber and his wife, strained unsuccessfully to catch the words. Barclay and the gringa were probably speaking English anyway. Even so, Montoya saw that they weren't the only ones interested in the argument: everyone had stopped to watch, even if they couldn't understand the words.

The barber's wife said quietly, "That gringa is not good for him. He should just walk away from her."

Montoya knew that the last thing his wife cared about was the Englishman. What she meant was that the gringa would be bad for *him*, and she was warning her husband to stay away from the blonde explosive.

Montoya said nothing, watching with interest to see how the argument would play itself out. He too wished that Barclay would simply walk away: Barclay had not been himself ever since the gringa had descended from the bus. Privately, he agreed with his wife: the gringa was not good for Barclay. But it soon became clear that the argument, whatever it had been about, was over. Barclay and the gringa turned and together headed towards Barclay's house. People began to move once more. Montoya moved toward the place where Señora Delgado and her daughter were standing. His wife reluctantly followed.

The señora saw Montoya approaching. She smiled graciously, as she always did, at the man's wife. The señora, normally so garrulous, had always kept her opinions about Montoya's wife firmly to herself. There was no point in making trouble. She treated the barber's wife with

113

unstinting and unexceptionable politeness, as if there were no source of tension between them.

"Good morning," said Montoya.

The señora and her daughter fell into step beside the barber and his wife, heading north along the *Calle*. Montoya continued, "Did you hear what that was all about? It looked for a moment like she was going to leave him."

"They were speaking English," said Isabella, the expression on her face clearly communicating her frustration. Neither Isabella nor her mother spoke more than a few words of that language.

"Good morning, señora," Señora Delgado greeted the barber's wife. "Father Emilio did well this morning, don't you think?"

She began to walk more slowly, forcing Señora Montoya to match her pace and allowing Montoya and Isabella to move on ahead so they could talk without being overheard.

Señora Montoya understood full well what was happening, but she was powerless to do anything about it. She glared at the back of her husband's head. She would talk to him about this later. How could he be so insensitive?

It was the first opportunity Montoya had had to be alone with Isabella since the arrival of the American *gringa*. He wasted no time. "What do you think of her?"

He did not really need to ask: one look at the set of Isabella's face was enough to tell him exactly what she thought.

"She's an American student, infatuated with his book."

"Do you think she's going to stay much longer?"

Isabella did not answer his question. Instead, she said, "He took her up into the mountains to see Xloxratl. Xloxratl says they will be lovers."

Diego Montoya nodded. Like most residents of Tecimal, the barber knew of Xloxratl and her purported mystic powers. And, like everyone else except Barclay, he tried to pretend that she did not exist, or that her so-called powers were no more than simple tricks. Only Barclay *believed*. If Xloxratl told Barclay that he and the American were to be lovers, then lovers they would be — simply because Barclay *believed*.

"Did he tell you anything else about what Xloxratl said?"

"Nothing that made sense. He spent half the night trying to explain it to me, but I never understood. Sometimes I wonder if Barclay isn't *loco*." She tapped the side of her head meaningfully.

114

"He's English. Worse, he's a writer. So of course he is *loco*. Surely it hasn't taken you nineteen years to understand that? Did he say anything else?"

"He's trying to write another book. Did you know?"

"He's been trying to write another book since before you were born. At one time he used to tell me about his progress. Then, when he went back over his words and read what he'd written, he would throw everything away. He must have written half a dozen books in the past twenty years, and thrown every word away. He's given up talking about it now. I think he knows it will never happen."

Isabella shook her head forcefully. "No, you're wrong. He knows it *will* happen, and that's the problem."

"What do you mean?"

"It's all the shaman's fault. She's told him he will write a second book."

Montoya considered this for a moment. "But that's good, isn't it? Anyway, what does it have to do with the gringa?"

"When they were in the mountains, Xloxratl told Barclay that he couldn't write the book without her. Barclay thinks Xloxratl told the gringa the same thing."

"They're going to write it together?"

The barber looked at Isabella incredulously to see if she was as disbelieving as he. It was impossible for Montoya to imagine Barclay — eccentric, lazy, drink-befuddled, intelligent, set-in-his-ways, stubborn Barclay — allowing anyone else even to see, much less collaborate on, a work in progress.

"Xloxratl says they need each other. I can't believe he'll really let her work with him. He also said that Xloxratl told him something else."

"What?"

"The gringa will leave, but...."

But behind them the barber's wife had had enough. She didn't like the way her husband was talking to Isabella. It was obvious they were talking about something they both thought important. Excusing herself abruptly, she increased her pace, leaving Señora Delgado with a bemused expression on her face.

"Diego," she called, "we've passed our street."

Taking hold of his arm, she pulled her husband away. They had gone no more than a dozen paces before she began to tell him what she thought of his behavior. Montoya's eyes grew vacant as he let his wife's tirade wash over him.

———————————

Donna opened the cupboards and stared forlornly at their meager contents. She didn't know quite what she had been expecting. Perhaps she had hoped that her last inspection of Barclay's kitchen had caught him at a bad time; or perhaps his offer of lunch had been premeditated, and therefore he might have improved his stock of food in anticipation of the meal. At least he might have gone to the effort of cleaning the kitchen. But as she cast her eye over the room itself, and then the almost-empty shelves, she saw that nothing had changed.

The floor and most of the exposed surfaces were still patterned with random dark splotches of food spilled long ago. A new pile of dirty plates had begun in the sink. She noticed only one change for the better: the blackened fruit had been thrown out, its place taken by half a dozen red apples. The cupboards still held only cans of spaghetti, vegetables and corned beef, as well as the ubiquitous bottles of tequila. Once again it was the refrigerator that produced the raw materials for the meal. And once again the meal was omelets.

While she was cooking, Barclay came into the kitchen. He stood beside her and nodded approvingly.

"When you find something you can do well, stick with it," he said. "I approve."

"You mean the omelets? For your information, there isn't much else I could do. This isn't a kitchen, this is a...." But words failed her.

"What you mean is, this isn't a woman's kitchen. It suits me perfectly."

"You're just trying to get me riled again, aren't you? Well it won't work this time. I'm leaving tomorrow, and I intend to have enough material for my thesis when I go. I'm not going to let you give me an excuse for losing my temper."

"And there's always that book of yours."

Donna fell silent. She poked at the omelet unnecessarily, so that just like last time it began to resemble a kind of corned beef and scrambled egg hash.

"You want a drink?"

She shook her head.

"But you don't mind if I do?"

"Of course not. It's your house." But her mind was on the manuscript she had given him before coming into the kitchen. She began to think about how badly it was written. She'd been stupid to let Barclay see it. How could she ever have thought it was any good? She should have destroyed it before she ever came to Tecimal. She wondered how much of it Barclay had read. Not much; she had been in the kitchen only a few minutes. Maybe half a dozen pages. But even that would be enough for Barclay to realize she had no talent.

Barclay poured a large measure of tequila into a glass and took a couple of swallows. "It's burning," he said.

It took her a moment to realize that he was talking about the omelet. Her mind had been elsewhere. Taking the pan off the heat, she divided the omelet into halves, decanting them on to a pair of plates.

Without a word, he picked up one of the plates and took it to the table that stood in one corner of the kitchen. He sat and, without waiting, began to eat.

As Donna took a chair opposite him she said pointedly, "You're welcome."

Barclay seemed to consider this for a moment, and then said, "You know, it's not bad. Not wonderful, but certainly not bad."

"Well, thanks for the vote of confidence. Sorry about the burnt bits — if you've noticed them; I was thinking of something else when I should have been paying attention."

"What? Oh! The food. Mm, yes, very good. No, I was talking about your manuscript."

Donna's fork halted halfway between plate and mouth. Slowly she lowered it. She waited for Barclay to continue.

She realized that her mouth was dry and her heart was pounding. It was like waiting for the results of an exam.

Wordlessly, Barclay kept eating, as if he had nothing more to add. He finished his omelet, and took two more swigs of the tequila; then he looked at her. Donna stared into his eyes and tried to read the thoughts that were going on behind them. It was no good; she never had been very expert at reading other people.

"You have your Dictaphone or whatever it's called?" he asked.

"Yes, in my handbag."

"Perhaps this would be a good time to get it out."

She scrambled quickly to get the machine out before he could change his mind. From somewhere outside came the shouts of children playing noisily: some game with a ball. She thought about closing the window, but the kitchen was already hot and closing the window would only make it worse. She placed the tape recorder on the table close to Barclay, and sat with her back to the window to block the noise.

"How do you want to do this? Questions and answers?" Barclay asked.

"Sounds reasonable."

She paused, trying to think of a good place to start.

"Why don't you think more?" Barclay suddenly asked.

Donna was taken aback. "What?" she said, sure that she must have misheard.

"Why don't you think more?" he repeated. "I mean, you're obviously capable of it. So why don't you make the effort?"

"I thought I was asking the questions."

He shook his head.

"That doesn't make much sense. How could you possibly know the right questions to ask? I thought it was me you wanted to write about."

"It is."

"Then obviously I should ask the questions. How else can you hope to understand how I think? So: why do you spend so much time reacting to circumstances instead of analyzing them? You've got a good brain. Why not use it?"

Donna searched Barclay's face for some indication that he might be joking. But there was none. Apparently, his absurd, insulting question was sincere.

She flushed with anger and was on the point of asking if Barclay was saying she was a fool, but too much was at stake. She bit back the retort and contented herself with thinking that all she had to do was to keep her temper for the next few hours and then she would have more than enough material for her thesis. If she worked quickly, she might finish a year ahead of schedule. That was worth any number of insults. And still, somewhere at the back of her mind was the thought that Barclay might help her with her book. She tried to gather her thoughts.

Barclay continued, "Sir Joshua Reynolds — the painter — once said something to the effect that there is no expedient to which man will not resort to avoid the real labor of thinking. He was quite right, of course. That's why writing is so operose. It's not the actual putting of words on paper that's difficult, it's the thought that's necessary to choose exactly the right words.

"Everyone thinks he can write. After all, how hard can it be to tell a story? It's not until one actually sits down to commit that story to paper that the awful truth becomes clear: that to tell a story properly, one has to think. And not just once, but for hours, and days, and months on end, writing and reading, rewriting and rereading, until the story is *right*. And all that time one is thinking endlessly about the book. It consumes every moment, waking and sleeping. For months, a writer reifies his work until it becomes more important than real life.

"So it's easy to think one could be a writer. That takes no effort at all. But to *become* one, that's something else entirely. Belief is just the same. Admit it, you think I'm crazy to believe in God, don't you? Don't be shy; you do, don't you?"

"Yes," she nodded, unsure how they had suddenly started talking about religion.

"But have you really given any thought to the question? If there's no God, how can you be satisfied with life? Since I believe God exists, at least I know that ultimately there's a reason for everything, even if that reason is beyond my meager understanding. Without God, isn't everything reduced to a mish-mash of happenstance, coincidence and inexplicable events?"

"Nothing's inexplicable. Some things just seem so because we don't have all the facts."

Barclay shook his head. "Like a conjuring trick? Everything's smoke, mirrors and misdirection? You can't really believe that... can you?"

"Of course I can. Give me one example of something that's happened to you that's truly inexplicable."

"Xloxratl," he responded instantly, as if that one word proved his point.

"That shaman? I've said it before: I don't understand you, Barclay. How can you be taken in by her? All she did was to give us some sort of hallucinogenic drug. What's so inexplicable about that? And anyway how can you possibly reconcile belief in that old Indian woman with belief in your Catholic God? I was watching you this morning: you really believed everything the priest said. I wouldn't be surprised if you told me you believed in transubstantiation. And one more thing: if everything you've said is true, if you really believe in this God of yours, how can you slap him in the face by spending Saturday night with Isabella and then going to Mass on Sunday as if you were as pure as the driven snow?"

Donna leaned back in her chair, satisfied that she had made her points without losing her temper.

A slow smile spread across Barclay's face, as if she were but a child who, no matter how hard she struck her parent, could inflict no real damage. Without speaking he leisurely finished his drink, then got up and poured himself another. Through the window came a sudden squeal of half a dozen voices shouting, "Goal!" A fly buzzed into the room and began to investigate the apples. Barclay returned to his seat, took a sip of tequila, and leaned back in his chair. He paused for a moment to gather his thoughts. Then he began to talk.

Rosalinda

The Dictaphone clicked, and Barclay stopped talking.

"That's the end of the last one," said Donna. "I'm sorry. I should have brought more."

Barclay drained his glass. "How many is that?" he asked, looking at the empty glass.

"Tapes or drinks?"

"Both."

"Three tapes, which means six hours."

"And drinks? Don't be shy. I'm sure you've been counting."

"Seven, I think. Maybe eight."

Barclay turned the glass thoughtfully in his hand. He slammed it on the table with a sharp bang.

"You're right," he declared. "I drink too much. When I first came to Tecimal I didn't have seven drinks in a week. Now I have that much in an afternoon and I don't even notice."

He looked out the window. It was dark outside. Night had fallen somewhere near the beginning of the last tape. "What time is it?"

"You don't wear a watch?" She had not noticed before.

"What use would I have for a watch? There's a clock on my desk to keep me from working too long, but that's the only timepiece in the house."

"I can't imagine living without knowing the time. But I suppose you're right; in a place like this...."

"So what time is it?"

Reflexively, she looked down at her wrist, but before she could register the numbers, she looked back up at him and smiled. She unstrapped the watch and put it face-down on the table between them. "It's late evening," she said.

"Tired?"

A slight frown wrinkled her countenance. "Is that a proposition?"

"Of a sort. Want to go for a walk?"

She nodded, relieved that he hadn't meant more. It would have spoiled everything. And ruined her objectivity.

"Yes. That would be nice. Especially if there's a chance we could get some food somewhere."

"I'm sure that Ana at *José's* would oblige us. Or there's always *El Presidente*. As long as you don't mind eating outside," he added mischievously.

Donna shivered, remembering her confrontation with Barclay inside the bar. "Please don't remind me."

"Come on then, you're making me hungry."

But once they were outside, Barclay wordlessly turned right, away from the *Calle de Generalissimo Javier Felipe Duarte*. They had gone a hundred meters, and the shabby houses along the *Avenida La Guardia* had given way to mean shacks before Donna realized that Barclay had linked his arm through hers.

She must have reacted, for at that moment Barclay stopped and freed his arm. He pointed up at the sky. "Have you ever seen anything like it?"

Tecimal at night, once one left the *Calle*, was a dark place. Here and there, lights in the closer shacks cast a dull yellow glow that barely touched the darkness. The only real light came from a waxing moon, early in its cycle, halfway to the western horizon. The sky was cloudless: the Milky Way arched overhead like a phosphorescent band reaching from horizon to horizon. Away from the hazy band, the stars hung in the patterns used by nomads, travellers, explorers and sailors for thousands of years.

"It... it's beautiful," said Donna. "I'd never realized."

"No. One of the many curses of civilization is that it has separated us from nature. Progress has a lot to answer for."

For a while they said nothing, sharing the silence of the night and the grandeur of the sky. To the north, above *Las Montañas del Cielo*, occasional lightning flashed, its thunder too distant to be audible.

A shooting star sped across the sky.

Donna said, "They say that if you wish on a shooting star, your wish will come true."

"So what's your wish?"

"They also say that if you tell anyone your wish, it won't come true."

"My wish will never come true anyway."

She looked at him sharply and he turned away, hiding his face from her.

"I'm sorry. It slipped out," he said. "Blame it on too many drinks."

"What's the matter? I don't understand."

For a long moment Barclay did not reply. Then he said with the abruptness of a man who had just made a decision, "Come with me. It's the only really important thing I haven't told you."

He strode away, and Donna had to move quickly to catch up. He turned left, heading south, and they soon reached the place where the houses stopped at the edge of the wide annulus of bare ground surrounding the church. Barclay led the way across the bare earth and around to the far side of the church. Donna had not ventured here before, and she was momentarily taken aback to see that Barclay was opening the gate of Tecimal's cemetery.

The cemetery was perhaps sixty meters square, separated from its surroundings by a low wooden fence. The graves were arranged in a loose grid; many of them were in clusters, showing where several generations of a single family were buried. Most of the graves were marked with a simple wooden headboard; only a few of the more pretentious boasted an engraved stone; many of the low mounds were marked with only a cross.

Wordlessly, Barclay led the way to an undistinguished area near the western edge of the cemetery. He halted in front of a pair of graves, each marked with a simple cross. One of the pair was small: a child's resting place. On the far side of the child a space had been left for a grave as yet undug. A single rose, desiccated by the heat, lay on the ground in front of the larger cross. Barclay pointed, and Donna saw that words were engraved on the crosses.

She leant closer, trying to make out the words in the exiguous light of the westering moon. ROSALINDA, she read, and the years of birth and death, 1950 – 1969. On the child's cross was only a single date: JULY 12, 1969.

She heard a sound and turned to look at Barclay. He was gazing at Rosalinda's grave; a tear was trickling down his cheek.

"Who was she?" Donna asked.

"My wife."

There was a long, empty silence.

"Your wife?"

"Rosalinda was the most beautiful woman I've ever known. I came to Tecimal in February of 1968, expecting to stay only a few days while I did some research for my second book. Rosalinda was the reason I stayed."

"How did she die? I'm sorry; I shouldn't pry. Don't tell me if you don't want to."

"No, it's all right. I wanted to show you. Now you know why my one wish will never be granted. For thirty years I've wanted only one thing: for Rosalinda to be restored to me. I know it can never happen, but that doesn't stop me from wanting it, even after all this time. Every hour of every day I think of her and pray to God that we will be together again."

"The rose? Is that yours?"

"Yes. It's the one extravagance I allow myself. Every week, a rose comes on the bus from Chiclahan, and I bring it here. To show her I haven't forgotten."

Donna indicated the smaller cross. "A child?"

Barclay nodded. He opened his mouth to speak, but for a moment his grief overcame him, and it was a while before he could bring himself to explain.

"She was stillborn. There was nothing anyone could do, at least not with the facilities available in Tecimal in those days. The midwife did the best she could. The placenta wrapped itself around the child's throat while my wife was in labor. In the process of delivering, Rosalinda ruptured herself. She died from loss of blood less than an hour after the child was delivered. We were holding hands when she died. Her last words were, 'I'm sorry. I love you.'"

He turned away, unable to say any more.

"I'm sorry," said Donna. "I didn't know."

"How could you have known? She was my life. When she died, I fell to pieces. I can't remember much of what happened afterward. For weeks I wandered around in a kind of daze. I thought seriously about killing myself, but Father Emilio talked me out of that, although even he could do little to assuage my grief. It was Rosalinda's mother who came up with the solution that gave me the strength to go on."

"What was that?"

"She told me to go to Xloxratl. Rosalinda believed in the old woman, you see. I'd tried to argue her out of it many times. All the arguments you've thrown at me the past few days I used long ago to try to convince my wife that a good Catholic — and like almost everyone in Tecimal, she *was* a good Catholic — that a good Catholic could not believe in the powers of an Indian shaman living like a hermit in the hills.

"She was immune to all my arguments. She just said that one day I would believe and left it at that. I realize now that Xloxratl must have told her that. Anyway, when Rosalinda died I completely forgot about Xloxratl until her mother came to me and suggested that I go into the mountains and discover the truth for myself.

"Nothing else had worked, so out of pure desperation I agreed. I wanted Rosalinda's mother to come with me, but she told me I must go alone. I was in no state to argue. So I went to see Xloxratl."

It was late afternoon as the Land Rover came to a halt. Barclay surveyed his surroundings dubiously. On the far side of the clearing stood a tin hut, hard against the scarred mountain, close to a tall tunnel that, he guessed, was one of the old mine workings from the days when this mountain was the source of more than half the world's silver.

He could see the remains of half a dozen other huts, some tin, some stone, all of them tumbled and halfway to ruin. A tidy vegetable garden hugged the one hut that was in good repair. A goat was tethered to a stake; the animal looked up briefly to examine the interloper before it resumed chewing the thin grass near to the entrance of the tunnel.

Overhead, the massed clouds grumbled, and Barclay got out of the Land Rover as the first drops of rain began to fall. The goat retreated into the tunnel and disappeared from view as Barclay walked across the clearing towards the hut. There was no sign of the woman he had come to see.

A rickety door hung open at an awkward angle. He halted in the doorway and peered into the gloom, letting his eyes adjust to the darkness. Behind him, a spear of lightning flashed to the ground somewhere not far away, the sharp crack of thunder hard on its heels. Heavy rain began to fall.

As the thunder died away, he heard a grating voice inside the hut: "Come in, come in. I've been waiting for you."

He took a step inside, but in the tenebrosity it was a moment before he spotted the owner of the voice. Sitting in one corner, motionless, was an old woman whom he had first mistaken for a pile of discarded clothes. It was impossible to guess her age. "Ancient" was the only word that sprang to his mind as she sat there without moving, scrutinizing the intruder.

She beckoned. "Come here, and let me see you." She spoke slowly, in a thick Chiclahan accent.

Barclay crossed the dirt floor and knelt in front of the old woman. She looked at him, and he returned her gaze, too startled at first to look away. Her eyes were the strangest he had ever seen, one green and one yellow, and they moved independently of each other, so that one eye examined his face while the other roved over the rest of his body.

"I'm glad you came. Your name is Barclay?" the old woman said.

"Yes. My wife... Rosalinda... she...."

"She is dead."

The old woman caught him off guard with her matter-of-fact statement, delivered as if she were talking about someone who had died long ago.

"Who told you?" he asked.

The old woman made an odd gurgling sound in her throat, and it was some time before Barclay realized that she was laughing to herself.

He shouted, "You find it funny that my wife is dead?"

He turned to storm out of the hut, but she replied, so quietly that he could hardly hear, "Please, Señor Barclay, accept my apologies. I am an old woman, and I have lived here for many more years than you can remember, my only company the words of Javí when He chooses to speak them. Please know that I mean you no harm and your wife no disrespect. I assure you that your wife meant more to me than you can possibly know. There are few left who believe, and I mourn deeply the passing of every one."

"Then why were you laughing?"

"You are suspicious of me, Señor Barclay. But perhaps it is for the best. Your wife told me the story of the man you call Saint Paul, and it has the ring of truth to it."

Barclay felt more disoriented every second. Not only was the old woman apparently incapable of holding a rational conversation, but there was something in the air inside the hut that was making him feel giddy, as if he had drunk a little too much.

"Please, sit."

It was framed as a request, but Barclay understood that it was really a command. His limbs obeyed the order of their own volition, and he found himself sitting on the ground a meter or so in front of the shaman. She looked into his eyes searchingly, as if looking for something she expected to see there but which she had so far failed to find.

The hut seemed suddenly oppressively quiet. To break the silence, he asked, "How many people still believe in you?"

She smiled. He had never seen a smile like it except on the faces of young children. It was coy and almost infectious, as if she were about to share a delightful secret she had never told anyone before. He wondered again if he were slightly drunk.

"One, Señor Barclay."

Barclay did not know what to say. "Does he visit you often?" he eventually asked.

The smile broadened, seeming to expand beyond the confines of the shaman's face until it included everything in the hut. Barclay realized that he, too, was smiling, sharing in some secret joke of which he was unaware.

"I have seen him only once. But he will return... many times."

"What's his name? Perhaps I know him."

"Oh, yes, you know him. But not as well as his wife did, and not as well as I do."

Suddenly he understood.

Barclay scrambled angrily to his feet and shouted down at her, "I came here because my wife believed in you and I always ridiculed her. She said one day I would understand, but now I know I never will. For my wife's sake I won't tell you what I think of you, except to say that I'm profoundly sorry you deluded her for so long. I'm leaving now. I won't be back."

He had taken two steps toward the door when the woman uttered a single syllable. "No," she said, so quietly that it was barely more than a whisper.

Barclay halted in midstride, but not because he wanted to. The muscles in his legs simply refused to obey his command to leave the hut. He strained, but they would not move.

"I'm sorry. You will turn around and sit down. I cannot permit you to leave until I have finished."

Straining against his own muscles, Barclay turned and lowered himself to the ground.

"What are doing to me? How are you doing that? What kind of a witch are you? "

"You are a civilized man. Surely you are not so gullible as to believe in witches?"

"Only a fool does not believe in the power of the spiritual world."

The old woman nodded in agreement. "You speak sense. Of course I knew you would. The spirit world is just as real as the physical one, do you not agree?"

Barclay nodded.

"And yet you find it impossible to believe in one to whom the spirits tell their secrets?"

"The Church speaks of spirits and demons as real beings, so I have to believe that they're just as real as I am. But the Church also warns us to stay away from those who claim to speak to the spirits."

"And yet the one you call Jesus, did he not speak to spirits?"

"That's different."

"Why? Because it was so long ago? You know that is no answer. But I will not argue with you. I will simply tell you... and show you. The rest is up to you. Did your wife tell you beforehand that she was going to die?"

"Rosalinda? Of course not. How could she have known? Everything went perfectly until the very end of her labor. There was no way any of us could have guessed what was going to happen."

"But I tell you that she did know."

"You're *loco*. How could she have known? I tell you, it's impossible."

"She knew because I told her."

"Impossible." Barclay made a half-hearted attempt to rise, but his legs still refused to obey.

"Just now I told you she was dead, and you asked who told me. I will tell you: the spirit of Javí told me. The spirit told me, just as the spirit told me many months ago that she was going to die. The last time she visited, I told Rosalinda what Javí had revealed to me. She is a strong woman, Señor Barclay. Even though she knew she was going to her death, she still returned to you. She loves you very much."

Barclay noticed that the shaman was using the present tense. "Don't try to make me believe she's still alive, like some kind of ghost. That's a shoddy trick to try to play on someone grieving for a loved one."

"Señor Barclay, you do not understand. My name is Xloxratl. Do you know what that means?"

"The One who tells the Truth."

"That is true, but it means much more than that. Perhaps a better translation would be: The One Who Cannot Tell a Lie. If I were to permit a falsehood to escape my lips, Señor Barclay, I would fall over dead before I could finish the sentence."

Barclay held his tongue. It was quite clear that the woman believed everything she was telling him, and equally clear that he could say nothing to change that belief.

"The spirits talk to me. Most of what they say, I keep to myself. But sometimes they use me to send messages to others. I told your wife her future because the spirit of Javí Himself, the greatest of all spirits, told me what her future held."

"Why? What was the point of telling her she was going to die?"

"The point, Señor Barclay? To test whether her love was strong enough to overcome her fear. Once I'd told her, she had a choice to make. I have not told you all I told your wife, all that Javí had revealed. She could return to Tecimal, in which case she would die soon. Or she could leave you forever, in which case perhaps she would deliver a healthy baby and live a long life of her own."

Barclay shook his head. "You're talking nonsense. You tried to scare her and failed, that's all."

"I told her the truth. I told her what would happen. There are few things more terrifying than a glimpse of the future."

Barclay declared triumphantly, "But if you'd told her what was going to happen, there wasn't much point in her trying to change it, was there?"

"People always have free will, Señor Barclay."

"I don't. You won't let me leave."

The old woman rocked backward on her heels, as if he had slapped her hard across the face. For a moment, he wondered if she had lost consciousness and was about to collapse, but then she said weakly. "You are right, señor. I should not have done this to you. You are free to go."

Barclay discovered that he had regained control of his legs, but before he could stand the old woman continued, "Perhaps I can help you understand about choice and free will. The one whom you call Jesus knew he was going to die, did he not?"

"Yes."

"And the night before he died, did he not pray that Javí, whom he called Father, would let this death pass from him?"

"Yes."

"And do you not think it was within his power to escape death?"

"Of course it was. He could have left Jerusalem and hidden in the hills. But if he'd done that, everything would have been different."

"Quite so. If he did not die, he could not come back from the dead. And if he didn't come back from the dead, then all of human history would have been changed."

Puzzled, Barclay said, "Do you mean... do you mean you believe?"

"That Javí has a son whom he sent to die? Why should I not believe that? It is no more incredible than many other things that are certainly true. But the point is that your Jesus knew what the future held, and still he did not walk away from it. He exercised his free will to meet his future, painful though it was. Your wife did the same, and she did it because she loved you

130

and could not bear to leave you. She knew how much it would hurt you if she left."

Barclay shook his head. "I'm sorry. I know you mean well, and I'm sure you believe everything you're saying, but I'm afraid I can't believe any of it."

"You want proof? Is that it?"

Barclay got to his feet. "I'm sorry. Thank you for everything you did for Rosalinda. I know you meant a lot to her. But I think I'd better be going now."

The old woman sighed. "I wish it had not come to this. But you are a stubborn man, Señor Barclay. I shall give you your proof."

———

"She told me something she could not possibly have known," Barclay said, his watery eyes on the cross that bore his wife's name.

"What did she say?"

Barclay shook his head. "Not now. Perhaps not ever. But it was something I'd never mentioned to Rosalinda, something that had been tearing me apart ever since she had died. Something that only one other person in the entire world knows, and which no one else could possibly guess."

"Perhaps that person told the old shaman."

Barclay smiled a tight smile. "That's even harder to believe than that the spirit of God told her."

"So that's why you believe in her powers?"

"No. Not any more. That's why I started to believe. But that was all a long time ago. As the years passed I gradually realized that the old woman was right all along. She is Xloxratl, and indeed she is the One who tells the Truth."

He looked sharply up at the sky. The moon had disappeared below the western horizon. To the north, the lightning had flickered to an end, leaving the distant hills a barely discernible shadow on the horizon. Only scattered starlight and the faint luminosity of the Milky Way lit the cemetery.

"Come on," said Barclay. "I'm hungry. Let's go find something to eat."

PART II
LETTERS

September 8

Dear Andrew

You can't imagine how many times I've tried to start this
letter and then gone back and deleted what I've already
written. Even the salutation has given me no end of grief.
"Dear Mr. Barclay" is so disgustingly formal. "Dearest
Andrew" seems presumptuous — which is ridiculous really,
isn't it? Considering that last night, I mean.

I could say it would have been easier if you'd already
written me, giving me a pattern to copy; but of course you
warned me not to expect much in the way of correspondence
from you. And, as you pointed out, I have the luxury of a
computer, which means that I can simply let my fingers get
carried away and be as verbose as they wish (can fingers be
verbose?) while you insist on conducting correspondence
by writing every word by hand. You will note, however,
that I have taken your advice and I am printing this in a
monospaced typeface.

Oh dear, this is worse than any of my previous drafts. My
words are coming out so stilted. I'd better get on and tell
you what's been happening before you wonder if I've been
drinking too much. Which, I assure you, I haven't.

I got back to LA on the Wednesday after I left Tecimal.
The only memorable thing that happened on the way back
was that someone in Chiclahan tried to steal my bag, but
fortunately a police officer had been watching me and
managed to thwart the dastardly deed. When I arrived back
home, I had intended to get straight to work on my thesis,
but what with one thing and another it was Monday before I
had time to begin to sort through my notes. (I know what
you're thinking, but honestly it wasn't because I was
putting off the "labor of thinking" — there was simply too
much to do. Travelling for two straight days is incredibly
tiring, and then I had to restock the apartment with food
and get myself organized for the new semester.)

Just listening to the tapes takes most of an entire day, of course. Incidentally, I had an odd experience when I listened to them the first time. I had all kinds of memories of things one or the other of us had said, but when I heard the tapes I kept discovering that what we'd actually said was something quite different.

This happened so many times that at first I half wondered if Xloxratl had somehow magically altered the tapes. But eventually sanity prevailed and I decided that my memory is simply untrustworthy.

Anyway, I've spent most of this week trying to construct some sort of coherent outline of what I'm going to write. It's been a stinker of a week here (literally), with temperatures in the high nineties and smog alerts nearly every day. The air is so polluted that it's sometimes hard to see more than a quarter of a mile, and it catches at the back of the throat like a glass of your raw tequila.

Remembering our visit to the cemetery, I went out one night to look at the sky, and it was terribly disappointing. In Tecimal, it was impossible to count the stars. Here you can count them on the fingers of one hand.

To get back to the point of this letter, and at the risk of having you bite off my head, here's the outline I've come up with. I'd be interested in what you think of it (but I don't promise to change it to suit you).

1. Outline of *The Condition of Love*, emphasizing the symmetry between the backgrounds of Adrian and Fiona and what brought them to the commune.

2. The cultural milieu of the 1960's: experimentation with drugs; the Beatles and other "pop" groups; the rise of hippiedom; experimental communes.

3. Your own background. I'll need a lot more help here. When I started listening to the tapes, I realized that you'd told me almost nothing about your family.

136

4. Belief systems: communism/capitalism; theism/atheism; the difference between stated belief and belief as reflected by actions.

5. Parallels between the commune in *The Condition of Love* and your residence in Tecimal (I hope that won't make you angry. But don't you see them both as an escape?) There won't be enough of this to make a complete chapter, but I want to slip it in somewhere.

6. A short section on the failure and eventual dissolution of the commune in the book, and the assimilation of Adrian and Fiona into what they called "uncivilization."

7. A conclusion. But I'm not really sure what the conclusion should be. On one hand, the commune appears to be a failure, since it dissolves and the members all go their own ways. On the other hand, Adrian and Fiona's love overcomes the failure, and their belief system remains essentially intact despite everything that has happened. Please don't tell me what *you* think the conclusion should be. I want to work out a sensible one for myself. Afterwards, we can talk about whether it agrees with what you really intended.

Does any of this make sense to you?

Knowing how you feel about word-processed letters, and especially how they tend to go on (and on and on), I think I'll call it a day for now.

I do hope you can find time to reply, even if only briefly.

Yours ever (see, I have just as much trouble here as I did with the salutation)

PS You needn't worry. Just in case you have been, I mean.

September 16

Dear Andrew

Don't expect a letter every week. I just thought you'd like
to be kept up to date with what's happening here. I know
you've probably only just received my last letter. I do
hope you'll reply to it, though.

I talked with several people who use tape recordings a lot:
a couple of graduates in the school of journalism, and also
some people in the law school. They all told me the same
thing: that people's memories are notoriously unreliable.
Apparently it's quite common for people to wonder if their
tapes have been tampered with because what the tapes play
back is so different from what they remember.

Of course, I never really thought Xloxratl had anything
to do with it. For one thing, I can hear the children
playing outside. And anyway you know how I still feel about
Xloxratl and her purported powers, despite what happened
to us. But perhaps what happened was simply inevitable;
I don't know. I don't intend to demean it by analyzing it
(or *thinking* about it, as you would probably say). What
happened happened, and of course I regret none of it.

There's one more thing I must tell you before I leave
this subject completely. When I was sorting out the
clothes I wore in Tecimal, I came across something that had
completely slipped my mind.

When we were with Xloxratl, she gave me something while you
were outside getting some water. (At least, that's the way I
remember it; given my confused recollection of the entire
trip, it could have happened at almost any time really —
the whole twenty four hour period is little more than an
indistinct haze. I didn't understand it at the time, but
now its symbolism is obvious. She fashioned a pair of grass
stalks together into a Y and then turned it upside down and
handed it to me. She told me to keep it, and that I would
come to understand what it meant. Obviously, it was meant

138

to symbolize our coming together as lovers. I've taped the grass to the wall above my computer, so that every time I look at it, I can't help but think of you.

I'm sure you're thinking as you read this that I am being terribly soppy, and particularly womanish. All I can tell you is that sometimes I find myself wondering if my whole time in Tecimal was nothing but a dream; but then I catch sight of Xloxratl's intertwined grasses and I know it all happened, that you and I really did spend that night in each other's arms, and that it was the *right* thing to do — that in some sense it was all preordained.

Please forgive me. I'm getting hopelessly sentimental. I feel like simply deleting everything I've written so far and starting all over again. But I won't. No doubt it will do your ego good (and, quite frankly, your ego could do with some building up after the battering you've been giving it about the second book) to know that you can make a slip of a girl like me go all gooey-eyed and muddle her thinking.

Anyway, I'm waiting to hear from you what you think of the outline I sent you last week. Professor Andover gave it her blessing (although she still makes no attempt to hide her opinion that my choice of thesis topic is questionable). Anticipating no great objections from you, I've begun padding it out.

I haven't told you much about Professor Andover, have I?

She's a rather mousy woman in her early fifties. She wears half-moon glasses on a chain around her neck — an affectation that more or less sums her up, in a way. She has the unnerving habit of looking elsewhere when she's talking to you, except when she's just asked a question: then she peers over the top of her glasses with an expression that I'm never sure about — it could be either skepticism or simple curiosity.

I'm afraid she's one of those terribly old-fashioned professors who believes that Jane Austen marks the

apotheosis of the novel, and after *Persuasion* the art went
to hell in a handbasket, with only occasional lapses into
readability by authors like Dickens and Trollope. You can
imagine how she reacted when I first told her I wanted to
write a thesis on you. I have to hand it to her, though:
although she initially tried to talk me out of it, once
she realized I wasn't going to be moved, she accepted my
stubbornness reasonably gracefully.

She's been in England most of the summer, researching
the private letters of John Sweet (an obscure
nineteenth-century English novelist, in case you didn't
know), and yesterday was the first chance we'd had to
get together to talk about my thesis. The idea was that I
would bring her up to date with what happened in Tecimal. I
suppose I have to tell you that I was terrified in case she
asked outright if we'd had a physical relationship of any
kind. No, let me rephrase that in the words she would use.
(Professor Andover is not one to beat about the bush.) I was
scared she would ask if we'd slept together, and then fix
me with that stare of hers over the half-moon glasses. It
would have been pointless to lie: my blush would have told
her the truth. And then, of course, she would have forced me
to change my thesis topic, citing lack of objectivity. So
you can imagine how I felt as I entered her office.

Professor Andover cleans out her office once a year, just
before she takes her annual trip to England. When she gets
back, it stays pristine for a day or two, but then the slow
but inevitable accumulation of papers begins, like the
first powder of the season in the mountains, a harbinger
of the drifts to follow as the year progresses. By the end
of the year, there are piles of papers and books covering
almost every square inch of her desk and table, and even the
floor sprouts unstable stalagmites of printed matter.

Anyway, since she'd just returned from her trip, her
office was almost immaculate. There was a small pile of
departmental flyers on the corner of her desk, but that was
all. She told me to take a seat and, to try to pre-empt the

embarrassing question I was afraid she was going to ask, I got in first with, "How was your trip this year, Professor Andover?"

She looked tired, probably still jet-lagged, but she nodded enthusiastically. "Good. Very good, actually. I spent several days at the Bodleian in Oxford. They have several hundred of John Sweet's letters there, and I think I learned enough from those to make the beginnings of a synthesis of his writings. Enough for a journal article or two, anyway; perhaps even a monograph. I trust that your visit to, what was the name of the place again?"

"Tecimal."

"Yes. I trust that your visit to Tecimal was as productive, if not more so."

I recounted more or less the highlights of my visit, except that I'm afraid I rather emphasized the difficulties you gave me early on. I never did tell her much about the last twenty four hours, in case that set her mind to wandering in directions I wanted to avoid.

Was that subversive of me, do you think? I really don't think my objectivity has suffered. I certainly don't intend to praise you unstintingly in my thesis. (Does that surprise you? Annoy you? Or perhaps it simply amuses you?) My little deception must have worked. Either that or she is more perceptive than I give her credit for and she's decided she'd rather not be told. Anyway, whatever the reason the fateful question remained unasked and I escaped half an hour later with her blessing to continue with my thesis as planned.

This letter is becoming over-long. I won't write again until I hear back from you. By then I hope I'll have made enough progress with the thesis to have more questions that need answering. Incidentally, I've temporarily given up writing fiction. I decided I had to prioritize my life, so I'm going to keep my fiction-writing on hold until I've got my thesis out of the way. You know, you never did give me much of an idea of what you thought about my book. I suppose it's not important just at the moment, but sometime I'd really like you to tell me what you think of what I've written so far and whether I should keep going.

I hope your writing is going well, and your long-standing difficulties are now behind you. Also, of course, I hope you are well. Have you cut down on the alcohol? (I sound like an anxious mother hen, don't I?) Sorry; I'd promised that I wouldn't ask. But I have to know. I care for you too much.

Yours ever

Dear Donna

You have forced me to break with my principles. It has been, until now, a firmly held belief that personal letters should be handwritten. However, your letters are so long — and demanding of a similar response — that you have forced me to abandon the practice of a lifetime.

Since you have been honest with me, I suppose I must be equally honest with you: I confess that I almost did not write this letter at all. When you left Tecimal that morning, I stood looking at the road long after the dust had settled and I could no longer see the bus. You youngsters can have no idea how disconcerting it is to have one's comfortable late-middle-age life uprooted by an unlooked-for, if not entirely unexpected, intrusion.

For a while, as I stared into the distance, I almost convinced myself that I had a choice: that, if I desired, I could simply walk away and return to my old life. I almost made myself believe that with your departure things would return to normal; that I had given you what you had come for; that there was no reason why I could not now consign you to my past, a mere bump in the laminar flow of my days.

But of course I was deluding myself, and I knew it even at the time. Xloxratl has made it perfectly clear that you are going

142

to help me write my second book. Unfortunately, in the manner of oracles and prophets in all times and places, she has given no indication of <u>how</u> you are going to accomplish that task.

I admit that I had been hoping that your participation would be merely catalytic, that having met you and undergone the agony of self-revelation that you forced on me, I would be free to write again as I once did. In short, to put it bluntly, I had hoped that I would never have to interact with you again. (I was going to write "have intercourse", which is undoubtedly the correct phrase, but in these depraved days with their debasement of the language, I fear my meaning would be too easily misunderstood.)

Perhaps my hopes will still be met, but I fear not. Something tells me that our interactions (awful word; makes us sound like a physics experiment) are not yet over. And so I fear that I cannot ignore your letters, much though I might wish otherwise.

In a typical Tecimalian fashion, your letters, despite being written more than a week apart, reached me on the same day. You will have to make do with this one reply to both of them, since I see no reason to prolong my agony by formulating distinct responses to your two missives.

Your thesis outline seems almost unexceptionable. The symmetry between Adrian and Fiona to which you refer was unintentional (at least insofar as I recollect my thoughts after so many years). One of the early reviews (the <u>TLS</u>?) mentioned it as an example of (if I remember the phrase correctly) "the author's subtle brilliance". I don't remember that any other examples of my subtle brilliance were given, and in this case the brilliance was so subtle that it had evaded my own notice. (Perhaps one could argue that true brilliance need neither be conscious nor even recognized by its possessor. The existence of idiots savant would seem to support such a view.)

My only other comment on your outline is that no, I don't see Tecimal as an escape, at least in the sense I suspect you mean. I came here simply in search of background for what I had hoped would be my second book. Once I met Rosalinda, the question of my returning to England never really arose. And after she died.... Well, I suppose that by then I had become accustomed to the pace of life here. The only things I truly miss after more than quarter of a century are the rain and the concomitant verdancy of the English countryside, and the occasional scratch game of cricket.

Looking back, I am fairly certain that I would never have had the courage to "escape" civilization, had that been my aim. If it were not for Rosalinda, I would have continued my brief tour of central America and returned home within two or three months. Doubtless I would have finished my second book, and the rest of my life would have been completely different from the one I have actually experienced.

Is it not strange how a life contains such pivotal points? If I had not chanced to visit Tecimal; if I had stayed only a day or two, and not seen Rosalinda; if Rosalinda had not been as smitten with me as I was with her; if her parents had not been so understanding... these and countless other "if's" had to occur before you could disembark from that bus and walk across the street and into my life.

I'll tell you a secret, Donna. When I saw you standing on the other side of the street after getting off the bus, I was certain that the Devil had sent you to perform some mischief of his own. But now I look back on everything that had to happen for that moment to occur and I find it hard to believe that even the Devil could be so circuitous. But perhaps the Devil is simply an opportunist, and took advantage of what God had already done.

Where was I? Oh, yes. (You see, unlike you with your confounded machine, I can't go back and erase my meanderings.) I was going to tell you that I detest the busyness of "civilization" not, I think, out of prejudice but because it seems to me that what society terms "civilization" is in fact nothing but a system for keeping everyone so busy that no one has time to consider the important things in life. To live a life without a foundational belief system — a theology if you will, although I suppose there's no specific requirement that God make an appearance — is an empty, inhuman thing. Yet that is undoubtedly how most "civilized" people live, no matter what they profess. The really unfortunate thing is that they probably don't even realize what they're missing.

144

If you doubt me, just consider your own reaction to the sight of the night sky here in Tecimal compared to the disappointment you felt when you tried the same experiment in Los Angeles.

I have no other comments on your outline. I have never read a thesis, and have no intention of ever doing so, so any advice I might offer would be simply the opinion of a layman. The only insight I offer is that at the time that I was writing <u>Condition</u> there were, in effect, no pop groups other than the Beatles. At least, that was the way it was in England. What the Beatles did today, America did tomorrow; then, the day after, it returned to England transformed and amplified, and was quickly adopted by the youth of those days, only to be picked up by the Americans again. In these sordid literal days when Britain has lost not only its Empire but even its adjective, it is hard to believe how optimistic we once were and how ready the whole world was to follow where we had shown them the way.

Enough. I am in danger of indulging in an examination of the British national psyche, for which I have neither the training nor the stamina.

I am now nearly at the end of your first letter. Your cryptic PS ("You needn't worry. Just in case you have been, I mean.") had me stymied for a while before I decided that you were trying to tell me periphrastically that you aren't pregnant. Would you be terribly let down if I told you that the thought had barely crossed my mind? Worrying never changes facts; I long ago decided to give up worrying about the future or regretting the past. The present is where we live, Donna. Today is the only day that matters.

I don't know what to make of the grass Y that Xloxratl gave you. It's my experience that she rarely repeats herself; yet if your interpretation is to be believed, her gift was simply a repetition of what she had already told us individually: that we would be lovers. I suspect, therefore, that there is more to it than you have concluded; but what she had in mind I have no idea.

Your Professor Andover is full of hogwash, and you are perfectly welcome to tell her so from me. Jane Austen was popular simply because she wrote escapist fiction. Compare the events and the settings of her stories with what was happening in England at the start of the nineteenth century. Her novels are the early-nineteenth-century equivalent of those expensive escapist movies that did so well during the Second World War.

You are wise to concentrate on your thesis at the cost of your fiction. Fiction is a folly for rich men and unoccupied women. Your thesis will advance your career; once you have established yourself in a college somewhere, you will have time to write fiction — if you still have the inclination. But remember the exercises I gave you. If you practice them assiduously in the intervening years, they will make the operose task of writing a novel almost bearable. Almost.

Yours

———————————

October 6

Dear Andrew

Thank you for your letter. I count myself honored that you broke the tradition of a lifetime by using your typewriter. Although, now I come to think of it, it seems odd to be honored by a typewritten letter instead of a handwritten one.

A couple of carry-over threads first. I see that you did not answer the personal questions I asked at the end of my second letter. (You can't fool me; the computer keeps a copy of my letters, so it's easy for me to check whether you've answered all my questions.) How is the writing going, and how is your health? Have you cut down on the drinking? Doctor Pasquale was most insistent that you are in danger of drinking yourself to death. Please, Andrew, I don't want to nag or to preach, but do try to look after yourself better. I don't want anything to happen to you.

Regarding Jane Austen: I'm sorry, but I just can't accept that she was no more than a kind of primordial Danielle Steel. While I certainly don't share Professor Andover's enthusiasm for Austen's books, I have to concede that at

146

least a couple of them belong on any list of "top hundred"
books. On the other hand, I think that my professor's
devotion to John Sweet borders on the ridiculous. As far as
I can tell from the two novels I've forced myself to read,
his oblivion as a writer is entirely deserved.

Now, before I go any further, I have what I hope is good
news. I've decided to come back to Tecimal for Christmas.
I hope that *is* good news. I think I'll have a first draft of
my thesis ready by then, and I'd very much like you to take a
look at it and tell me what you think.

I haven't dared tell Professor Andover about this, partly
because it once again raises the risk that she'll ask
about the two of us, and partly because I know she would
balk at the idea of your seeing a thesis that is supposed
to be independent and objective. She'd be certain I was
submitting it for some kind of vetting. I hope you don't
think the same thing. Your comments would be invaluable,
but please don't imagine I want you to do my work for me.

Anyway, when the time is right, I'll just tell her I'm
going away for a couple of weeks' vacation over Christmas.
Assuming it's all right with you if I come and visit again,
that is. Please tell me if you don't want me to come and I'll
abide by whatever you say.

The thesis is going well, I think. I've drafted all the
first chapter, as well as half the second and odd bits of the
others. Computers make it so much easier for a disorganized
person like me to produce a reasonably coherent product
from a veritable mish-mash of notes, jottings, tapes and
ideas.

Maybe you should get a computer. I'm sure it would make the
job of writing easier. These days you can buy dictionaries
and thesauruses that work on computers; they're much faster
than the printed versions, and I'm sure they'd save you a
lot of time when you're trying to find exactly the right
word. And if your spelling is anything like mine, you'd find
a spell-checking program invaluable.

There is still one aspect of Andrew Barclay that I am having
trouble with (apart, that is, from the fact that more
frequently than I like to admit I wonder I'm infatuated
with him and over-concerned about what he thinks of me).
The Andrew Barclay I know seems to drag religion into even
the most mundane of conversations, yet there seems to be
no trace of religiosity in *The Condition of Love*. Was your
faith something that came to you after you wrote the book?
Or did you simply think that it had no part in your writing?

I will tell you that you are without doubt the most
religious person I have ever met, and your religiosity
is the most confusing thing about you. I still don't
understand how you can embrace both Catholicism and
shamanism at the same time, nor do I understand your
cavalier attitude to acts that your church teaches to be
sinful. Yet one thing that became clear in the brief time
we spent together is that without your beliefs you would be
a very different person. Please bear with me while I try to
understand this. You must understand that to an enlightened
liberal woman such a resolute faith in something inherently
unknowable and unprovable as God is as troublesome as if
you'd said you support slavery.

Trying to come to grips with all this, I went to church last
Sunday. (There, that surprised you, didn't it?) It would
be hard to imagine a greater contrast with what I saw in
Tecimal. The church here was an enormous modern edifice of
steel and glass with a ceiling so high I swear you could have
taken your church and stood it on end and still not hit the
roof.

There must have been two thousand people at the service. The
seats (not a trace of a pew) were similar to the ones they
have in movie theaters. They were even arranged in terraces
so that each person had an unimpeded view of what was going
on at the front of the church.

The service in Tecimal left me with the feeling that I'd
witnessed a kind of arcane religious ritual, the purpose of

which was never entirely clear to me. (So tell me, please: what exactly *is* the purpose of going to church on Sunday?) I'm afraid that the purpose of the service I went to on Sunday was all too clear: it was a carefully orchestrated theatrical show, with the pastor as both emcee and star performer. The support act was the choir, a hundred strong and wearing immaculate robes and intricately embroidered stoles that probably cost more than it takes to feed the entire population of Tecimal for a year.

The pastor, unlike poor Father Emilio, was blessed with a voice that was deep and sonorous; it also benefited from a hi-fi sound system that ensured his words reached every corner of the enormous sanctuary. And just in case someone missed the pastor's sermon, the whole show was videotaped. ("Video and audio tapes of the service are available at 2pm on Monday," according to the church bulletin.)

I won't bore you with details, except to say that I'm sure you would have been disgusted with the whole sorry spectacle. I may not understand your faith, but I do understand the importance it has to you, and I also understand that I need to understand it better before I can understand you. (Five "understand"s in one sentence. Oh dear!)

I won't say any more about this; it's not really the sort of thing we can discuss in letters; but I hope you won't mind talking about it more at Christmas.

One more thing about Christmas: if I do come, should I stay with Señora Delgado again or do you want me to stay with you? You know Tecimal's mores and I don't, so I leave that decision entirely in your hands. Although, since I absented myself from Señora Delgado's for my last night in Tecimal, I don't imagine it would do much further harm to simply admit everything and openly move in with you. But I'll abide by your decision.

I think that's just about all for now, except to say that for the last week or so, LA has been baking under an unseasonal

heatwave. Everyone has been complaining and waiting for
the weather to break; but I assure you that this is nothing
compared to Tecimal in August. I'll never again complain
about it being too hot in California.

Love

----

15 October

Señorita Donna

*Please excuse me writing to you like this. I do not know exactly
the relationship you have with Señor Barclay, but I do know that you
are exchanging letters. Living in a place such as Tecimal does have its
consolations: it was easy to get your address from the post office, copied
from one of your own envelopes. Since you are still communicating with
Señor Barclay, I retain some hope that perhaps you might also have
some influence with him.*

*Señorita, I do not know what Señor Barclay has told you about his
condition, if indeed he has told you anything. I shall do my best to relate
to you, verbatim, what happened earlier today.*

*Perhaps you are aware that as well as functioning as Tecimal's doctor,
I am also its only veterinarian. It was in this capacity that I was working
this morning. A boy had brought in one of his pet rabbits; he had had
half a dozen of them, but somehow they escaped in the night. Five had
been killed by a wild dog, but this one, although it was badly mauled and
little more than a bloody mess, was still alive.*

*I was trying to save the poor creature's life when suddenly the door
of my office was thrown open, and someone shouted my name.*

*I looked up and saw Diego Montoya standing there. He was panting
and his hair was wild, and he just kept shouting my name over and over.
All thoughts of the rabbit flew from my head. I told the barber to calm
down and tell me what was the matter.*

*"It's Barclay," he said. "He was in my shop just now and he fainted.
Before I knew what was happening, he fell over and I couldn't wake him
up. Come quickly, Enrique! Please!"*

*Stopping only to tell the open-mouthed little boy to stay where he was
and to try to keep the rabbit comfortable, I grabbed my emergency bag
and ran outside with Diego.*

150

D. R. EVANS

You know how far it is between Diego's barbershop and my house, maybe a hundred and fifty meters. By the time we got there, perhaps a couple of minutes had passed since Diego had burst into my office. Señor Barclay was lying on the floor awkwardly on his back. He was so pale, and his breathing so slow and shallow, that for a moment I thought he was dead; but when I knelt down to attend him, I realized that he was merely unconscious. His pulse was even and quite strong, and before I had prepared the shot of adrenalin, his eyes flickered open of their own accord. Slowly he came around.

It was a few minutes before he was strong enough to stand. He seemed embarrassed by the whole incident, particularly because Diego had summoned me. At first he insisted that there was nothing wrong with him, and that he had simply been working too hard and had suddenly been overcome by the heat. But this is November, and it was a relatively cool day, and in any case his breath smelled of tequila, so I doubt that he had been writing. Barclay might be able to convince himself that he was a momentary victim of overwork and heatstroke, but he cannot convince me. I waited until he was strong enough, then forced him to come back with me to my office.

The rabbit had died while I was away, and I am afraid I will have to work long and hard to regain the trust of that little boy. He went away, cradling the dead body of his last pet, with tears dribbling down his cheeks.

I subjected Señor Barclay to a thorough physical. I'm afraid that it produced no surprises. Señor Barclay is a very sick man, señorita. His liver is almost nonfunctional, and if he continues to poison it with alcohol it will surely stop working entirely before long. When I asked him some pointed questions about his recent physical history, Señor Barclay admitted that he has been suffering from many of the classic signs of advanced liver disease. He is readily tired, his ankles are noticeably swollen, and his hands are beginning to tremble. The blackout which he suffered this morning was simply nature's way of giving him one last unignorable warning. If he does not change his ways immediately, he will surely be dead before long. To tell the truth, señorita, even if Señor Barclay were never to touch another drop of liquor, his liver might still betray him at almost any moment.

Needless to say, I am telling you nothing I have not told Señor Barclay himself, although I was much angrier with him since I have already warned him many times that his drinking will kill him. I was

151

prepared for almost any response save the one I actually received. I had been hopeful (but, to be honest, not expectant) that this blackout, along with my words of warning, would be enough to cause him to mend his ways. My greatest fear was that he would simply shrug and say that life without alcohol would not be worth living. In the event, his response mystifies me. Perhaps you understand it.

He simply looked at me and shook his head.

"I'm sorry, Doctor Pasquale," he said, "but I'm afraid you don't understand."

"I understand enough to know that if you don't change your ways, you're going to die. What else is there to understand?"

"It's out of the question that I could die just yet," he replied firmly. "You see, I know that I won't die until I've finished my second book."

"Your second book?"

"Yes. Let me try to explain. You know that I wrote a book a long time ago, before I moved here."

I nodded. Of course we all know that.

"Well, ever since then I've been trying to write my second book. I've made so many starts that I've given up counting. Four or five times, I've made it all the way through to the end, only to realize that what I'd produced was so much toilet paper, so I threw it all away and started again. The last time I threw everything away was a few weeks ago, when the gringa was here." (That's the name you are known by here, señorita. Everyone simply calls you "the gringa." I hope you are not offended.)

"I thought that this time it would be easier, but it isn't. Whenever I go back and read what I've written, I despair of ever actually finishing the book, but I know that I will. You look skeptical, but it's true. I'm as certain that I'm going to finish my second book as that I'm standing here and that I need a drink."

It was my turn to shake my head. "You don't need a drink. I've already told you: if you carry on drinking this way, we'll be burying you inside of six months whether you've written another book or not."

"You're wrong, doctor."

I saw the certainty on his face, and I thought I understood.

"You think you've received some sort of message from God, don't you?" I challenged him to deny it.

"No," he said. "I've never put much stock in direct messages from God. I'm more than fifty years old, and not once have I encountered a bona fide *example of God speaking directly and unambiguously. If I*

152

thought God had spoken to me about this, I would be full of doubt. As it is, I have none. You see, Doctor Pasquale, it's not God that told me, but Xloxratl."

Señorita, I don't know what you think of the so-called seer who lives in the mountains, but I have to say that for a man as otherwise intelligent as Barclay to put his faith in the words of a mystical Indian shaman is one of the most preposterous things I have ever heard. It's bad enough that he believes in a God for whom there is not the slightest shred of physical evidence — but that particular delusion is a common one and its sheer popularity makes it at least acceptable, even if it remains incomprehensible to skeptical logicians such as myself. I confess that Señor Barclay's statement about Xloxratl left me speechless.

There is not much more to tell. When I finally regained my tongue, I tried to convince him that he was a fool to trust Xloxratl. I confess that I became quite angry with him. He let my tirade flow to its conclusion, then looked at me with what seemed to be pity, and said, "I know you care for me, Enrique. And I want you to know that I appreciate you and I'd never do anything to hurt you; but in this matter you are wrong. Perhaps it's true that drink will kill me, but it won't happen until after I've finished my second book. And once I have finished the book, there will be nothing for me here anyway. I feel old, Enrique, and sometimes I feel so tired. And it would be so good to see Rosalinda again."

With that, he turned and left. I am certain he was telling the truth, at least as he sees it. He truly believes everything Xloxratl tells him, and nothing I can say is ever going to change his mind.

So, señorita, now you know everything. If you have any influence with Señor Barclay, I beg you to use it. I am sorry if you feel that I have placed a heavy burden on you. To the extent that I have done so, I apologize. But it is a doctor's duty to care for his patients, even when they do not want to be helped. And each man has to live with himself, and I know that I could not do so had I not written to you to make you aware of all this.

Sincerely yours

October 25

Dear Andrew

The enclosed arrived here earlier today from Doctor
Pasquale. I am sending a copy of his letter because I want
you to know that if what he says is true (and I'm sure it is)
I want you to promise me you'll stop drinking NOW!

Andrew Barclay, you're an ornery SOB, and I don't
understand a tenth of what makes you tick, but I can't let
you do this to yourself. So please, please, *please* will you
do this for me? If you won't, I'll drop everything and come
to Tecimal now instead of waiting for Christmas.

Yours desperately

October 25

Dear Dr. Pasquale

How can I ever thank you for writing and telling me? I have
not heard from Barclay since the incident, but I am sure
that, left to his own devices, he wouldn't have mentioned
anything about it to me.

I hope this won't make you angry, but I sent him a copy
of your letter. I thought it might make him understand
the depth of your worry. I had been planning to visit
Tecimal again at Christmas, but I've told him that I'll come
immediately unless he promises to stop drinking.

Your letter took ten days to reach me. I don't know if it
is feasible, but if you need to reach me more quickly in
future, you can call me at 213-555-0132.

Thank you again for everything. Rest assured that I very
much appreciate your concern for Barclay and I'm doing

**everything I can to make Barclay understand the seriousness
of his condition.**

Yours sincerely

Oh, bloody Hell!

Do what you like, Donna, but it won't change anything. I've
known Xloxratl for more than a quarter of a century, and in all
that time she's never been wrong. She's not wrong this time,
either. If she says you're going to help me write the damned
book, then that's what's going to happen. I thought I would
have a rough draft ready by Christmas, maybe not all the book,
but at least a good portion of it. When you wrote saying you
would be here for Christmas, I planned for us to go through
it and make the first series of edits. After that I thought I
could do a revised draft, which would take maybe another three
months. Sometime around Easter we could get together again and
put together the final product.

So much for plans.

Maybe Enrique is right: maybe my liver is going to give
up the ghost; but it's not going to happen until the book is
finished, and the way things are going right now my most recent
timeline is proving to be laughably optimistic, so his fear
that I'm going to die at any moment is completely unfounded.
I've started the book three times since you left, and as of
yesterday I'm back to staring at a blank sheet of paper. Maybe
your job at Christmas, or whenever you decide to come down here,
will be simply to help me plot the damned thing. I keep setting
the story in England, but before I know it the scene shifts to
an imaginary town in central America that bears a disturbing
resemblance to Tecimal. Even Xloxratl managed to worm her way
into one of the drafts.

So come down now if you want to. Maybe it will help move the writing along. Of course, by doing so, you will perversely be hastening my demise. I leave the decision entirely up to you.

Yours

P.S. I just made the mistake of rereading this letter. I'm sorry if I'm being too hard on you. This bloody book will kill me without any help from my liver. Don't take my anger too personally. I need to vent my wrath, and you're just the person who happens to be in the way. I think my original plan is best: come down at Christmas and we'll work on whatever I've done by then. If you come down now, it will probably only make things worse.

November 16

Dear Andrew

I received your undated letter two days ago, and this is the first time I've felt calm enough to sit down and write you. Your letter reduced me to tears and it's taken me this long to calm down enough to try to think sensibly.

Do you know that you're the most pig-headed, stubborn, and simply impossible person I've ever met? The trouble is, knowing you, you'll take that as a compliment, which is *not* my intention.

Anyway, I've made my decision. My head keeps telling me I should catch the next plane down there and show up on your doorstep next Monday, and not leave until the "bloody book" is finished. I even picked up the phone yesterday to make the plane reservation.

But that's not what you want, is it? You want me to understand your faith, whether its object is your oddly distant God or that funny old shaman who lives in the mountains. And it seems to me that the only way to

156

understand faith is to exercise it. And so, because I'm
trying to understand you, and because I want to demonstrate
a faith I don't have, I won't be coming until Christmas, and
I promise not to mention your drinking again in my letters
unless you bring up the subject.

And having got that off my chest, I'll try to make the
remainder of this letter as normal as possible.

Work on my thesis has almost ground to a halt these past
few days. I haven't been sleeping well because of worrying
about you, and I'm finding it impossible to concentrate on
work. Every time I sit down to try to get something done,
I find my mind wandering off to Tecimal. In my mind's eye
I keep seeing you lurched forward unconscious over your
typewriter with no one to help. I keep trying to tell myself
I'm being silly, but half of me refuses to be convinced.

Yesterday, out of sheer desperation to get you out of my
mind, I went to the beach; but even there I was reminded of
you. There were half a dozen games of beach volleyball and
two or three impromptu Frisbee games under way. I just sat
and watched, and for a while I emptied my mind of everything
except the breeze, the tang of the sea, and the ebb and flow
of the games.

But after a while I realized that the games were nothing
more than a kind of ritualistic mating dance. From the
glances the players were giving each other it was obvious
that their minds were only partly on volleyball and
Frisbee; the real games were going to be played later in
bed.

One guy invited me to join his game, but I demurred, and
only partly because I had no desire to be picked up by some
stranger on the beach. Since I got back from Tecimal, I
haven't felt like the company of others my own age.

It was about half an hour before it dawned on me that when
you were their age (they seemed to be all more or less in
their mid-twenties) you had already published *The Condition*

of Love and had moved to Tecimal. A few minutes later I
realized the obvious truth that I, too, have accomplished
nothing worthy of note in my twenty-three years. Like most
Americans, I was raised to believe that going to school and
studying are worthy attainments, but I realize now just
how hollow and empty school really is. Here I am, plodding
through the first draft of a thesis whose basis is a book
written by someone my own age a generation ago.

I couldn't stay at the beach any longer. I came back to my
room and spent the next three hours working on my thesis
like a crazed woman. I have to get it done; I have to get it
behind me, because only then will I be free to do what I want
to do. I want to write. I want to write your second book with
you, and when that's done, I want to write another book, and
another.

Before I went to bed last night, I picked up a copy of *The
Condition of Love*, and I opened it at random. My eyes landed
on this paragraph:

When Fiona came to her senses, she discovered she was on
the top of a double-decker bus, seated in the front seat,
gazing blindly through the rain-marred window. A hundred
shifting dribbles of vertical rivulets rendered the city
a distorted, multicolored, unstable place of peculiar
beauty. Spires and tall buildings grew pseudopodia and
magnified evanescent limbs, defying gravity in violation
of physical laws. At the level of her eyes, a large red shape
quickly grew from nothing until it filled half her view;
then, just as suddenly, the other bus was gone. Looking down
at the street, she watched a shifting particolored carpet
weave itself into and out of existence as the London traffic
passed by.

That's what I want to do: to draw pictures with words,
bringing people and worlds to life. I know it won't be easy
— my memory of you dumping six months' work in the trash
is too recent for me to think otherwise — but it's what I

want to do. So let's promise each other to make Christmas a working vacation. Let's get my thesis and your book both knocked into shape, no matter how hard we have to work.

And now, even though it's late I'm going to finish this letter and put in another half hour on the thesis before bed.

Love

Dear Donna

Unlike you, I don't have the luxury of a copy of my letters. Perhaps that is a blessing, since it is quite possible that what I actually wrote a few days ago was even worse than my memory of it.

I am sorry. I should not have lost my temper with you. And having done so, I should not have written to you while I was in such a state. And most unforgivable of all, I should never have mailed the resulting letter. The one mitigating factor in my favor is that I did try to recover it from the post office — but of course it was Monday and the mail was already on its way to Chiclahan.

Please do not think that I don't appreciate everything you are doing. However, it really is unnecessary for you to come down any earlier than you had planned. I will make a conscious effort to limit my drinking to two or three small glasses per day. To be honest, I find it increasingly difficult to write the next day if I drink any more than that, so it will help both my health and my writing if I cut down a bit. I still hope to have a good portion of a novel written by Christmas, even though I realize that that's only a month away now.

Since I did not respond to any of your outstanding questions last time, I'll try to answer at least some of them in this letter.

Of course you must stay with me. We shall be working late into the night, and having to go back to Seora Delgado's would simply be an unnecessary impediment to our work.

159

All right, then; I admit that my last paragraph was no more than a rationalization, and I don't suppose it fooled you any more than it fools me. Please stay with me. No one in Tecimal cares, and please believe me that it does a middle-aged curmudgeon good to know that a pretty young blonde thinks he's worth bedding. Whatever you do, don't disillusion me and tell me it's really my mind you're after.

I'm looking through your letters as I write this, and I see that you wrote "...I just can't accept that Jane Austen was no more than a kind of primordial Danielle Steel". Please enlighten me: who exactly is Danielle Steel?

Now to the serious matter of writing.

I'm afraid I'm too old to change my ways. I know nothing at all about computers; I expect that they are every bit as helpful as you suggest, but I am content with the way I have always done things and see no reason to complicate matters by introducing yet another barrier to finishing the damned book.

A couple of your comments give me pause. You suggest that computers would make the job of writing easier. I would be the first to admit that writing is difficult. But do you not think it a mistake to try to make writing "easier"? Writing is <u>supposed</u> to be difficult. Every word has to be pored over, argued about inside one's head, and committed to paper only when one is certain it is the correct one. Can a computer make that process any easier? I think not.

Your suggestion about thesauruses and dictionaries is horrifying. I would not dream of using such devices, whether in the form of books or of computer programs. When I use a word in a novel, it is a word I know intimately, and it has been chosen because it conveys the precise shade of meaning I intend to convey. If you feel the need for such artificial aids, then I urge you to read more; it is only by reading that one can ever truly understand the meaning of words.

Your comment about spelling isn't even worth the dignity of a reply.

Diego just walked in. You will doubtless be pleased to hear that he was worried when he went over to <u>El</u> <u>Presidente</u> and I wasn't in my habitual spot. Since I've had only one drink today I think I am permitted another, so I shall close now and join my friend at the bar. I think I deserve it: I wrote eight pages today, and even when I reread them I thought almost everything worth keeping.

And no, there weren't any spelling mistakes.

Yours

December 2

Dear Andrew

Of course I forgive you. And I'm so pleased that you're limiting yourself to just a few drinks each day. I'm sure you're feeling better because of it, and it certainly eases my mind.

This will probably be my last letter before I see you again. I'm leaving here on the eighteenth and I should arrive on the bus on the twentieth barring the kind of scheduling disasters that are always possible when travelling in central America. (I sound like a seasoned traveller, don't I? In fact my visit to Tecimal last summer was the first time I've ever been outside the States.)

This will be a short letter. Most of what I have to say can wait until we are together again. I hope you are looking forward to our time together with at least a fraction of the expectancy that I feel. I think it's going to be a good time and we're going to get a lot accomplished.

I've finished the first draft of the thesis. I can't decide whether to let Professor Andover see it or whether I should wait until I've had a chance to incorporate some of your suggestions. I think I'll probably let her have a copy. That way, we will have the benefit of her thoughts when we work on the next draft over Christmas.

In the meantime, I'm taking your advice and spending a lot of time simply reading. It's been years since I've

had an extended period of time to read, and I must say
it's wonderful to have the time now, even though it's only
for another week or so. I reread *Pride and Prejudice* and
Mansfield Park to try to make up my own mind about Austen.
I decided that the former is as overrated as the latter
is underrated. But you're certainly right, the settings
of both books seem to be a far cry from the conditions
prevailing in England at the time she was writing. But I'll
wait until I've got my degree before arguing the point with
Professor Andover.

Despite your advice. I've done a little writing of my own
in the past week or so, but reading so much has made me
dissatisfied with my own efforts, so I think I'll start
on something new in the New Year. Perhaps we can talk at
Christmas about some plot outlines I've made.

That's all for now. Given the quality of the mail service
between us there probably isn't time for us to exchange any
more letters. See you soon.

Love

PART III
TECIMAL REVISITED

Arrival

The journey from Los Angeles to Tecimal takes about a day and a half, and by the time I boarded the bus in Chiclahan for the last leg of the trip I was exhausted.

Everything had gone wrong; beginning with a rare LA downpour that caused me to miss the plane, my luck had remained stubbornly bad right up until the moment I climbed the steps of the bus and saw Isabella watching me intently from a seat near the back of the bus. To my surprise she gestured for me to join her.

"Señorita Donna," she called down the length of the bus, "please sit with me."

I had no choice. I had been hoping to try to get some sleep before seeing Barclay, and the last thing I wanted was to spend two and a half hours in Isabella's company. But what can one do? I made my way past the empty seats and sat next to her, struggling to keep my feelings off my face.

Part of me whispered that I had no right to judge Isabella. Barclay had made it clear more than once that it was a cardinal mistake to apply my American mores to Tecimal in general and to Isabella in particular. And at some level I knew that he was right: Isabella performed a valuable service for the men and women of Tecimal. But none of this changed the way I felt about her. I plopped down on the seat beside her and threw her an artificial smile.

She was more heavily made up than I remembered, perhaps because it was cooler now, or perhaps because a journey to Chiclahan was a special occasion. Her mascara was cheap, and dark streaks edged the corners of her eyes; her bright red lipstick was smudged at one corner of her mouth.

"Señor Barclay's been looking forward to seeing you again. The last couple of times I've seen him he's been like a little boy waiting for Christmas."

An uncharitable question sprang to mind — whether his excitement had affected his performance in her bed — but I grunted a noncommittal reply.

The bus started: the engine spluttered noisily, coughing twice; then the driver crashed the gears and with a jerk that sent my bag crashing to the floor from the seat in front of us where I'd put it, we were on our way.

"And he's not the only one looking forward to your visit," Isabella continued while I jammed the bag more securely under a seat. "We've all been worried about him recently. Doctor Pasquale told me he wrote to you asking if you could come earlier, but you said you couldn't get away until now."

I felt a sudden chill in my stomach as I regained my seat. Had I underestimated the danger from Barclay's sickness? Accompanying the chill was a frisson of guilt. It would have been inconvenient to leave LA earlier, but it was hardly impossible. The real reason I had delayed was to demonstrate a faith I did not feel in Xloxratl's predictions.

Unwilling to speak, I simply nodded.

"You and Señor Barclay have been writing to each other?" Isabella asked.

"Yes."

"Has he told you how sick he has been these last few weeks?"

The chill in my stomach became an icy fear.

"No, he's said nothing. Doctor Pasquale wrote to say that Barclay had a blackout, but I haven't heard anything about his health from Barclay himself. He did say that he's cut down his drinking, though. But whenever I ask him directly about his health, he ignores the question."

I began to wonder if Barclay was keeping something from me. I vowed to myself that he wouldn't get away with evasions once we were together and I could look him in the eye while I asked some very pointed questions.

"I worry about him," continued Isabella earnestly. Her expression confirmed her words. Her forehead was furrowed with worry lines, and

I wondered if something had happened that I didn't know about. Had there been more blackouts? I felt a sudden urge to confront Barclay, to find out the truth.

The bus was picking up speed as it clattered through the outskirts of Chiclahan. Another five minutes and the paved road would give way to a dusty highway. Half an hour more and we would be following a track across the desert. The first stop would be in a village an hour or so later. The second, another hour after that, would be at Tecimal. I would just have to be patient.

Isabella abruptly changed the subject: "I know what you think of me, señorita." I felt myself coloring with embarrassment as she continued: "Señor Barclay told me how you look down on me."

The look in her eye challenged me to deny it, but how could I? It was the truth. My feelings for Barclay flip-flopped as I felt a surge of annoyance because he had told his whore something he had no right to share; but then I realized that I should have known he wouldn't be able to keep anything, even something so personal, from Isabella.

"It's all right, I understand," Isabella said. I imagined that a sympathetic priest might use the same tone of voice in the confessional: understanding, compassionate and forgiving, all at the same time. I tried to detect any hint of patronization in her voice. I couldn't. She was, apparently, sincere.

"I know what I am, and I know I could never be like you. I'll be honest with you, señorita. I was hurt when Barclay first told me about you. I didn't want to share him with you. You already have everything. Why should you have him as well?

"I could never compete with you, but that doesn't stop me from loving Barclay. If you're as clever as he says you are, then you must know I have feelings too."

I looked at my bag, trying desperately to will into oblivion the flush that I could feel spreading across my face.

"Señor Barclay helped Momma once, when everyone else turned away. Please believe me when I say I love Barclay. Not the way you do, because he's clever and a famous writer, but because he's the only real man in Tecimal. The others strut and like to show their machismo; but to me only Barclay is truly a man. Do you know that he's the only man I've ever seen cry?"

I remembered our last evening together, when we'd gone for a walk and Barclay had stood at his wife's grave and I had seen the tears trickle down his cheeks in the moonlight. So I shared something with Isabella: Barclay was also the only man I'd ever seen cry. I wondered whether Isabella and I had been specially honored, or was it Barclay that was special: a man honest enough to be unafraid of tears when the occasion demanded them, regardless of who might see them.

"Please let me worry about him, señorita. I know I can't understand him the way you do. I know I can't talk to him the way you can. But please believe me when I say that I love him and I'd do anything to help him, no matter how much it hurts me.

"I'll tell you, señorita, that I'm scared what might happen if you leave again. This time you must stay, for his sake. You're the only one who might be able to influence him. The rest of us have all tried: myself, Momma, Doctor Pasquale, even Diego Montoya, his best friend, we've all told him to stop drinking. But he doesn't listen. He doesn't drink as much as he used to, but he says that's because he promised you, and the doctor says it's still too much. Please, señorita, will you promise me something? Will you promise not to leave Tecimal until Barclay has agreed to stop drinking completely, forever? I'll do anything I can to help you. Please."

I tried to think of a way to explain why it was impossible for me to stay in Tecimal. There were at least another six months of hard work still to be done on my thesis. And there was something I had not yet told Barclay because I wanted to see his face when I gave him the news: Professor Andover had written me a strong letter of recommendation to a liberal arts college in Iowa. Although we had heard nothing official, she had told me only the day before I left LA that I was almost certain to be offered the post of assistant professor for the next academic year.

I examined Isabella's face, but the only thing I read there was a trusting belief that if I wanted to I could convince Barclay to stop drinking. Personally, I doubted I had that power, but to appease her I nodded and said, "I'll try to work out a way to stay. But I can't promise anything. I have work to do back in the States."

Having won this concession, she seemed to lose interest in me. She fell silent, looking out the window at the desert.

Despite the jolting of the bus I nodded off. I slept through the first stop, and only woke as we were approaching *Las Montañas del Cielo*. They looked dark and brooding, shadowed by an enormous thunderhead massing above them. Even as I watched, two large, black, mushrooming growths extended from the ominous-looking cloud, reaching away from the mountains and groping toward us.

"We will have rain soon," said Isabella, the first words she had spoken since our conversation about Barclay.

I remembered that this was the season for rain in the high desert. "Does it rain much in winter?"

"No, usually just a few times. But when it does rain, it sometimes seems like God is so angry with us that he intends to cover the Earth with water again, just like in the days of Noah. That cloud is a bad one. You wait, señorita, it'll grow into a storm this evening, and evening storms at this time of year usually stay all night and last into the next day."

I watched the brooding cloud for some time. I thought of Xloxratl up there somewhere, in her dingy hut, readying herself for a deluge that would last all night. I wondered if Barclay would take me to see her again this time.

Then I remembered something Barclay had said when we took our leave of the old woman. "This is the last time I'll see you, then?" he had said. The old woman had neither confirmed it nor denied it, but Barclay must have had some reason for thinking that he would never see the shaman again. Perhaps she had died since the summer, and I thought of asking Isabella, but then I realized that if something had happened to Xloxratl Barclay would surely have said something in one of his letters.

"Have you ever met Xloxratl?" I asked, trying unsuccessfully to get my tongue around the clicks. "She lives up there, you know, in a hut on one of the mountains."

Isabella shook her head emphatically. "She's a crazy old woman. Everyone in Tecimal says so except Barclay. He's never talked much about her to me, but I know she means a lot to him. I heard that after his wife died, it was Xloxratl who got him back on his feet again. But that was before I was born, so I don't really know the truth of the matter.

"He did invite me to go with him once, about four years ago, but Momma thinks the old woman has an evil spirit, and when I asked Father Emilio he told me it would be better if I didn't go."

She paused for half a minute before continuing. "I'm sure you and I are the only people he's ever invited up there. After I refused, Barclay hardly ever mentioned her until he took you up there last summer.

Tell me, señorita, did you really meet her? And did you think she was evil?"

"Yes I met her. She was certainly peculiar, but I don't think it's fair to call her evil. She lives in a small hut near the entrance to one of the old mines. Her hut's not much bigger than your kitchen. She brewed us a kind of tea from herbs. I thought we were up there for only a few hours, but actually we stayed more than an entire day. It was only after we got back to Tecimal that I realized I was missing a whole day of my life."

Isabella looked at me in amazement, then quickly crossed herself. "Did she cast a spell on you?"

I smiled. "No, nothing like that. There was some kind of drug in the tea she made for us, that's all. No magic. Afterwards, when it was all over, it was hard to remember very much about the visit at all. At the time I felt angry at the way she tricked us. Now I just feel sorry for her." I shrugged. "That's all there was to it, really."

But I was lying; that wasn't all there was at all. There was Xloxratl's prediction about Barclay's second book, and her prophecy that we would become lovers, and the intertwined grass that I had brought with me from LA. But those were private matters between Barclay and me, and not for Isabella's ears.

We left the mountains behind, but the clouds spread quickly across the sky, almost but not quite keeping up with us. My first view of Tecimal as we approached was of the town bathed in light from the westering sun filtered through the edge of the rain-pregnant clouds. In the peculiar yellow-brown light, Tecimal seemed almost ominous, as if it were a ghost town — literally, a town from which all living souls had fled, and which was now populated only by ghosts. Nothing moved; the sunlight glinted with a peculiar luminosity from the distant church tower, and was swallowed by the dark shacks on the edge of town.

We passed the first house, and saw the first signs of habitation: half a dozen children who had been playing in the street scattered before the clattering bus.

Half a minute later we were in the *Calle de Generalissimo Javier Felipe Duarte*, the houses on the edge of town giving way to the stores I remembered so well. We passed the post office and the service station; on the far side of the bus through the dirt-streaked window I could just make out the façade of Diego Montoya's barbershop. The bus squealed to a halt.

As I rose from my seat, I looked across the street to see if Barclay and Diego Montoya were seated outside the barbershop, waiting for us. But the rocking chairs were empty. It was well past siesta and it was more likely that Barclay was waiting to greet me when I got off the bus. Or perhaps he was at home, working on his book in an unnecessary attempt to impress me.

Clutching my bag, I made my way to the front of the bus and stepped down with Isabella a few steps behind me.

Doctor Pasquale was at the bus stop. I looked around for Barclay, but there was no sign of him. The doctor stepped forward to greet me. Behind him, Diego Montoya hovered uncertainly in front of the food store.

The doctor opened his mouth to speak, but the bus driver engaged first gear and revved the engine as he pulled away, making conversation momentarily impossible.

I glanced from Doctor Pasquale to Diego Montoya, and the look on the barber's face caused the blood to drain from my face. By the time the bus was far enough down the *Calle* for the doctor to speak, I already knew he was the bearer of bad news. Isabella must have seen it too, for she had halted beside me and, after glancing at the doctor and the barber, she threw me a single horrified glance. She shook her head.

"No!" she shrieked.

Doctor Pasquale spoke. "I'm sorry, señoritas. There was nothing anyone could do. I'm afraid Señor Barclay is dead."

No one moved. I remember the moment perfectly, indelibly etched in my memory like other moments of unforeseen catastrophe whether private or shared: coming home from school and my father telling me my dog had died; the *Challenger* explosion; the Loma Prieta earthquake. There was no one else on the *Calle*, just the four of us standing in an untidy knot outside the food store. The bus noisily changed gear for the last time, and then its clatter gradually diminished into nothingness. From somewhere to my left, momentarily distracting me, came a flicker of lightning. Tens of interminable, silent seconds later, the distant dull rumble of thunder reached us.

Isabella found her voice before I did. "I saw him last night," she said.

Her words were ambiguous, and I wondered whether Barclay had spent his last night in the arms of his whore. "He didn't seem any sicker than usual," she said.

Diego Montoya said, "I didn't see anything unusual either. He was at *El Presidente* yesterday as usual and I didn't notice anything. Of course he's been looking thin and ill these past few months, we've all noticed that, but he didn't seem especially sick last night."

"He was much sicker than any of us knew," Doctor Pasquale said. "Even I didn't realize how ill Señor Barclay really was. If I'd had any idea, I'd have insisted that the señorita come sooner."

For a moment I wondered who "the señorita" was; but they all looked at me and I understood: I had crossed a line: I was no longer "the gringa" but "the señorita."

He continued, "The fault is all mine. I was his doctor, and I should've known how sick he was and done something about it. I didn't."

His eyes wetly reflected the yellowing sun, as if he were about to cry. Hiding this embarrassing lapse, he looked away for a moment, sniffing and wiping his hand hurriedly across his face. When he looked at me again, his eyes were still sad, but they were no longer damp with unshed tears.

"When did it happen?" I managed to ask, still trying to absorb the news. Barclay? Dead? It couldn't be.

"I found him," said Diego Montoya. "He didn't appear at the shop for siesta, so I went to his house. I found him on the floor of his study as if he'd just fallen out of his chair. At first I thought he'd had another blackout, but when I saw the color of his face I knew he had to be dead."

The doctor finished the brief tale. "Señor Montoya fetched me, and I confirmed what he already knew. The body was still slightly warm. Señor Barclay must have died late this morning, not long before noon."

Involuntarily I glanced at my watch. It was nearly three.

Doctor Pasquale said something about the funeral taking place in the morning but by now I was oblivious to everything. I watched, without taking anything in, as Isabella walked away in the direction of her house. Diego Montoya must have left as well, although I did not notice. When I became aware of my surroundings once more, only Doctor Pasquale remained. The odd-colored glare from the filtered sun had become even more harsh as it bathed the *Calle*. The outlying clouds from the storm were almost overhead. The air was heavy and sticky and ominously still. The taste of salt in my mouth told me I had been crying.

172

"Señorita, it's going to rain soon," said the doctor gently. "Please, you must come inside before the rain starts." He touched me lightly on the arm, and I struggled to smile through my tears.

"Please, stay at my house tonight," he continued. "Tomorrow, you can decide what you want to do. You're welcome to stay with me as long as you like. But if there's somewhere else you'd prefer to stay — at Señora Delgado's, or at Barclay's house; or if you'd rather just leave Tecimal and go home — then I'll certainly understand. Now, please, you must come with me."

He picked up my bag and, carrying it in one hand and guiding my arm with the other, he led me down the *Calle* toward his home.

The doctor's wife, Francisca, greeted us as we entered the house. She was a pretty woman in her early thirties. A boy of about ten peered at me from behind the safety of her frame.

Francisca repeated her husband's offer to let me stay as long as I wanted. There was a spare room that was sometimes used for patients. She led me to the room, briefly showed me around, then left me to my grief.

As soon as Francisca Pasquale had closed the door, the dam broke. I collapsed on the bed and began to cry. I cried for Barclay, for the extinguishing of his mind and what he could have given to the world had he lived to complete his book; I cried because his faith in Xloxratl had proved false when I had so much wanted it to be true; but mostly I cried for myself. I'd never admitted it before, even to myself, but a future without Barclay seemed blank and meaningless. I loved him. For the first time, I admitted something I had for months been trying to pretend hadn't happened. Without consciously realizing it, I had constructed a future for Barclay and me. I would help him write his second book, which would be an instant success. A third book and then a fourth would follow. Barclay would overcome his addiction to alcohol. He would leave Tecimal, perhaps to join me in Iowa, where I would spend my days teaching English Literature to fresh-faced students, and the evenings and weekends would be spent working and loving with Barclay.

Now none of it would happen. I would stay in Tecimal only until the next bus, and then I would leave forever. Gradually this whole episode would recede into the past. I would finish my thesis; I would move to Iowa; and I would never again dream of writing a great book. My bookshelves would hold only one novel by Andrew Barclay; never would it be joined by a second.

Hugging the pillow as if it were a giant teddy bear, I heaved and sobbed until at last I cried myself to sleep.

I was startled awake by an explosive crack that shook the room. Rubbing the sleep from my sore, caked eyes, I glanced at my watch, thinking from the darkness that it must be late evening. But my watch told me it was barely five o'clock. I went to the window and witnessed an extraordinary sight.

My room faced the *Calle*. To the south I could see beyond the town to the desert, which now was a dishrag gray instead of its usual burnt sienna. In the opposite direction, I could see most of the length of the *Calle*, past the stores and as far as the *Avenida La Guardia*. My view beyond the *Avenida* was blocked by what looked like an immense gray curtain that stretched up to the sky. As I watched, the curtain advanced along the *Calle* at walking pace.

In moments, the entrance to the *Avenida La Guardia* disappeared behind the curtain. As the gray sheet passed the first of the stores, I heard the spang of raindrops hitting the hard ground like bullets. There was a flicker of lightning somewhere high above me, lost in the grayness, and, less than a second later, the sharp crack of proximate thunder. The sound was stifled almost instantly by the sheet of advancing water.

The curtain advanced past Diego Montoya's barbershop; it kept coming, as remorselessly as a tidal wave. It passed *El Presidente* — for the first time in my memory no one was standing outside — hiding the manic señorita with her outsize *Cerveza de Chiclahan* from my gaze. I became aware of a new sound, as if a hundred thousand feet were pounding the ground at some frenzied sports event.

And then the rain reached the doctor's house.

I was forced to step back from the window as a sudden draft sucked air from the room with a violence that tugged at my hair. In moments, the temperature in the room dropped several degrees, and it became so dark that it might almost have been night. The feet pounded the ground just outside my window. Above the roar, I heard a single, quickly muted report, and I thought for a moment that some crazy person had gone out into the street and fired a gun into the rain. Then I realized that what I had heard was thunder, its sound absorbed by the wall of water.

The breeze died down, and I returned to the window. For perhaps half a minute, I could see no more than a few feet into the downpour. Gradually, the grayness outside became perceptibly brighter and the

174

sound of drumming diminished. I heard my door opening, and I turned to see who had entered the room. Señora Pasquale held a baby in her arms, and the boy I had seen earlier trailed close behind her.

"Señorita," she said with a warm smile, "I thought I'd better make sure you weren't worried by the storm. We sometimes get violent storms like this in winter. The thunder and lightning will pass and the rain will decrease, but it will be a day or more before we see the sun again. Afterwards, next week sometime, the desert will bloom for a week or two. It will beautiful."

"The thunder woke me up," I said stupidly.

Her eyes flickered over my face and she nodded. "Men are so foolish," she declared, seemingly for no reason. "They think it a sign of manliness not to cry when they are hurt. Even my husband will not cry, no matter how much I know he is hurting inside." She moved to the bed and sat down, rocking the child in her arms. "We women know better. We know that to cry is to offer oneself for healing; we know that grief is just as much a part of life as happiness, that sadness is every bit as important as joy.

"I didn't know Señor Barclay well, señorita, but do I know that he was a good man who cared greatly for the people whom he adopted."

"Just like your husband," I suggested, and she paused to consider this as if she had never noticed the parallel before.

"Perhaps," she admitted. "But selflessness is expected of my husband. After all, he is a doctor. No one expects a famous writer to go out of his way to help people the way Señor Barclay helped so many of us. Did you know that if it weren't for Señor Barclay my husband's practice would have failed and we would have been forced to leave Tecimal?"

"Yes, I've heard the story." I paused, struck by something the doctor's wife had said. "You know, Barclay really isn't... wasn't a famous writer. I suppose he was quite well known for a while after his book came out. But he never wrote anything else, and I think that used book stores and libraries are the only places you can find copies of his book in the States nowadays. I doubt that one person in a hundred would recognize his name. That was part of why I wanted to write my thesis about him. One of the reasons everyone's forgotten him is because he never wrote a second book. One of the things I originally came to Tecimal to find out was why he'd never written another one."

"Maybe if he hadn't died, you might have been able to help him write that second book," Francisca said.

I looked at her, wondering for a moment if she knew about Xloxratl's prophecy. But I could not imagine Barclay sharing that with anyone except me. He would have kept it a secret from everyone, even Isabella.

The thought of Isabella brought a question to mind, one I had always been too scared to ask in case I got the answer I dreaded. But suddenly it was important to know. I had to know how to remember Barclay. Was he a great man who had lost his way, or was he simply an unprincipled vagabond who had drunk himself to death? I couldn't know without an answer to the question that had haunted me since summer.

I took a deep breath and blurted, "I'm sorry if I'm being too inquisitive, but could you tell me something? Do you know if Isabella is Barclay's daughter?"

"Isabella?"

She could not suppress a laugh, which caused the baby to open its eyes and let out the beginnings of a cry. The doctor's wife opened her blouse and offered a breast to the child, who sucked at it greedily.

There was a clap of thunder. The storm was more distant now, the rain reduced to an ordinary drencher. The thunder rumbled and growled for some time before being lost in the rain.

She shook her head decidedly. "No, Isabella isn't Señor Barclay's child. She was born long before I moved to Tecimal, of course, but most people think that her father is Diego Montoya. You know him, of course? The barber?"

"Doesn't anybody know for sure who her father is?"

"How could they? Not even Señora Delgado could know for sure. In any given month, Isabella's mother probably slept with two dozen men. Any one of them could be Isabella's father. But not Barclay. You only have to look at her to know that he couldn't possibly be her father; even though, from what I hear, Barclay was the señora's favorite."

"But Barclay told me once that Diego Montoya sleeps with Isabella." I was unable to keep the disgust out of my voice.

The boy, apparently bored with the conversation, climbed on to the bed beside his mother and placed his head in her lap. The baby had fallen asleep in her arms. Francisca patted the bed for me to sit next to her.

She said, "You're disgusted at the idea of a father sleeping with his daughter? Yet you thought it at least possible that Señor Barclay was doing so?"

176

"Not really. I never really thought she could be his daughter. It's just that the timing was right, that's all. And I suppose I wanted to be sure." I struggled to keep the relief from my voice.

"You mustn't think less of Diego Montoya. His wife knows all about it. I'll tell you something that might surprise you, señorita. Señora Montoya, like half the wives in Tecimal, is far more afraid of you than she is of the likes of Isabella or her mother."

"Me?"

I was astonished. Why would anyone be afraid of me?

"Señorita, please don't be angry. You must remember that things are different here. Just now you were shocked at the thought of a man sleeping with his own daughter, yet no one here thinks much of it. Isabella is a beautiful girl. It is only natural that men would want to sleep with her. Why should her father be exempt? Especially if no one knows for sure who her father really is?"

Her argument was logical, but that did not make it palatable. "But why would Señora Montoya be afraid of me?"

"Because she sees you as a threat to her marriage. You are exotic, señorita. I cannot remember the last time a blonde gringa came to Tecimal. And you snagged Señor Barclay, whom everyone knows was the most dependable, the most upright, the most unassailable and the most unattainable man in Tecimal. Barclay belonged first to Rosalinda, and after that to Consuela Delgado, and most recently to Isabella, everyone here knows that. And yet he took you into the mountains, alone. Somewhere he has never taken Isabella or Señora Delgado. And you spent the last night you were here with him. If Barclay could fall prey to your feminine wiles, what other man — and therefore what wife? — was safe?"

"But it wasn't like that at all," I protested. I was going to go on to try to explain that at first Barclay and I had been undeclared enemies, that it was only later, when we realized that we needed one another, that other, gentler feelings had arisen to take the place of the animosity between us. But before I could say anything we were interrupted by a gentle knock. The doctor poked his head around the door. Francisca immediately declared that it was time she was preparing supper. She got up and, taking her children with her, left the room.

"Señorita, permit me once again to say how sorry I am," the doctor said when we were alone. "I know it must have come as a terrible shock. But there's something I must discuss with you before you make any plans for the future."

177

I looked at him quizzically.

From his pocket he withdrew a single folded sheet of paper. On the outside, in Barclay's handwriting, were the words: *For Doctor Pasquale.*

"This was on his desk beside his typewriter," said the doctor. "I think you should read it."

I accepted the sheet and unfolded it. Barclay's compact handwriting covered most of the paper.

Dear Enrique (I read)

If you are reading this, it means I am gone. If I am right, I have no time now to explain why I believe I am about to die. Ask the gringa later, after she has been into the mountains. I hope she will be able to explain.

My dear friend, by writing this I am trusting you to handle a delicate and important matter for me. I apologize that my request will doubtless cause you some trouble. I am afraid that all I can do is apologize; there is no time to make reparations or correct the situation.

When I married Rosalinda, I made a will naming her my sole beneficiary. This will was deposited with my family solicitors, Messrs. Turpin, Waterhouse and Watson, whose address and phone number in England I will append to this note. I have never invalidated that will, but I wish to do so now. You will find another sheet of paper with this, on which I have written and signed my new will. As you are probably aware, in order for this will to be valid, my signature must be witnessed by two disinterested parties known to me. I have no time to find you. I ask that you and Diego sign it as if you had witnessed my signature.

I feel time closing in, and there are other things I must do. Please do what I ask, Enrique, and you will have more than repaid any debt you may think you owe me.

Beneath Barclay's signature was taped a dog-eared, yellowing business card on which was printed the London address and telephone number of Messrs. Turpin, Waterhouse and Watson, Solicitors and Commissioners for Oaths.

"The will, señorita," the doctor said, handing me another sheet. This note was much shorter. It said simply:

Being of sound mind, I, known as Andrew Barclay and residing in Tecimal, bequeath all my worldly goods without let or hindrance to Donna E———, widely known in Tecimal as "the gringa". This document supersedes all prior wills.

Next to his signature was today's date and the time: 9:30 a.m. Below that were two more signatures where the doctor and the barber had countersigned.

I shook my head. "This isn't legal. You weren't there when he signed it."

The doctor took both sheets from me. One he carefully folded and replaced in his pocket; the other he slowly ripped to pieces in front of my eyes.

"Señorita," he said, patting his pocket. "This is the will that my friend made this morning. Diego and I saw him write it, and after he signed it, we affixed our own names. If you wish to contest this will, both Diego and I will be forced to repeat this statement before a judge in Chiclahan." Seeing the look on my face, he added, "Please, señorita; it was the wish of a dying man. Do not fight it."

I supposed he was right. I had no right to contest Barclay's will just because of a technicality. But even though I appreciated their gesture it was inconvenient just the same. What use could I possibly have for the rundown house on the *Avenida La Guardia*? Once the funeral was over, I would leave Tecimal forever. Barclay's will, though doubtless he meant well, only complicated matters. He probably had relatives in England; there would be difficult explanations of a relationship that I had never really understood myself. And to what purpose? To the best of my knowledge Barclay's "worldly goods" comprised the house and the trickle of royalties brought in by occasional foreign-language printings of *The Condition of Love*.

"And now," the doctor said, "I think it's better if I don't remain." With that, he turned and left the room.

I sat down on the bed and it began to sink in at last.

Barclay was gone. Forever. And now, too late, I said the words out loud. Words that he would never hear. Words for which I would have given anything just to be able to say them to him.

"Barclay... Andrew... I love you."

The tears returned.

The Funeral

Barclay's funeral was at nine o'clock next morning.

I had brought nothing remotely appropriate for the occasion, but not long after sunrise Isabella appeared briefly at the doctor's house with a black dress in my size. I thanked her for her thoughtfulness, but it wasn't until later, when I saw her wearing a dress two sizes too large, that I realized that the dress she had given me was her own and she had been forced to borrow another one for the occasion.

The bell began to toll at eight thirty. Light rain had continued through the night, and a warm drizzle still fell, deadening the sound of the bell and enveloping everything in a ghostly gray mist. Señora Delgado and Isabella knocked on the door of the doctor's house and invited us to join them in the walk to the church.

We were a silent group as we walked up the *Calle*. As we approached our destination, we were joined by other knots of people, all equally silent. It was almost as if the gray, spirit-sapping drizzle had been brought into being by our mourning. The streets were slick with mud, and twice I slipped and would have fallen were it not for the doctor's quick reflexes.

The plangent tolling became clearer as we neared the church. Turning the last corner, I saw an enormous clump of people standing outside, despite the rain. There must have been more than two hundred people just standing there, many with heads bowed. Everyone was utterly silent, even the children. A few heads swiveled as we came into view and as I saw the expressions on their faces it dawned on me that something had changed.

Wherever I went in Tecimal, I had become accustomed to the stares of the townspeople. Barclay had said it was the color of my hair that attracted attention; I had always thought suspicion (the women) or lust (the men) more likely causes.

But this morning I was one of them, one *with* them. People glanced my way, but then they looked away again and in their eyes was sympathy, not suspicion or lust. I began to realize what Barclay had meant to these people — not just his circle of close friends but everyone in Tecimal.

"Why are they waiting?" I asked the doctor in a whisper.

"It's the custom. No one enters the church until the family arrives."

As we passed in front of the waiting crowd I wondered whether it was I or Señora Delgado and her daughter whom they recognized as Barclay's family.

Father Emilio was waiting at the door. He was, oddly, it seemed to me, the only person not dressed in black. He wore a white cassock and an intricately embroidered stole, but the set of his face showed that he too was in mourning.

Without saying a word, the priest ushered us to the front of the church. Some secret signal must have marked the moment when we sat, for as soon as we had done so the people began to filter silently into the church behind us.

The bell stopped tolling, leaving a sudden, ominous void. I looked around: the church was completely full.

Father Emilio stepped to the front of the church, and after pausing for a moment to look slowly over the amassed congregation, he began the service.

No doubt the Catholic church prescribes a particular form for a funeral service, but that form, whatever it might be, was ignored that day in Tecimal. Father Emilio began with a eulogy to Barclay, dwelling on his strength of character and his willingness to help others no matter the cost to himself.

When the priest had finished, Doctor Pasquale rose and, with all eyes on him, strode to stand beside the priest at the front of the church. Father Emilio was so taken aback by the unexpected intrusion of the avowed atheist that he made no attempt to stop the doctor when he turned to face the congregation.

"My friends," Doctor Pasquale began. His voice was loud and confident, unlike the squeaky tones of the poor priest. "We all know that everything Father Emilio has said is true, but few of us, perhaps none of us, know the true extent to which Barclay touched life in Tecimal in the thirty years he spent among us."

The doctor proceeded to recount the story of how Barclay had forced him to visit *El Presidente* one night when he was on the verge of packing his bags, and then making him drink until he collapsed, unconscious, under the table. "It was a lesson I never forgot," said the doctor. "A doctor's patients must see him as a human being, as weak as they, before they can fully trust him.

"I could tell you many other tales of what Barclay has done over the years. But one will have to suffice. We are a poor town. Not one among us is rich. I discovered very quickly that many of my patients cannot afford even the cheapest of medicines. At first, I tried to pay for medicines out of my own pocket, but it wasn't long before I discovered I was spending almost as much money on medicines as I was making from my fees. For a month I fretted and worried how I could help my patients obtain the medicines they needed even though I couldn't afford to pay for them.

"Then one day Barclay came to see me. I asked him what was wrong, because as far as I could tell he was in perfect shape. 'With me?' he said. 'There's nothing wrong with me. I came to find out what's wrong with you. You look like you're carrying the cares of all Tecimal on your back.' So I told him my dilemma. He just sat there and listened, and when I finished he left without saying a word. I wondered if I'd said something to offend him, but those of you who knew him well can guess what happened next.

"A few days later, Barclay walked into my office without knocking. I remember I was examining a patient, and my first reaction was anger at the interruption. But before I could say anything, Barclay placed a bulging envelope on my desk. 'It's to buy medicines,' he said. He left without saying another word.

"When I opened the envelope, I discovered it was full of money, enough to buy medicines for an entire year. Every year since then, he's done the same thing. Never has he asked for anything in return.

"My friends, Señor Barclay was a great man. I doubt there is a family in Tecimal that hasn't been touched in some way by his presence among us. We will all miss him. I will miss him."

The doctor sniffed once, drew his hand across his eyes, and walked slowly back to his seat. As soon as he sat down, Diego Montoya stood up and took the doctor's place at the front of the church. The barber looked embarrassed, and he kept his eyes on the floor as he spoke.

He spoke quietly, and I'm sure that those sitting more than a few rows away could hear little of what he said. But perhaps they didn't need to hear his words. The look on his face was enough.

"Señor Barclay was my friend," he began. "When no one else in the town would speak to me, he came to my shop one day and offered to share his drink with me at siesta. Next day he came again. Soon afterward, he got two rocking chairs from somewhere and put them outside my store. After that, he came to see me every day at siesta and we would sit and drink and enjoy each another's company. It seems impossible now, but that was twenty years ago. Except for the occasional day when one of us was sick or he was away in the mountains or in Chiclahan, yesterday was the first day he didn't come to visit me. Tomorrow, siesta time will come, and there will be no Barclay. But I will sit in my chair and I will offer a silent toast to a great man."

By now several other people were standing, and some of them began to move toward the front of the church as the barber finished. Father Emilio looked upward and smiled silently at heaven. He knew that he had lost control of the service; but he had sense enough not to care.

One after another they came forward and told their stories. The stories were short and long; concise and rambling; pointed and ambiguous. But one thing they all had in common: they were told from the heart, and it was not long before I realized that the greatest thing Barclay had done was not to write *The Condition of Love*: it was to live among these people and to show them how much he cared.

It was more than two hours before the last person finished speaking and Father Emilio regained control, and nearly midday before the priest led us out of the church and into the cemetery, where we gathered in a crowd around Barclay's open grave.

The drizzle had stopped and the clouds had thinned, but the sky was still overcast as the priest began the final part of the service.

The open grave lay between Father Emilio and the rest of us. The grave was shallow, only about three feet deep, and I could clearly see the dark, rain-stained wood of the coffin. Next to it lay two other graves, thirty years old. At last Barclay was reunited with his beloved Rosalinda and their daughter.

Throughout the morning's eulogies I had managed to remain calm. The stories I had heard, although they were all about Barclay, were about a Barclay I never knew. But once we were outside and I found myself staring at the dark wood of the coffin and the two graves next to it, it all became personal. Barclay was inside that coffin. I would never see him again. Never again would he make me laugh. Never again would he infuriate me. Never again would one of his peculiar, skewed comments cause me to stop and think about a subject in a way I had never considered before.

Thinking about Barclay I began to cry, and it was some time before I regained my composure sufficiently to be aware of my surroundings once more.

"This," Father Emilio was saying, "This is the last resting place of our friend Andrew Barclay."

As the priest intoned Barclay's name, the torn clouds chanced to part and a ragged shaft of sunlight shone down and struck the coffin. The sun reflected directly into my eyes, so that for a moment it seemed that the coffin itself was shining with celestial brilliance. The light began to spread outwards from the coffin, touching first Father Emilio, then those of us at the front of the crowd, and then those farther back.

A gray wisp rose from the coffin, ascending a few feet before evaporating into the drying air. The symbolism was too much for me, and I surrendered to my tears once more.

While I cried, Father Emilio brought the service to a conclusion. Some of the younger children had been making their boredom heard for some time, and the priest rushed through the last few prayers. He pronounced a benediction and the crowd began to disperse, the people going home to exchange their funereal garb for their everyday clothing. Within an hour Tecimal would be as it always was, the men tending the stores and lounging in front of *El Presidente*; the women performing their daily rituals of shopping, cooking and looking after the children; the older children playing outside in the drying streets, kicking soccer balls and playing cops and *bandidos*; the strays curled up in sunlit corners. The only difference between Tecimal yesterday and Tecimal today was an empty house and a new grave in the cemetery.

I wanted to talk to Father Emilio. As the crowd drifted away and a lanky, shock-haired youth appeared from somewhere to shovel the glutinous earth back on top of the casket, I thanked the priest for everything he had done.

Father Emilio took my elbow and guided me away from the graveside.

"You will be with us long?" he asked.

"I don't think so, no. I'd been planning to stay for Christmas. But now...." Now what? I had no idea. I'd had a vague notion of leaving Tecimal on the next bus, but Barclay's will complicated matters.

We reached the door of the church. "I must go inside and tidy up," said the priest. "At times like these, señorita, one sometimes needs a sympathetic ear. My house is never locked. If you need someone to talk to, I'm always available."

I thanked him again and began to walk away. Not far away Doctor Pasquale and Diego Montoya were talking quietly, their eyes on me as I approached.

"Señorita," said the doctor. "If you have the time, would you please accompany me to Señor Barclay's house? It's important."

Puzzled, I agreed, and we set off together. Diego Montoya soon left us, and in silence the doctor and I made our way to the *Avenida La Guardia* and the shabby pink and white house that had been Barclay's home for more than a quarter of a century.

It was strange to walk inside. The doctor stood to one side and let me enter the house first. The front door was unlocked, and, despite myself, I had to restrain myself. I wanted to call Barclay's name, and I was overwhelmed for a moment with a mad certainty that if I were only to do so Barclay would answer from the study, "I'm in here."

The feeling passed, but it left me shaken. Uncertainly, I led the way into the study.

It was exactly as I remembered it. It looked (*but of course*, I thought, *how else would it look?*) as if Barclay had left it a moment ago, gone to the kitchen in search of a drink. In a minute or two he would return, glass in hand. Then he would sit down at the desk, frown at the sheet of paper in the typewriter, and go on with his work.

"Señorita?" Doctor Pasquale gestured toward the armchair in which I had once spent the night reading *The Condition of Love*. I sat, and waited for the doctor's explanation.

There was a long silence while the doctor seemed to be gathering his thoughts. Instead of sitting in the chair behind the typewriter, he leant against one of the bookcases.

"Señorita, this is a difficult time for you. I won't waste my breath telling you yet again what we both know: that Barclay was a great man who ravaged his body and, in a sense, took his own life despite our best efforts to prevent it. I brought you here because that was Barclay's request. The letter I showed you yesterday wasn't the only one he left. Before he died he wrote two others, one for me and one for you. He left them on the table next to the typewriter for us to find after his death.

"Here's your letter, señorita." he placed a hand inside his coat and withdrew a folded sheet of paper. He passed it to me. On the outside it said: "The Gringa — not to be read until after the funeral." I began to unfold it, but Doctor Pasquale stopped me.

"No. Please, in the letter he left for me, he gave explicit instructions that you weren't to read it until you're alone."

"Do you know what it says?"

He shook his head. "No, señorita, I cannot guess. But my own instructions were clear enough." From his coat he extracted an envelope. Opening it, he took out a single sheet of paper and began to read.

Dear Enrique (he read)

Three things only I ask of you, not as my poor doctor, abused and ignored for too long, until now I fear it is too late, but as a trustworthy friend.

First, see that my message reaches the gringa, but she is not to read it until after the funeral. If it can be arranged, try to ensure that she is alone when she reads it. I prefer for her not to have to mask her feelings because someone else is present.

The second matter is more delicate.

I trust, my dear friend, that you have seen to the matter of the will. I ask that you also see to it that the gringa contacts my publishers and my solicitors in London as soon as possible. She is to speak to them in person and inform them of my death. One of you must also make my solicitor aware of the terms of my will. I cannot stress the importance of this enough.

I look to you, Enrique, to ensure that my wishes are carried out. I have no living relatives, so I believe and hope that no one will contest my will, but I apologize now if the matter causes you any difficulty.

And my last request, I hope, will not be onerous. It may be that the gringa will want to visit Xloxratl. If so, please accompany her. I am afraid of what she might find if she goes alone.

Finally, I want you to be reassured that you bear no responsibility for my death. The responsibility rests entirely with myself. The truth is simple: I should have listened to you, my doctor and my friend. I am sorry it has turned out this way.

The doctor folded the paper and replaced it in the envelope. "That is all," he said. "My telephone is at your disposal when you need it, señorita, although connections are not always reliable. If there is nothing else, I shall leave you now, so you may read in private, as he wished."

I nodded, not trusting myself to speak, and Doctor Pasquale stole from the room. The front door closed, and for a long while I sat in Barclay's chair, fingering the envelope that was all that remained of the man I had loved.

I opened it carefully, afraid of ripping the sheet within. The handwriting was recognizably Barclay's, but more ragged than usual, as if the letter had been written in a desperate hurry.

Dearest Donna

Perhaps I am suffering under a delusion — in which case, you will never read these words. But I fear the future as never before. I thought I had tamed that monster when Xloxratl made the future — or at least the part of it that matters — known. But now I am afraid that all this time I have been wrong about Xloxratl.

And if I was wrong about Xloxratl, I fear an even more terrifying possibility: that everything I have held to be true is but an uncertain shadow with no more substance than a wishful daydream.

I fear I am about to die, and worse, for the first time since I embraced Catholicism as a teenager, I fear that my faith is without foundation. Xloxratl was wrong. There will be no second book. There will be no shared future.

There is no time to say all that needs to be said. I have only one last hope. Go and see Xloxratl. Perhaps she understands what has happened....

The letter ended there.

Back to the Mountains

I wondered if we would ever be able to find the place.

There were three of us in the borrowed Jeep: Doctor Pasquale, Isabella, and myself; but I was the only one who had travelled the road before, and at the time I hadn't been paying much attention to the route.

The doctor was driving, which was a terrifying experience in itself. Sometimes I wondered if he'd ever driven before, and only my determination not to hurt his feelings prevented me from wresting the wheel from his hands and taking charge of the vehicle myself. His spectacles refused to stay in place, and after only a few kilometers he took them off and handed them to me for safe keeping. For the rest of the journey he peered through the windshield as if it were a dense fog.

I tried to ignore the sudden swerves and jerks that marked our progress up the mountainside, and to concentrate instead on keeping us on the right road. I noted the flat rock where Barclay and I had stopped to eat, but after that we drove for a long time without any obvious landmarks that I recalled. Then I recognized the place where we had spent the night, and I knew there was not much farther to go.

Not long afterward, with the sun halfway down to the western horizon, I shouted "There!" and pointed to the narrow track that led to the old mining camp.

We bounced crazily down the track for a hundred yards, then Doctor Pasquale halted the Jeep with a stomach-wrenching jerk and turned to us with a triumphant smile.

"That's it over there," I said when I had recovered sufficiently to speak.

The hut looked even smaller and more dilapidated than I remembered. There were no signs of life: no smoke rose from the metal chimney, even though it was chilly in the shadowed clearing.

As we got out of the Jeep I paused, feeling a knot of foreboding in my stomach. There were no chickens pecking in front of the tunnel, and the goats were nowhere to be seen. The small vegetable garden that abutted the hut was still there, but it had been some time since it had last been tended: weeds sprouted thickly among the vegetables, and several bushes were weighed down with unpicked fruit.

"Is that where she lives?" asked Isabella. She had been adamant about coming, and neither the doctor nor her mother nor I could dissuade her. She wanted to see for herself, she said, what Xloxratl was like.

"Yes," I replied. But I was becoming more certain with each passing second that we were too late.

"You look worried, señorita," said the doctor.

"I am. The garden hasn't been tended in a long while, and there used to be chickens and goats...." I left my sentence unfinished, leaving them to draw their own conclusions.

We stood there for several moments, clustered not far from the entrance of the hut. But having come so far we had no choice. I moved to the doorway. Isabella and Doctor Pasquale followed a few steps behind.

I halted in the doorway, partly to give my eyes time to adjust to the darkness inside, but mostly because the stench made me want to retch. I stood there for some moments, eyes smarting, before I saw a movement in the gloom at the far side of the hut.

"You've come," said a raspy voice, weak and barely audible.

I swallowed once, and stepped inside.

I reached the old woman in five paces. She was huddled in one corner, under a thin blanket. That was all I could make out. Too little light reached the corner for me to see anything except the gray outline of Xloxratl lying on the floor.

"He is the doctor," she said, her voice gaining strength. "Send him away."

"What's going on?" Enrique asked as he moved to stand beside me. Behind us, holding back, Isabella's silhouette filled the doorway.

I knelt beside Xloxratl's head, and she turned to look at me. In the gloom, I could see only that she was old and weak and fading. I remembered the unnerving eyes that had evaluated me so piercingly the last time I had been here. Now they were reduced to two narrow slits of gray.

"Is this the shaman?" asked the doctor.

"Send him away," repeated the old woman with surprising petulance. Her annoyance made her voice stronger, although it still cracked with age.

"Maybe he can help you," I suggested. She didn't look like she had long to live.

"He couldn't help Barclay," she replied, her voice sharp and distinct. The words hung in the malodorous air for several long seconds before any of us said anything.

I wondered how she could have known about Barclay, and felt the hairs on my arm prickle. Doctor Pasquale began to defend himself, saying that he had tried to save Barclay from himself.

The old woman interrupted him with surprising vigor. "I have no interest in what you tried to do. I simply tell you the truth: you could not help him. Neither can you help me. Now leave."

But the doctor was not to be browbeaten into leaving so easily. "When's the last time you ate?" he asked her quietly, kneeling beside me. "We must get you out of here. This is no place for a woman in your condition."

The shaman appealed to me. "He is no fool, yet he acts the part. Tell him to go, gringa. I am too weak to argue."

I hesitated, vacillating. Doctor Pasquale lowered his head so that it was close to Xloxratl's ear. With one hand he felt her wrist, judging the strength of her pulse. "Please," he said even more quietly, "I only want to help."

Staring up at the ceiling with her gray eyes, the shaman said, "Then leave me to die in peace."

Suddenly, Xloxratl turned her head sharply toward the doorway, where Isabella was still standing. The old woman seemed to look at Isabella intently, although to her Isabella could have been nothing but a dark silhouette against the light that leaked in from outside. A smile spread across the shaman's face, and with it her weariness seemed to fall away like a discarded garment. She relaxed, as if nothing mattered any more. She said something in a language I did not know; whether she was speaking to herself or to Isabella I could not tell.

Isabella took a step inside the hut, but the shaman's eyes remained on the doorway as if someone were still standing there. She said something else in the same language; then she turned abruptly to look at the doctor.

Now that Isabella was no longer blocking the doorway, more light entered the hut. I could see that the shaman was wearing a peaceful smile.

"He's come for me," she said, speaking more strongly than before. "But he insists that the doctor must leave."

Doctor Pasquale glanced at the doorway to assure himself that no one was there, then he shook his head as if to say, "She's slipping away. She's seeing things and there's nothing I can do for her now."

The old woman cackled suddenly, filling the hut with eerie laughter. "You're blind, all of you. You don't see him, do you? But I see him. I've spent a lifetime speaking to him, but only rarely has he shown himself, and never more clearly than at this moment. He says your time has come, Señor Pasquale."

"My time? I don't understand."

"He says you've spent a lifetime denying his existence. This is the last time he will prove himself to you. If you still refuse to believe, then he will have nothing more to do with you. But he says you must go outside."

The doctor looked at me pleadingly. I didn't know what to say.

The impasse was resolved by Isabella. In a shaky voice, she said, "Doctor, please. We should do as she says. We should leave."

"Not you, my dear. Just the doctor. You have faith. It is clear in your heart, if not in your head. What Javí has in mind is for the señor only."

Isabella nodded. "Yes, of course. I understand. Please, Doctor Pasquale, leave us. Wait for us outside. I don't think we'll be long."

The doctor looked at each of us in turn: first Isabella, then me, and finally the shaman, who was now lying with her eyes closed, facing the dark roof.

With a sigh, he heaved himself to his feet. "All right," he said. "I'll wait outside. But if anything happens to her, shout for me. I'll stay within earshot."

He left the hut, and a heavy silence fell.

The End of Xloxratl

"So Barclay has gone," Xloxratl said, although none of us had confirmed the fact. "I tried to warn him the night before he died."

Isabella and I exchanged puzzled glances, but neither of us said anything. We waited for the shaman to explain.

"I went to him in his dreams," she said. "But he didn't want to believe. He tried to tell me it wasn't time. He thought he couldn't die until he'd written another book." The woman cackled. "As if Death can be manipulated by mere mortals. Wasn't it enough that I gave you a warning last summer, gringa?"

I was taken aback. I remembered no warning.

She must have seen my confusion. "The grass," she said. "I gave you a figure made of grass."

I recalled the Y she'd crafted, and suddenly its meaning became clear. I was angry at myself for not seeing it earlier. I should have known that Barclay had been right: Xloxratl did not repeat herself and she did nothing without meaning. The Y had nothing to do with me. She knew I had seen her turning it upside down: she had been trying to tell me that two who had been divided were going to be reunited: Barclay was going to be reunited with Rosalinda.

"He is with Rosalinda now," she continued. "His child is called Maria. She has waited a long time to be with her father." She looked at me sharply. "You think my mind is touched, señorita."

I smiled weakly, wondering if it was really so easy to guess my thoughts.

"But if I can visit Barclay in his dreams cannot he and his family visit me in mine? Last night I told him you would be coming to see me, and he gave me messages for both of you. He wants to thank you, Isabella, for the many nights when you comforted him. He says he knows he was a difficult man, and he is sorry for any pain he caused you or your mother."

Isabella mumbled something inaudible, then the shaman shifted slightly to look at me. A shaft of late afternoon light stole into the hut as she smiled, exposing her rotting teeth.

"And he has a message for you too, señorita. He asks you to forgive him for misleading you, but he could not resist. He says he will be watching your face when you discover the truth."

Before I could ask the maddening old woman what she was talking about, a loud cry from outside interrupted us. Footsteps pounded, and Doctor Pasquale burst into the hut. He stopped and began to cough as the foul air caught at the back of his throat. He was trembling as if from fear. He wiped a layer of sweat from his brow.

Isabella gasped, but not because of the doctor. She pointed at the old woman and I turned in time to see her body spasm once and her eyes roll backwards so that only the rheumy whites were exposed.

"Xloxratl?" I cried. But she could no longer hear me.

The blood fled from her face with remarkable rapidity, and in a few moments there was only a pale, lifeless shell.

"Let's get out of here," said the doctor urgently behind us. He passed his hands several times through his hair, adding to his disheveled look.

I hesitated. "Shouldn't we do something about the body?"

"Let's just go," the doctor replied. "Please. There's nothing for us here any more. We shouldn't have come."

Without waiting for a reply, he turned and hurried from the hut. Glancing first at me and then at the dead shaman, Isabella followed. Pausing only for one last look at the old woman, I went after them.

The drive back to Tecimal passed in taut silence, each of us busy with our own thoughts. The doctor drove like a man possessed, as heedless of the potholes as he was of the crashing gears. More than once I gripped the Jeep in true fear as we careened around a corner on the way down the mountain, coming within centimeters of sliding off the road and down the steep hillside. But by some miracle we reached the desert floor unscathed, and from then on the Jeep raced through the gathering gloom like a demon of the night late for an appointment in Tecimal.

It was dark well before we reached our destination. We dropped Isabella outside her house, then the doctor parked the Jeep outside his own house. Following him inside, I was surprised to see him head straight for the room that served as his surgery. He emerged a few moments later holding a small glass containing a clear liquid. The smell of raw tequila reached me, and I looked at him interrogatively.

"Just once, purely for medicinal purposes," he said, emptying the glass at a gulp. The unaccustomed taste of the raw alcohol gave him a brief coughing fit. When he had recovered he looked at me conspiratorially and whispered, "You won't tell my wife, will you?"

Relieved at my negative answer, he called out, "Francisca, darling, we're home."

The doctor was subdued as we ate a late supper half an hour later. Afterwards, I excused myself and went to my room. Downstairs, I could hear the muffled drone of conversation. I wondered what he was telling his wife.

I slept badly, my dreams filled with distorted images from the day. At one point I woke up shaking at the image of Barclay reaching out to the old woman as she lay on her deathbed. Behind Barclay stood a strikingly handsome, dark, long-haired woman, and by her side was a mulattress whose face shone with a dusky beauty. The mulattress gazed reverently at Barclay, as if she were in awe of him.

Barclay's hand touched the shaman, and I woke up sweating.

I passed what was left of the night restlessly, too afraid to sleep for more than a few minutes at a time in case I was visited by more dreams of the same kind.

Next morning, the doctor came to see me after I had showered, but before breakfast.

"You must think me *loco*," he said without preamble.

I shrugged. "It's none of my business."

"Was it all real, do you think? At the time I thought so. Now, today, in the light of a new morning, I'm not so sure."

"What happened after you went outside?"

For more than a minute he did not reply. At last he said, "I thought she was just a crazy old woman. I've seen it before, you know. Just before they die, some old people begin to hallucinate. There's a

194

perfectly logical explanation, of course: the brain gets less oxygen than it needs, and begins to shut down. It's like a kind of waking dream."

"So when she thought she saw her spirit god in the doorway, she was just seeing things?"

"That's what I thought. It seemed best to humor her. There was nothing I could do to save her, and there was no point in distressing her by arguing."

He fell silent again.

"So what happened?" I prompted.

"I went outside and waited beside the Jeep. After a couple of minutes I began to get this feeling that I wasn't alone. You know the feeling?"

I nodded.

"So I began to look carefully at my surroundings, and at last I saw him, hiding in the shadows near where the trees grew against the mountain, near the entrance to the old mine workings.

"I smiled and waved to show I'd seen him. He responded by drawing nervously farther into the shadows. Intrigued, I began to walk toward him. He waited in the shadows until I reached him."

"Who was it?"

"He didn't tell me his name," the doctor replied. "He was very young. Only about twelve or thirteen. A Chiclahan Indian, by the looks of him. He asked me if I was a doctor."

"How could he have guessed that?"

"That's what I asked, and he told me that he'd been told to wait until a doctor came to visit Xloxratl. 'The old Xloxratl,' he called her. He said he was from Chiclahan, and at home his father was dying from a fever. A man had come to him in a dream and told him that to save his father's life he had to trek by himself up *Las Montañas del Cielo* to the place where Xloxratl lived, and then he was to wait until a doctor came. Then he could go home again and his father would be well again. He said he'd been waiting two days."

"Had he been in to see Xloxratl?"

"He said not. In his dream the man told him he must talk to no one except me."

"And what were you supposed to do?"

"Nothing. Apparently it was enough that he see me. Nothing else was needed."

"It's certainly odd," I said noncommittally.

195

He shook his head. "There's more. I asked him to describe the man who had come to him in his dream."

I felt a premonitory chill.

"Exactly," the doctor said. "'A white man with a wide brimmed hat who spoke Spanish with an accent: quite old, with a long, lined face' was how he described him."

"Barclay," I said, hardly able to breathe.

"Barclay," he nodded. "You can imagine that it shook me as well. I looked away for a moment, toward the hut. I heard the boy thank me, but when I turned back to look at him again, he'd gone. I called out, but there was no answer. It was as if he'd never existed. That was when I decided I'd had enough."

The Second Book

After breakfast I tried to call England on the doctor's phone. To my surprise, the call went through the first time. An English voice came on the line, scratchy and echoing, but clearly audible.

"Adams and Gilt," a none-too-young-sounding secretary said.

I asked for Mr. Adams and after invoking Barclay's name I was put through. Mr. Adams made no attempt to keep his curiosity from his voice as he asked me my business.

"I'm calling from Tecimal, Mr. Adams. I'm afraid I have some bad news. Andrew Barclay is dead."

An ambiguous snort came down the line. I couldn't tell whether the publisher was surprised, disappointed or relieved.

He seemed uninterested in any of the details surrounding Barclay's death; after a brief and not very satisfactory conversation, I hung up.

The second time I was not so lucky with the phone. It took three attempts before I successfully connected with Barclay's lawyer, an elderly-sounding but not unfriendly man by the name of Turpin.

Once more I went through the rigmarole of explaining who I was and the purpose of my call. This time there was no ambiguity about the reaction. Mr. Turpin expressed sympathy at my news before adopting a more businesslike tone. "Regarding the matter of the will. You're certain it's legal?"

I suppressed a frisson of guilt. "Yes. I have one of the witnesses here if you'd like to talk to him."

There was a break while the lawyer located someone who could speak Spanish, and then there followed a two-minute conversation between Doctor Pasquale and the London lawyers. At the end of it, the doctor handed me the phone. "They seem satisfied," he said.

They were. Mr. Turpin said, "It's hardly standard procedure, and we'll want confirmation in writing at the earliest opportunity before we can provide full details, but insofar as I feel able, I'm willing to discuss my client's assets in general terms."

"I wasn't really aware he had any assets," I said.

There was an extended silence that lasted so long I thought the connection had been cut.

"Hello?" I asked. "Are you still there?"

"I'm sorry. Perhaps I misunderstood. Did I understand you correctly? You are unaware of the extent of Lord Barclay's holdings?"

"Wh... what?"

"I asked if you were unaware that when last audited, Lord Barclay's estate came to roughly twenty million pounds. Excluding the house and lands, of course. Naturally there will be death duties to pay, which may require the sale of some assets. However, even after all taxes have been met the value of his estate should run well into eight figures. In pounds, of course."

I clutched the phone desperately while the room swam crazily around me.

"I had no idea," I said, stupidly.

"Yes, well, I'm afraid His Lordship always was rather on the eccentric side. Now, if you'll just send me certified copies of the will and the death certificate as soon...."

I put the phone down. I looked around sharply at the sound of laughter, but the only person I saw was Doctor Pasquale, who was eyeing me anxiously, as if afraid I was about to faint. He certainly wasn't laughing.

He says he will be watching your face when you discover the truth.

"Are you all right?" the doctor asked. "Is something the matter?"

"No. Everything's all right. If you don't mind, I'd like to be alone for a while. I think I need to get some air. I'm going for a walk."

Against his better judgement, the doctor let me go. Without thinking where I was going, I found myself a few minutes later standing on the *Avenida La Guardia* outside the pink house with the white shutters.

I stood there for some time, not daring to go inside, thinking about Barclay's final joke. A joke against himself as much as against me.

I wondered what poor Mr. Turpin must have made of an English peer who abandoned both title and fortune to eke out a living in an impoverished town in central America.

And Barclay had left me everything. It slowly began to sink in that I was rich. I could do whatever I wanted. There was no need to go to Iowa now, not unless I wanted to. If I didn't want to, I didn't even have to go back to the States. I could stay here and write. I could even live in Barclay's house.

I stepped forward and pushed the door open. Without thinking, I entered the study.

I'd left my computer back in LA. But if a typewriter was good enough for Barclay, perhaps it would be good enough for me. I sat down at the desk, Barclay's desk, knowing now what the future held.

There was a sheet of paper in the machine, with a few lines on it. I read what Barclay had written and knew immediately that this time he'd gotten it right. It was the first paragraph of his second book. He'd begun it, and now it was up to me to finish it. I had to. Xloxratl had said we would write the book together, and so we would.

I rested my fingers on the keys and read the paragraph again.

It was afternoon, the hottest part of the day on one of the hottest days of the year, and Tecimal was at siesta. On the south side of the Calle de Generalissimo Javier Felipe Duarte Barclay sat under the awning of Montoya's barbershop, rocking slowly, watching from beneath his wide-brimmed hat the cloud of dust that presaged the arrival of the bus. On the table between Barclay and Montoya were two glasses holding the smooth curving remnants of ice and a centimeter-deep layer of water.

Colophon

The main body of the text of this book was typeset with the pdfTEX digital typesetting system. The typefaces used are mostly from the Latin Modern family, set at 10·5/13. Letters from Donna to Barclay are set in Courier Bold, and those from Barclay to Donna in Computer Modern Typewriter.

The paper stock used for the body of the book and for the cover depends on the particular printer that created the book you are holding.

The VEDIT PLUS text editor was used to create the original text.

The cover was created with the Scribus desktop publishing system and the GIMP image manipulation program.

Computer processing for this edition of *The Second Book* was performed on an Intel quad-core system running the Kubuntu 12.04 64-bit distribution of the GNU/Linux operating system.

www.ingramcontent.com/pod-product-compliance
Lightning Source LLC
Chambersburg PA
CBHW050531260626
47157CB00004B/1552